A green two-door Ch_____
the drive. When J.J. _____ _____ side of
the car from the rear, he saw a body in front of the
vehicle, covered by a sheet. One gnarled, pale hand
peeked out from under the edge of the fabric, fingers
curling, as if the corpse beckoned the police chief
to come closer and look. He resisted, preferring to
finish his circuit before checking the body.

The driver's door was open. Inside, J.J. noted a
woman's black patent-leather purse on the front seat.
It had fallen forward, presumably when the driver
hit the brakes. Most of the contents spilled across
the floor on the passenger side of the car. It was
interesting to note that there weren't any skid marks
until after the point of impact.

★

JULIE WRAY HERMAN

Three Dirty Women
and the Shady Acres

TORONTO • NEW YORK • LONDON
AMSTERDAM • PARIS • SYDNEY • HAMBURG
STOCKHOLM • ATHENS • TOKYO • MILAN
MADRID • WARSAW • BUDAPEST • AUCKLAND

To the Caretakers who live the 36-hour days

THREE DIRTY WOMEN AND THE SHADY ACRES

A Worldwide Mystery/August 2006

First published by Silver Dagger Mysteries.

ISBN-13: 978-0-373-26574-9
ISBN-10:   0-373-26574-3

Acknowledgments

Thanks to all the people who answered my endless questions during the writing of this book. If I got things wrong, it certainly wasn't for lack of knowledgeable help.

To Daniel "Chipp" Bailey for informing me of the finer points of North Carolina law enforcement—and for lending me his name.

To the staff at Garden Terrace of Houston, particularly the staff on D, for sharing their shining example of nursing care with my mother.

To Dean James and Megan Bladen-Blinkoff for helping me through this book, even without a manuscript to critique.

To the Teabuds for the laughter, chocolate, and friendship.

To Gloria Herman for the cover photograph.

To Sgt. Michelle Scheibe of the Houston Police Department for answering questions in my hour of need.

And last—but never least—to Sherry Lewis, Karin O'Brien, and Beth Wright at Silver Dagger/ The Overmountain Press. Thanks for making all my dreams come true—again.

CHARACTERS

Babbitt, Lyndsey: nurse's aide at Shady Acres

Bailey, Daniel: fine Southern-gentleman police officer in Charlotte

Bascom, J. J.: Pine Grove Chief of Police; Janey Bascom's husband

Bascom, Janey: partner in Three Dirty Women Landscaping; married to J. J. Bascom

Falkirk, Maris: former resident of Shady Acres

Fontenot, Carly: charge nurse, Alzheimer's Unit at Shady Acres

Harris, Sylvester: political wannabe in Pine Grove

Hawkins, Mrs. Ethyl: cook at the Penny Whistle Café; Juanita June Osborne's mother

James, Darryl "Doc": Pine Grove physician

James, Marlene: police dispatch clerk; married to Doc James

Jenkins, Hank and Sarah Jane: Pine Grove mayor and his wife

Jurik, Hazel: Shady Acres Nursing Home administrator

Klein, Buster: hardware store owner; Korine McFaile's current beau

McFaile, Cal: Korine's brother-in-law; Charlie's younger brother; Dora's son

McFaile, Chaz: Korine's son; attorney; recently relocated to Savannah

McFaile, Dennis and Katie Anne: Cal's estranged son and daughter-in-law; Korine's favorite nephew and his wife

McFaile, Dora: Korine's mother-in-law; mother of Cal and Charlie

McFaile, Korine: senior partner in Three Dirty Women Landscaping; mother of Chaz McFaile; widow of Charlie McFaile; Cal's sister-in-law; Dora's daughter-in-law and caretaker

Merriweather, Jett: not-so-up-and-coming police officer in Pine Grove

Olmstead: Korine McFaile's calico cat

Osborne, Juanita Jane: owner of the Penny Whistle Café

Smith, Lorraine: formerly the Whittier's housekeeper, currently Dora McFaile's sitter

Taggart, Jack: Olan Taggart's son from Charlotte

Taggart, Olan: bagpiper; Shady Acres resident

Taylor, Colleen: Doc James's pretty young nurse

Whittier, Amilou: partner in Three Dirty Women Landscaping

Winters, Leon: up-and-coming police officer in Pine Grove

ONE

"OH, FOR GOODNESS' SAKE, hold your pants on, Mr. Taggart!" Hazel Jurik's voice descended into irritation at the sight of the man standing by the broken concrete birdbath.

The wizened old man looked around, startled, his lips white around the mouthpiece of his bagpipes. Not waiting for Hazel to reach him, he inhaled deeply and prepared to blow. Until two years before, Olan Taggart had proudly marched with his pipes in the town parades. That last year had been a disaster and had clued all of them in on Taggart's condition. Memory impaired, he hadn't even begun to play two notes related to each other, much less something that could be called music.

Taggart's features settled into defiance, and he started to play. The wail that resulted confirmed what Korine McFaile, Amilou Whittier, and Janey Bascom had feared was about to happen. All three partners in Three Dirty Women Landscaping, Inc. covered their ears, Amilou muttering under her breath.

As Hazel closed in on the man, her high heels left dimples in the soft bare earth of the sparsely turfed lawn. For his part, Taggart glared furiously at her from under faded, bushy eyebrows. Still blowing on the pipes, he executed an about-face with military precision and marched away from the advancing woman. Spindly bare legs strutted beneath the hem of his kilt. Behind Taggart, hanging from a stout limb of one of the venerable white oaks which gave Shady Acres its name, an empty bird feeder swung time with his mournful step.

The stiff breeze coming off the ridge tore slivers of dull brown leaves from the trees and chased them across the lawn. Korine pulled the collar of her pea coat up around her neck as she watched the fuming woman who, a moment before, had been the sweetest, kindest administrator a nursing home could ever want to see.

Korine had arrived before the appointment she and her partners had with Hazel. She wanted to scope out the facility, and this seemed as good a time as any. The visit with the administrator had put her mind at ease with regard to her mother-in-law. Since the death of Korine's husband, Charlie, several years before, it fell to her to do his share of family things. When the time came that Dora McFaile needed more care—and she most certainly would—Shady Acres would be a good choice. Dora had moved in with her six months earlier, after setting the stove on fire in her own house. If Korine hadn't developed the habit of stopping by a couple of times a day to check on the woman, the entire building might have burned to the ground.

Dora's remaining son, Cal, had seen nothing wrong with his mother's behavior; and despite the signs, he had refused to stand behind Korine's decision to confiscate the old woman's car keys or to consider any medical care other than regular doctor's appointments. With Cal in Charlotte and the grandsons scattered to the winds, Dora's care fell to Korine. Most of the boys supported Korine—especially her son, Chaz, who now lived in Savannah, and her favorite nephew, Dennis, who lived with his sweet wife in Knoxville. The fact that Cal had no relationship to speak of with the sons he'd abandoned only made matters worse. He wouldn't listen to any of them, remaining argumentative every step of the way.

Korine's husband had once summed up Cal's personality by saying that his brother would debate the birds right out of the trees. Remembering Charlie's exasperation with his younger brother, Korine felt her lips twitch as she watched Hazel try to coax the bagpipes away from Taggart. Dealing with Cal had become more difficult than Dora's care itself. A move like this one might put him over the edge.

Taggart glared up at the ramrod-straight administrator as he jabbed his outstretched finger at her chest. Hazel retreated a step, then replied, her hands rigidly at her sides. She must have been good at talking people down, because whatever she said seemed to do the trick. The man's face lost some of the ruddy hue that had begun to alarm Korine. He hadn't completely relaxed, though; he whipped the chanter to his pipes out of Hazel's way when she reached for it.

"Hasn't lost his temper, has he?" asked Janey. She'd jammed her hands into the pockets of her red canvas jacket, trying to keep them warm in the fall breeze. The color complemented her creamy brown skin, while the cut emphasized her slimness.

Korine gave a thought to wishing she could look like she had in her thirties, but then she decided she would rather endure a few wrinkles and the smattering of gray gracing her brown curls than be thirty all over again. The past twenty-odd years held precious memories that she wouldn't trade for anything.

Hazel caught the unfortunate man by the elbow and steered him firmly back toward the building. The plaid of his wool kilt fluttered as Taggart stumbled beside the administrator, leaving Korine, Janey, and Amilou with a fit of the giggles. Stepping over the threshold, Hazel put her hand to Taggart's back, still urging him forward.

"Does that answer the age-old question, or do we need to check out a few more Scotsmen?" Amilou asked. One carefully darkened eyebrow disappeared under her honey-blond bangs.

The bright flash of baby-blue boxers had confirmed what Korine always suspected. At least one Scotsman wore something more than tartan between himself and the rest of the world.

Janey's skin acquired a rosy hue even as her lips curved into a shy smile. The subtle reaction warmed Korine. There had been a time when Janey wouldn't have dared smile at a joke like that; her disastrous first marriage had crushed much of her natural sense of humor. Fortunately, she had found the strength to escape Raynell's abuse. She'd exercised much better judgment the second time around. Janey called her current husband her knight in shining armor. Korine couldn't think of a better way to describe Police Chief J. J. Bascom.

Korine dragged her attention back to the matter at hand when she heard Amilou say, "Well, until Hazel gets back and can tell us what she wants out of all this…." Her friend gave up trying to finish the statement, evidently for lack of inspiration.

Years of poor upkeep by so-called lawn-care services had left what grass there was scalped and scanty. There were no ornamental plantings to speak of. The first owner had run out of money soon after putting down the imported marble on the floors of the home. Recently acquired by an out-of-town company—reportedly better at management than the previous owner—things were changing at Shady Acres, and it was hoped that Hazel would give them good news when she got to the budget part of the proposal.

"Maybe more to the point, what would a Scotsman like in his garden?" Amilou asked. "Mr. Taggart used to have a terrific vegetable patch alongside his house."

Janey shook her head. "I don't think the residents can handle that. My vote is for a nice walking path through a restful garden."

Hazel joined the three women once more. "Not all our residents are as challenged as Mr. Taggart," she said.

"I agree with you," Amilou said. "Just because these folks are retired doesn't mean they're dead and buried. Most of them had little garden plots at home—no reason they can't have them here as well. Although," she added judiciously, "perhaps you ought to make certain that Mr. Taggart's plot is well away from the building, in case he decides his plants need music to help them grow."

Amilou reached up and plucked her pencil out of her smooth ponytail. She made a note on her clipboard. "It's fairly level out by the staff parking lot in back. The soil isn't too bad. Truck in a little garden mix, put some borders up for raised beds, you'll be set." She paused and pointed down the hill toward the duck pond. "But Janey has a point. A relaxing walking space would be good here, too."

Korine added her voice to the chorus. "The pond would be a nice destination, but we'll need to do something more than plunk a path in to make it work. I'm thinking a series of benches and beds to draw them onward."

She was rewarded by a quick look of gratitude from Janey.

Amilou had a slight smile on her face as she made another note on the clipboard. She looked up, saw that Janey had gone with Hazel, and winked at Korine.

The two had been friends for so many years, it seemed they were always on the same page—or had been until the summer two years earlier when Amilou's husband, Greg, died mysteriously. Their friendship wasn't as close now as it had been, but moments like these gave Korine hope that they could finish mending the breach between them.

"There is one more thing," Hazel was saying to Janey as Korine and Amilou caught up with them. "We'd like a fenced area outside the door to the secure unit." She caught the tail end of a startled look on Amilou's face and must have interpreted it as censure. "We really do keep better tabs on our residents than you think."

Shady Acres had been placed on the state watch list due to the death of one of the residents during the first cold snap of the year. When Korine had asked about Maris Falkirk's untimely death, Hazel had been frank. The woman had wandered out an unsecured door. She'd been found hypothermic and unconscious under the tall weeping willow by the front gate to the property. Even though she was taken immediately to the hospital, she died two days later.

"I know, it sounds bad," Hazel continued, "not being able to keep track of our residents. Someone's been opening the locked door in the secure wing, and the residents take to the great outdoors like lemmings. It's happened so many times in the last month, I don't know what to do. At least if we had a fence there, it would be an additional hurdle for them to cross before they got out on their own."

"Buster Klein at the hardware store could help you, I'm sure," Korine said. Buster's store had recently branched out into various services, trying to compete with the big warehouse hardware store that had recently opened on the freeway. In the course of the previous year, he had gotten to be a good friend, and Korine wanted to give him more business. "You need his number?"

"Would you mind taking care of it?" Hazel replied. "Just get me a proposal I can give to the owner, Mr. Owens." She handed Amilou a folded sheet of paper. "Here's our budget. It's not as much as I wanted, but it's more than I thought he would let us do." She looked over her shoulder. "I'd better get back inside and see if they've managed to settle Mr. Taggart down. He's been pretty agitated today."

"I understand," Korine said. "Dora was having kittens herself this morning." She sighed, remembering the rush to find Dora's misplaced Bible so she could read her morning passage. Lorraine Smith, Dora's sitter, had finally found it under some old mail on the table in the downstairs hall.

Realizing that the others were waiting for her to continue, Korine smiled to show she was still paying attention. "We'll get the proposal to you by the early part of next week," she promised.

As Hazel reentered the building, the three women surveyed the lay of the land. A soft slope ran from the squat one-story building, down a short ridge, to the road. Falling away from the ridge on the north side was a tangle of tall evergreens and the usual accompanying forest under-growth. The south side had a cleaner look to it, having been cleared when Shady Acres was built. The lawn ran down to the pond at the bottom of the hill.

An oak lent its leafy bower to softening the look of the place. It stretched up and over the east wing of the building and reached down to welcome the drive. There weren't many oaks around the town of Pine Grove, which, appropriately enough, had more pines and other evergreens than hardwoods. This tree was significantly old. Probably planted by a farmer to shade his homestead, well over a century ago, it lent a serenity to the hill with its swaying branches. The property had a lot of potential.

"That needs a circular bench around it," Amilou said decisively, pointing to the tree. "And some of those limbs don't look too firm. Maybe we need to call Tom and have him come have a look?" Tom Cornelius was an arborist the ladies used from time to time when they needed a good tree consultant.

Janey nodded. "I'll do that," she said.

The women walked together to Amilou's car, where Amilou made a few more notes on her clipboard before un-locking the doors. "They really missed the boat when they took all the trees off that part of the ridge," she said with true regret. She checked the budgeted amount Hazel had given them. "We won't have enough to add any up there if we do all the rest we've talked about."

"It's actually better this way," Janey observed. "If we put trees there, it wouldn't be long before the garden plots you were talking about got shaded out. The other trees are beautiful all on their own." She turned to Amilou and said, "Can we meet tomorrow to go over things before I leave town?"

"Sure," Amilou replied. "Morning good for you?" she asked her partners.

"I may have to miss it," Korine said. "I've got Dora all to myself on the weekends."

"You packed yet?" Amilou asked Janey.

"It's been so long since I was home, I don't even know what to wear there. Memaw will kill me if I don't look nice for her friends."

Janey was leaving for Louisiana on Sunday to visit her grandmother. As long as Korine had known her, she'd never met Janey's family. In all that time, none of them had come to Pine Grove. No one came when Janey went through her divorce. No one came when she remarried. Korine had assumed that Janey was pretty much alone in the world. The announcement that she would be going home to visit her grandmother had been accompanied by an uncharacteristically chilly glance declaring the topic closed.

"You'll look fine no matter what the current style is back home," Korine assured Janey.

The tension eased slightly around the younger woman's brown eyes. "I'm sure you're right. I just want everything to be perfect."

"As it will be," Korine said again.

Amilou looked up from making a note on her clipboard. "I'll call Korine after you and I meet, Janey. We'll see what we can put together. You won't have a lot of spare time, getting ready for your mysterious trip back home, so we won't count on you."

Only Amilou can get away with talking like that to people, Korine thought.

"But if you have any great ideas," Amilou added, "you'll have our phone numbers with you, right?"

"I know them all by heart," Janey laughed. "And I'll have plenty of time to think about things while I'm driving."

Everything decided, the women got into their cars to head home. As Korine steered her way down the drive, she had a vision of Shady Acres as it could be, banks of azaleas alight in spring, crocuses popping up to greet the warming sun.

An oriole, heading south for the winter, flew overhead as Korine approached the pond, and left a reminder of the capriciousness of life splashed across the windshield. She hit the windshield-wiper-fluid button and made a mental note to add bird feeders and lots of berry-bearing shrubs to the mix. Dora spent an inordinate amount of time documenting the birds that visited her feeders each morning. Windshields notwithstanding, folks at Shady Acres might appreciate the same opportunity.

Korine turned onto the highway and accelerated. The clock on the dash read 5:08. Reaching down, she pulled her grocery list out of the pocket on her door—milk, butter, bread, and Dora's medicine. The latter made the trip necessary, even though she knew that Dora's sitter would be impatient to leave. Lorraine often stayed to chat a few minutes with Korine to let her know how the old woman's day had gone, but she had to stop on her way home from watching Dora to baby her due-any-day daughter.

Korine ran the contents of her freezer through her mind. They needed chicken to have with dinner, too. She took the turn-off into town. A quick stop at the Winn-Dixie, and soon she'd be home.

THE AISLES WERE CROWDED with folks getting ready for the weekend. Korine steered her cart around a woman pushing a basket with three raucous children hanging off the side. She saw Sarah Jane Jenkins at the end of the row and slowed down, hiding her head behind a stack of canned pumpkin. She didn't have the leisure to stop and pass the time of day with the biggest gossip in town. Once Sarah Jane was safely past, Korine grabbed the items she needed and ran her cart to the pharmacy.

Sarah Jane stood at the counter. She looked up from putting her wallet back into her purse and spied Korine. She picked up the small bag and waggled it in the air. "I've got to get up to Shady Acres and give this to the nurses," she said, as if Korine had accosted her. "I wish they'd give me more warning when they're going to change Mother's medicine. They want to start her on this tonight."

While Korine waited for the pharmacy worker to slap the label on Dora's pills, she watched Sarah Jane bustle toward the front of the store. Sarah Jane's mother, Mrs. Lawson, didn't have Alzheimer's. Far from it. Sharp as a tack and twice as spiteful, she gave her daughter daily hell for "putting her away." Mrs. Lawson stridently asserted that she was perfectly fine, conveniently forgetting that her arthritis was so debilitating that she needed help to do the littlest thing. Both Sarah Jane and Korine had their hands full. A flush of shame at avoiding the other woman bloomed in Korine's heart. On the other hand, she reminded herself as she signed the credit card receipt, she might be forgiven for thinking her own troubles were as much as any human being could handle in one day.

Turning, Korine ran into the person behind her in line.

Colleen Taylor, Doc's pretty, young nurse, spluttered an apology. "I'm so sorry, Mrs. McFaile. I didn't leave you enough room."

"I should have looked where I was going," Korine said. "How are things in the office?"

"Busy as anything. This flu outbreak is so early in the year, I don't know what winter will be like."

"You look a little peaked yourself."

Colleen leveled a look at Korine that would freeze a margarita in its glass. "Thanks."

"I didn't mean it that way," Korine protested.

"It's all right," Colleen sighed. "You're just the fifth person since I walked in the door to tell me that."

"I see you've got plenty of Tylenol in there." Korine indicated Colleen's basket. Three bottles rested next to frozen vegetables, a roast chicken, and a bag of chocolate candies.

Colleen laughed. "Not all for me, I can assure you. Doc's got me delivering medicines to some of the older folks who can't get out because of the flu. Tylenol is one of those things they can't do without." She consulted a prescription in her hand, then handed it over the counter to the pharmacist. Turning back to Korine, she asked, "How's the older Mrs. McFaile?"

Doc's nurse had always been a likeable young woman, very solicitous and helpful during Dora's office visits. But now, Korine thought Colleen's searching look seemed intrusive. The girl had hesitated slightly before she said *Mrs. McFaile,* as if she had started to say something else and changed her mind. Her thinly tweezed eyebrow cocked a little too sardonically for Korine's taste.

Taken aback, Korine had the irrational feeling that Colleen's friendly manner masked something mean-spirited. *Dora's paranoia must be catching,* she thought. She shook off the sensation. If she didn't, her next stop would be Klein's Hardware to pick up extra padlocks for the door.

Not that she'd need the locks once she finished talking to Buster. Soon after Korine had gotten back from Savannah the summer before, she had gone in for fertilizer and heard Buster telling one of the other customers that it had been over a year since his wife died. The manner in which he remembered his wife, Tilde, spoke volumes about his nature. When Buster had nervously asked Korine out a few weeks later, she'd said yes without reservation. Their dates weren't wildly exciting, but he had the unusual quality of stillness about him, as if he were at rest. Korine felt calmer when she spent time with him, something which now seemed to come to her in smaller doses.

"Not bad, considering," she said, hauling her mind back into the grocery store and out of the front seat of Buster's car at the end of their last date. To her delight, Korine found that she wasn't blushing. "It's been a fairly good week. I don't know what we'd do without Lorraine, of course."

"She stays with Mrs. McFaile when you're gone?"

This time there was no mistaking the intensity of Colleen's interest. Korine took a mental step back. Perhaps Colleen was so tired of working in Doc's office that she was eyeing this sort of job for herself. Korine had plenty of help, with Lorraine there five days a week. She didn't want to hurt Colleen's feelings, but she didn't want to give her false hopes either.

"Speaking of which," Korine said hastily, "I'd better get

on home." She turned away as Colleen mouthed a startled good-bye.

Rationalizing her unaccustomed rudeness, Korine reminded herself that she really should get home and relieve Lorraine. She pushed her cart to the checkout stand and unloaded the few groceries she had.

Collecting her change, Korine scooted out to her car and started the motor. The fifteen minutes she'd spent in the store wouldn't make that much difference, but she didn't feel any less guilty. She pressed on the gas and headed for home.

TWO

J. J. BASCOM'S POLICE CRUISER made it out to Shady Acres Saturday morning before the sun had cleared the horizon. He'd intended to take the day off to be with Janey before she left. So much for that notion.

He stopped his cruiser below the accident scene on the blacktop drive and got out of his car. There was a small group of people milling around, a significant number given that it was barely eight o'clock. Since most of them wore scrubs and white uniforms, J.J. figured they were Shady Acres employees.

He walked cautiously around the area to get a good feel for the overall scene. Leon Winters, the junior officer who had rousted J.J. out of bed early that morning, looked up from what he was doing and nodded to show he knew his boss had arrived.

A green two-door Chevy sat askew in the middle of the drive. When J.J. rounded the passenger side of the car from the rear, he saw a body in front of the vehicle, covered by a sheet. One gnarled, pale hand peeked out from under the edge of the fabric, fingers curling, as if the corpse beckoned the police chief to come closer and look. He resisted, preferring to finish his circuit before checking the body. Leon was a good man; he'd have taken care of things properly. Besides, J.J. wanted to wait for Doc to arrive.

The driver's door was open. Inside, J.J. noted a woman's black patent-leather purse on the front seat. It had fallen forward, presumably when the driver hit the brakes. Most of the contents spilled across the floor on the passenger side of the car.

It was interesting to note that there weren't any skid marks until after the point of impact. The comma-shaped stain on the pavement showed clearly enough where the victim had been struck.

Shaking his head, J.J. flipped his notebook shut over his notes and went over to Leon, who stood off to one side, away from the small crowd of folk, talking to a tall, neatly coiffed brunette. Her carefully applied makeup had smeared, tear tracks marked by traces of wiped-off mascara, but she answered Leon's questions quietly. He was doing a good job with the interview. J.J. was glad Leon had been the one to respond. His second officer, Jett Merriweather, wasn't worth a dime on fatality calls.

Waiting behind the woman as Leon finished his questions, J.J. hadn't recognized the administrator at first. The last time he'd seen her, J.J. was answering the call a month earlier when Maris Falkirk disappeared. Hazel had sported long hair then. The new look suited her.

Hazel stepped away from Leon, nodding at J.J. as she passed. Dark brows drew close together as she glanced toward the body. Turning her head, she marched resolutely up the hill, limping slightly due to a broken heel on one of her pumps. She looked appropriately glum. This fresh disaster wasn't going to do Shady Acres any favors.

"Leon," J.J. said by way of greeting.

"Sir," Leon acknowledged.

"Who is it?"

"You're not going to like this. It's Olan Taggart."

"Anyone else hurt?"

"No."

J.J. pursed his lips and stared down at the car. "And that's Dora McFaile's car?"

Leon nodded.

"Who was driving?"

"Mrs. McFaile. The older one." Leon confirmed J.J.'s incredulous glance.

"Korine took her keys away."

"Mrs. McFaile took 'em back today with a vengeance."

J.J.'s glare wiped the suspicion of a smile off Leon's face. "Where is Mrs. McFaile now?"

"Colleen suggested that we put her someplace quiet in the building."

"Colleen Taylor—Doc's nurse?"

"That's the one."

"You have a problem there?" J.J. asked, catching the reserved note in Leon's voice.

"No," Leon said quickly. "I went out with her a few times is all."

J.J. nodded to let Leon know he had registered the statement.

"According to the witnesses, Mrs. McFaile drove in and stopped at that point." Leon pointed to the spot where the blood started on the drive. "Taggart stepped out of the bushes there." Leon's finger swerved to the right to indicate the stand of forsythia beside the drive. "She stopped when she saw him. Rolled down the passenger-side window." Leon pointed at the car, and J.J. saw that the window was still open.

"Taggart leaned on the side of the car and spoke for a moment to Mrs. McFaile. He fell against the car. Must have rolled under. According to the witnesses, as soon as he hit the ground, she hit the gas. His clothes snagged on the underside of the car. He was dragged to where you see the car now."

"Wonder why she took off like that?"

Leon's shrug showed that he wasn't about to make any guesses on that one.

"Who are the witnesses?" J.J. had seen several familiar faces in the crowd as he drove up. Still, even in a town as small as Pine Grove, there were residents who were unknown to him.

"Sylvester Harris, Sarah Jane Jenkins, and Colleen. They're in the lobby."

J.J. turned to yell at a man wearing scrubs whose curiosity had gotten the better of him. He scrambled back away from the car pretty quick. Watching until the man had retreated to his satisfaction, J.J. said, "Did any of these folks see anything?"

"Nope. Just came out to have a look before they went home."

"In that case, why don't they go home?"

Leon met J.J.'s eye. They both knew that by a two-to-one margin, the average person's intellect was outranked by curiosity. Everyone felt they had a right to see what was going on. Reality TV without the cameras.

"You talk to any of the witnesses yet?" J.J. asked.

"Not really. Just a general idea of what happened. I thought it might be better to take care of things down here first. Colleen did CPR on the old man."

"Optimistic, isn't she?" J.J. said dryly.

"I think *dogged* might be a better word to describe Colleen." Leon stared toward the body.

In profile, J.J. could see what all the girls in town found so damned attractive about the young man. Long and lean, and dark of hair and eye. Hadn't been that long ago that J.J. sported those kinds of looks. He rubbed one hand over his thinning hair and wasted an ounce of regret over what had been.

Yanking himself off that train of thought, he took note of Leon's compressed lips. If expressions could talk, Colleen would have quite the reputation. J.J. filed it away under mental notes. With this second hint of a strain between the two young people, he decided it would be better if he dealt with Colleen personally. "In that case, I'd better go up and talk with her. Might as well do all of them while I'm at it." He nodded toward the hill.

"Sure." There was real relief in Leon's face.

A sheriff's vehicle turned in at the gate and parked behind J.J.'s cruiser. Two burly men got out, and Leon hurried down to let them know what had been done and where they could be the most help. Doc would arrive soon to take care of getting the body off to the morgue.

J.J. headed up to the building, following the impressions in the soft earth that signaled Hazel's original path down from the nursing home. Halfway up the hill, the impressions changed character. He stopped and retraced his steps a few feet down the slope and poked a finger in the dirt.

He nudged the missing heel from Hazel's shoe, pulled it free, and put one hand on his bent knee to help him straighten up. J.J. may have been as lean as Leon at one time, but his knees didn't remember being that young.

He resumed his course, lips pursed, and found Hazel sitting in the lobby with Sarah Jane. Neither Sylvester or Colleen was in sight.

"I told them they couldn't leave the accident scene when they were witnesses." Sarah Jane's strident voice bounced across the inlaid marble floor.

J.J. stopped. "Sylvester and Colleen left?" he asked. Nothing Sylvester Harris did surprised J.J. anymore. Even considering Leon's comments about Colleen, he would have thought that any nurse of Doc's would be more responsible. He was beginning to see why Leon had not gone out with the young woman for long.

Hazel leapt to the girl's defense. "Colleen went to pick up some medicine Doc called in for Mrs. McFaile."

"How'd she get back out on the road?" J.J. asked.

"The accident happened on the front part of the drive. The back entrance is over there." Hazel pointed out the window.

Sure enough, another ribbon of blacktop led out to the road farther down the hill. J.J. had forgotten that they'd put in a service entrance. With all the fancy fixing-up they'd recently done around the place, it stood to reason they wouldn't want the garbage truck coming up the front way.

He took a step closer to Hazel and placed the heel of her shoe in her hand. She looked at the grubby item and threw him a startled look of gratitude.

J.J. turned his head back toward Sarah Jane. "I'd like to

talk with Mrs. McFaile first," he said. "Can you stick around for a bit?"

"Of course I will." Sarah Jane settled back in the chair. "That poor woman."

J.J. nodded. "I'll be back in a few," he said.

Sarah Jane had the right of it there. Korine would be beside herself, and then some. She'd bent over backward to do the right thing by her mother-in-law, up to and including taking the woman's keys away from her when she had precious little support from that son in Charlotte. J.J. grimaced. He wasn't looking forward to that particular phone call.

Hazel indicated the hallway to a conference room. "She's sitting back here with a nurse right now. She was so agitated when she got inside—and who could blame her—that I decided seclusion would be a good idea."

"Thank you." J.J. opened the door and nodded at the young male nurse sitting in the chair next to the door. Dora McFaile sat in an armchair in the corner. A small neat woman with an apple-doll face, she stared blankly at the wall ahead of her. One hand stroked the sleeve of her jacket. Her hair, usually tied up neatly in a topknot, lay frizzed about her shoulders.

She looked up at J.J. as he closed the door behind him. Her eyes narrowed. "About time you got here. What are you going to do about this mess?"

J.J. didn't know quite how to respond.

"Eh!" she said sharply when he didn't speak immediately. "As usual, no answer."

Although he'd had teachers like Mrs. McFaile, J.J. had gone to school in Lufkin, Texas, far away from Pine Grove Elementary. The tone of voice was the same, no matter where the teacher taught. J.J. deduced that she thought he was one of her students.

He stooped in front of the woman so he could look her in the eye. "Mrs. McFaile, I'm J. J. Bascom, a friend of Korine's. I need to speak with you about Olan Taggart."

There was a twitch of life in her eyes, as if the woman she'd once been stirred behind the tangle of her thoughts. She blinked, tears dimming her focus. She glared at the wall behind J.J. and began to rock back and forth rapidly, a monotone cry issuing from her lips.

Angry with himself, even though he knew it wasn't his fault that he'd lost her, J.J. stood and stepped back, allowing the nurse to fuss over the woman. Obviously, he wasn't going to get anything close to coherent out of her right now—if he ever did. J.J. apologized and said he'd return later.

Walking back out to the lobby, he saw that Sarah Jane remained perched on her chair, a slight frown of concentration on her face. J.J. didn't know why some people thought that witnessing a violent act added importance to their lives, but Sarah Jane was clearly of this ilk.

"Are you up to talking?" he asked, as if unaware of her overly bright eyes and the way she inched to the edge of the chair so she could get closer to him.

"Certainly," Sarah Jane assured him. "I had finished feeding Mother her breakfast and was in the parking lot when Dora ran that poor man over."

"Do you remember what time this was?"

Sarah Jane looked taken aback. "No, I didn't check my watch," she said, biting her lip as if she had failed Credible Witness 101.

Not for the first time, J.J. wondered how his friend could

stand being married to this woman. It was a toss-up as to which J.J. found most inexplicable—Hank's career as mayor, or taking Sarah Jane as his wife. No accounting for tastes.

"Most people don't go looking at their watches, trying to set the time in their minds just in case they witness something interesting," J.J. said. "Simply one of many questions we ask. Sometimes we get an answer, sometimes we don't. Suppose you tell me who else was around when Mrs. McFaile drove in."

"That's all you want to know?"

"I may have more questions that will occur to me as you talk." J.J.'s dry tone was lost on the woman.

She nodded and put her hands in her lap. J.J. saw that she'd taken a fold of her skirt between her right thumb and forefinger and was pleating it. J.J. sighed. He hoped Sarah Jane would be as truthful as she was anxious to please.

"I don't know what Korine was thinking," she began, "to let Dora out in that car alone—"

J.J. interrupted, trying to help Sarah Jane clarify her narrative to exclude assumptions. And blame. "Did you see Mrs. McFaile driving alone?"

"She drove up that driveway by herself. Poor Olan Taggart stepped in front of her bumper. Dora didn't even slow down. Think if it had been me!"

J.J. frowned and went back in his mind to what Leon had told him had happened. He leaned forward. "She didn't stop at all?"

Sarah Jane's hand gripped her skirt so hard, he thought he heard fabric rip. "I don't think so." She lowered her lashes.

When she opened her eyes again, they skittered past J.J. and focused on something outside the window. She caught her bottom lip in her teeth and frowned. J.J. had time to count to five before Sarah Jane amended her statement.

"I suppose she might have stopped," she allowed. "I saw her coming in, then she went behind those trees down there. I was taking my keys out of my purse so I could get home before Dora got back on the road again."

Her shoulders lifted in a shrug as Sarah Jane spread her hands. "It seemed like she went behind the trees and then she came back into sight. If I had known that she'd kill someone, I would have timed her."

Was that sarcasm? J.J. inspected the earnest look on her face and let it go.

"Would you believe Korine isn't even home?" she said. "Some stranger's going to tell her all about the accident and upset her."

"You called Korine already?"

"Well, of course. Her mother-in-law is wandering the streets. No matter what Korine thinks, I try to help her keep up with things as best she'll let me." Her characteristically bitter words were accompanied by a tone very much at odds with what J.J. knew of Sarah Jane.

She looked up at him and caught his surprise. "Don't think I don't understand what Korine's going through. Wasn't so long ago that I had to fight with Mom to get her to see reason. It's the son who should be strung up. We all know Korine's tried her best. And no person in his right mind would hold Dora responsible."

J.J. had already come to the same conclusion. No way could he take Mrs. McFaile into custody. He didn't have the means to care for her. He would, he supposed, have to try to get some sort of statement from the poor woman. He refused to harass her. If talking with him upset her this much, then he would wait on her to be ready. It wasn't like it was murder.

"Was there anyone else around when all this happened?" he asked.

"That Harris person—Sylvester. He came out of the building as Dora pulled up the drive. He stopped to watch from the porch steps over there. Never made a move to help." Her tone made it clear that she thought little of his standing by while a man bled to death.

She continued, "Colleen came running up the drive behind the car. Poor girl was so broken up. She was the one who went down and pulled the poor man out from under the car. Some of the staff came out when they heard me yelling for help. They weren't much help. There was one man who seemed really upset, though, when he saw Mr. Taggart."

"Which of the attendants was it?"

"I was so far away. I don't think I could tell you for sure." Sarah Jane reached over and pulled a shabby brown purse off the floor. She tugged a plastic bag with some tissues in it from the side pocket. "Excuse me," she said, dabbing at her moist eyes. "It's just that…it could have been my mother or me down there."

"Thank you, Sarah Jane. I know this has been difficult for you. I'll call if there's anything else." J.J. reached out and helped the woman to her feet. He might wish she had actually seen more, but she'd witnessed with an eye for detail.

After Sarah Jane left, J.J. poked his head in the door of

the conference room. Mrs. McFaile had fallen asleep, looking more like a rag doll than ever. Cracker crumbs littered her blouse like confetti. The nurse sitting next to her rose, looking like he would skin J.J. alive if the police chief disturbed his charge.

J.J. backed out and went down the hall to the administrator's office. Hazel sat behind her desk. As J.J. came through the door, she looked up from rummaging in one of the drawers. Her shoe and the now-clean broken heel lay in front of her on the desk. She opened a tube of super glue and pressed the tip to both items, applying a goodly amount. Holding the two bits together, she asked, "You wouldn't happen to have any Tylenol on you?"

J.J. shook his head.

Hazel propped up the shoe between two books and used the pencil holder to keep the heel straight. "Do you mind waiting a minute while I go find something for this headache?" She was out the door before J.J. could respond.

While the woman was out of the room, J.J. borrowed her phone to call Korine.

Problem was, there wasn't an answer at her house. He then called home, opting not to leave a message when the machine came on. He called Amilou's house next, going on down the list of likely places he might find information about where Korine could be. The answering machine picked up. Frustrated, J.J. left a brief message that there had been an accident but he had Dora McFaile safe and sound. He rattled off his cell phone number and hung up.

Running his hand over his head, he wondered where the hell everyone was. Unable to reach any family, he thought he'd better go ahead and take extra measures with the woman. He picked up the phone again. Since Korine's son, Chaz, had moved to Savannah, Old Man Franklin was the only attorney left in town. Franklin said he'd meet with Mrs. McFaile out at Shady Acres and let J.J. know when she was ready to talk with the police.

Remembering the woman's reaction earlier, J.J. wasn't sure they'd be able to use anything she said as evidence, lawyer present or not.

Hazel came back through the door, carrying a medicine bottle and two cans of Coke. She put one drink on the desk in front of her and shoved one toward J.J. After flopping back in her chair, she pried open the top to the telltale red-and-white bottle and shook out two capsules. Pulling out the middle desk drawer, she dropped the bottle inside and shut it. She tossed the pills into her mouth, popped the tab on the can, and took a long swig of her Coke. She closed her eyes, swallowed, and then sighed deeply, letting her head fall forward on the desk blotter in front of her. She covered her neck with one hand and rubbed.

After nearly a minute, J.J. cleared his throat. He was afraid she'd forgotten he was there.

Hazel sat up quickly. Opening her eyes, she focused on J.J. "Sorry," she said. "Losing a patient is hard enough without having it be so…." Her pallor, already painful to see, worsened.

J.J. understood completely. Taggart's death had been graphic, to say the least.

Her green eyes narrowed. "Are you going to have to charge her?"

"I certainly hope not. We'll have to get some sort of comment from her, but I think it's fairly clear neither she nor the community is going to benefit if we take her into custody."

The lines around Hazel's mouth relaxed. "Good," she said, nodding. "Although, that's not what I expected you to say."

He raised his eyebrows.

"According to Mr. Harris, you'd stop at nothing to harass a citizen."

Mr. Harris being Sylvester, J.J. wasn't surprised at Hazel's statement. "Sylvester and I don't get on," he said shortly. "Don't believe everything he says about me." J.J. sat up straighter. "Had Mr. Taggart been acting odd lately?" he asked, thinking of the sudden way Leon said the old man reportedly had fallen.

"He's an odd sort, that one."

Okay, J.J. thought, *that was a stupid question.*

"Acting oddly how?" Hazel asked, apparently having understood him after all. "He's been delusional for almost as long as I've known him. People are after him. Complaining about his things being moved. He's right about that last one, by the way. The residents walk off with each other's belongings all the time. Drives the families nuts, but what can you do? These people don't remember it's not theirs to take."

"Any sudden loss of balance?"

Hazel thought for a minute. "I'd have to double-check with his nurse, Carly, but I don't remember anything like that offhand."

J.J. stood. "Do you have Jack Taggart's number? I need to notify him about his father's death."

Hazel's face softened. "Would you? I thought I had to.

I've been trying to get up the nerve to do it." She opened a folder, which lay on her desk, and wrote a number on the pad of paper she pulled out of the drawer. She shoved the paper across the desk toward him as if he might back out of his offer to make the call.

"It's my job," J.J. said. He picked up the slip and stared at it. The numbers blurred together. He looked up and nodded at Hazel while folding the paper into his shirt pocket. He was already tired, and the day had barely begun.

He walked back to the lobby, where there was a private room he could use to make his calls. He pulled his cell phone and the paper from his pocket, then punched in the number.

A male voice answered, and J.J. went into his soothing deliverer-of-bad-tidings voice. The reaction to the news was better than J.J. had hoped, but Jack Taggart was still appropriately stunned.

After receiving Jack's assurances that he'd be there later in the day, J.J. hung up and tried Korine's number again. Still no answer. His next call was to Cal McFaile. He wasn't nearly as calm as Jack had been. Things were bad enough now, but it would really be a mess when Cal hit town.

Neither Colleen nor Sylvester had returned, meaning J.J. would have to hunt them down to get their statements. He shoved the phone into his pocket and went down to see if Doc had arrived yet. J.J. knew the next few hours were going to be some kind of busy.

THREE

KORINE TOLD HERSELF LATER that she should have known something was wrong the minute she opened her eyes. The truth was, she didn't give it a thought. All she realized was that she had just enjoyed the first uninterrupted night's sleep in months. She stretched, catlike, and rolled over. The clock blinked solemnly at her. She threw back the covers and shot out of bed. It didn't matter how tired she was. Ten o'clock was far too late for her to have slept.

Thrusting her arms into her robe, Korine poked her head into the hall. The house was silent. Even the dust hung suspended, still in the air. Tiptoeing across the hall, Korine turned the brass knob of Dora's door. The blankets lay smooth across the bed; her flannel nightgown hung on the back of the bathroom door. The woman herself was nowhere to be seen.

Becoming frightened, Korine called down the stairs.

No answer.

It wasn't until she had checked the living room, dining room, and kitchen that she admitted defeat. Dora was not in the house. Heart racing, Korine flew down the back porch steps and across the damp stepping stones to the garage door.

Bare feet numb against the cold concrete floor, Korine

tried to keep from blasting herself. Both Dora and her car were gone. The phone on the garage wall began to ring, as if Korine had tripped a hidden switch on the threshold with her toes.

She reached the phone on the second ring. "Hello?"

"It's about Dora." Sarah Jane would have been the last person Korine would have called about her missing mother-in-law. But here she was, calling Korine, right on cue.

"Where is she?" Korine asked, fingers gripping the phone.

"You know I go up to Shady Acres every morning to help Mom with her breakfast? Well, Dora turned up, driving her car, and I've been stuck here ever since."

"She's at Shady Acres?" Korine grasped at the one piece of relevant information offered by Sarah Jane's recital. She really didn't care how much Sarah Jane was inconvenienced; she was concerned about her mother-in-law. "Is Dora all right?"

"I know you've tried to keep her from driving—and a good thing, too—"

Alarmed, Korine interrupted Sarah Jane. "She had an accident?"

"Didn't I just tell you that?"

"You know full well you didn't! What happened to Dora?"

There was silence on the other end of the line. Sarah Jane took a breath, then said, "Dora's fine. I've been trying to call you all morning so that you could hear this news from a friend; obviously I don't count as one in your book. Call J. J. Bascom. He'll tell you what your mother-in-law did."

Korine's ears rang from the force with which Sarah

Jane slammed down the phone. She leaned her hands on the potting bench, fingers splayed wide. Breathing deeply, too scared of what she'd hear if she called J.J., Korine took in the peaty smell, which clung to the wood, and the sharp scent of the bone meal she'd put in with her new stand of daffodils the weekend before. Honest smells. Soothing.

Korine let out a breath that she felt she'd been holding for months. Dora had finally done something she wouldn't be able to explain away. Cal would have to see reason. Straightening, Korine touched the underside of the right-hand front corner of her potting bench. Her fingers traced the heart that Charlie had carved next to his initials. For the first time, Korine was glad that her husband wasn't around any longer. The state his mother was in would have killed him all over again.

Giving the carving one last pat for luck, she picked up the receiver and punched in the number for the Pine Grove police. "Marlene," Korine said when the dispatch clerk answered, "I'm calling about Dora. Is everyone all right?"

"Hang on," Marlene answered. "J.J.'ll want to talk with you." She covered the receiver and spoke to someone in the room.

There was a pause on the other end of the line, then a click signaled that someone had picked up another extension.

"Korine?" J.J. said. "I've been trying to reach you."

"I've been here." How on earth had she slept through the phone's ringing? "Sarah Jane called me. She said there was an accident."

"That woman—" J.J. broke off what he had been about to say. Korine heard the creak of his oak desk chair. "She had no more business calling you than Mrs. McFaile had driving," he said. There was a weariness to his voice that Korine had never heard before.

"What happened?" Seconds beat out as she braced herself for J.J.'s reply. When he didn't seem able to find his voice, Korine continued. "How serious is it? Sarah Jane said Dora was fine."

"Mrs. McFaile is okay," he confirmed. "Hang on a minute, I've got a call coming in." Without another word, J.J. put her on hold.

Korine was suddenly aware that she was still in her pajamas. She'd need to put on some clothes before she picked up her mother-in-law.

When J.J. came back on the line, Korine tried to keep her voice steady. "You didn't answer my question. Was someone else hurt?"

"Cal will be here this afternoon."

"Someone was hurt." Korine heard her rasping breath echo on the line. "I did try. You know I did. Cal won't even let me say a word to him about his mother. Maybe he'll listen to you."

"Oh, he'll be listening—loud and clear."

Korine noticed that J.J.'s tone had altered. Not his usual friendly tone or even his police chief voice. The official J.J. was bad enough. This was far worse.

She shivered. Her hand once again sought comfort from the time-smoothed carving on the underside of the bench. "Sarah Jane wouldn't tell me what really happened. How bad is it?" Korine held her breath, hoping for reassurance.

"She hit a man up at Shady Acres. I'm afraid he's dead."

"Merciful Heaven!"

Korine's soft gasp was overridden by J.J.'s stern voice.

"I know you," he said. "Don't go blaming yourself."

Her stomach violently disagreed. "I'll be right there."

"Hold your horses," J.J. said. "Old Man Franklin is here right now, so she's not alone."

"Good," Korine said automatically, then registered who J.J. said was with Dora. "Franklin? The lawyer?"

"That's right."

That must mean they were going to charge Dora with something. Guilt shook Korine right down to her bones. She'd failed her mother-in-law. All she'd done to protect her from something like this was to hide Dora's keys and make her promise not to drive.

As if promises were reliable memory aids.

Korine had no idea how the woman had found the keys so carefully hidden away, but she had. Just as confounding was the fact that Korine had slept through both the sound of Dora's car and J.J.'s attempts to reach her.

"Do I need to have Chaz come home?"

"I don't think so. Franklin knows what he's doing. No need to pull your son out of whatever case he's working on just yet."

"You said Dora's fine. Physically or mentally?"

"If it's any comfort, she doesn't seem to grasp what happened," J.J. said. His earlier implacable tone of voice had relented. "You did try."

"Not hard enough. Who did she hit?"

"Ironically enough, the man she says she went up there to meet, Olan Taggart."

Korine felt the phone slip against the damp of her palm. She tightened her grip and closed her eyes. In the darkness of her mind, she watched an instant replay of Hazel Jurik chasing poor Mr. Taggart across the grounds.

Korine frowned. Opening her eyes, she checked her watch. "But I just saw him!"

J.J.'s voice softened. "I know. It's always harder to hear that someone's dead if you've seen him recently."

"No, I mean yesterday, when Janey and Amilou and I were out there. He was playing his bagpipes."

"Janey told me. This is going to tear her up."

"Janey will be fine. She's tougher than you think." Korine didn't bother to hide the bitterness from her tone. "I, on the other hand, have just found out that my mother-in-law is a pretty solid suspect in a case of vehicular manslaughter."

"Korine…."

She heard the apology in his voice. He wasn't ignoring Korine. J.J.'s need to protect Janey was so keen that he sometimes couldn't see how strong his wife really was. Or how shaken other people could be.

"Surely someone saw what happened," Korine said. "Maybe it's not Dora's fault at all."

The apologetic note was gone. "I do know what I'm doing, remember? I know all about Dora's illness, and I'll be careful with her. Come down to the police station. We'll talk more once you get here."

Korine nodded, then spoke out loud when she realized that J.J. couldn't hear her head rattling around on her shoulders. "Thank you for calling Cal. I don't think I could do that right now."

"It's my responsibility."

J.J.'s strained voice scraped Korine's frayed nerves. She pressed a hand to the back of her neck. Rope-like cords threaded their way under the skin all the way up into her hairline. The months of caring for her mother-in-law—

without stepping on her way-too-sensitive toes—had taken its toll.

Once again overcome by the sheer weight of her emotions, Korine closed her eyes and said, "I'll be there shortly." She replaced the receiver with exaggerated care. She had intended to have it out with Cal soon, but not like this.

Surely not like this.

Korine's hand fell to her side, the imprint from her sweaty palm clearly visible on the black plastic receiver.

She opened the door to the garage and walked quickly back over the paving stones. The ginger stray which had taken to hanging around Korine's place during the last week poked his head out from under the fothergillas by the porch steps. The cat took in Korine's expression and vanished.

Korine stepped onto the back porch and pulled a towel off the hook by the door. Quickly rubbing the worst of the dirt from the soles of her feet, she opened the door and went into the warm kitchen. The Felix the Cat clock on the wall above the sink said ten-thirty. She'd go put some sheets out for Cal; he could make his own bed when he arrived.

Pushing open the swinging door from the kitchen to the front hall, she grabbed her mother-in-law's faded pink overnight bag out of the downstairs closet, then went up to the older woman's bathroom. It smelled faintly of the Estée Lauder talc Dora liberally patted on every morning. Korine stepped onto the white tile floor and grabbed Dora's blue toothbrush and the tube of Crest out of the medicine cabinet.

Korine hoped she would be allowed to bring her mother-in-law home, but she wanted to be prepared for anything. She left the bathroom and went back into Dora's room. As she tried to decide whether to take the boar's-hair brush or the black comb from the dressing table, she admitted to herself that she was procrastinating. Shoving a change of clothes into the bag, Korine faced the possibility that the woman might never be coming home. She snapped the lock on the case. It wouldn't do to think about that now.

She went to her room and changed quickly into jeans and her favorite winter-weight shirt. She needed something comforting. Her son's faded college sweatshirt was as good as anything, right then.

She picked up the case and headed down the steps. When she got downstairs, she stumbled a little on the throw rug at the bottom. As she fell, she put out her hand to steady herself and connected with the solid oak of the front door. It gave under her hands, shutting firmly with a snap.

Frowning, Korine turned the knob. The door opened easily. She pushed it shut again and flipped the latch. Korine knew she had double-checked everything the night before. Dora must have opened the door that morning.

Korine never used to bother with locking the house at all. Even though it sometimes seemed like the big city was trying to reach out and swallow Pine Grove, she'd always felt safe enough. They'd begun locking the doors soon after Dora moved in, trying to assuage the woman's paranoia that someone was prowling through the house, moving her things.

Korine grabbed the latest Toni L. P. Kelner mystery off the kitchen counter. No telling how long she'd have to wait on J.J. to finish up his business. She would be grateful for the gentle humor to get her through those hours. She shut the back door and let the screen porch door slam behind her.

The stray cat shot out from under the bushes. Winding his thin body around her ankles, he darted off into the woods when they got to the garage.

Korine put the suitcase in the trunk and started the car. She cared deeply for the woman who had raised her husband, though it hadn't always been an easy relationship. Dora initially resented the fact that Charlie had left home and married a girl from someplace else. Among other things, it had messed up Dora's traditional Christmas celebration. Korine had talked Charlie into experiencing the joy of their first Christmas together with her family. Dora had never let her forget it. Shaking her head, Korine thought that if anyone had told her then that she'd be the one caring for Dora in her old age, she would have told them, in no uncertain terms, that they were crazy.

The two of them rubbed along far better together than anyone would have thought. Korine had done her best. Clearly, it had not been enough.

KORINE PULLED the Buick into a visitor's slot in front of the police station. Inside, she found Marlene taking a message.

"How is she?" Korine asked when the dispatch clerk got off the phone. She looked over Marlene's shoulder toward the office where she thought Dora would be.

"I'm fine, and so is Mrs. McFaile," Marlene replied.

Korine refocused. Marlene looked exhausted. "I'm sorry," she said, and meant it. "I'm a little preoccupied. How is Megan?"

Marlene came around and gave Korine a hug. "I shouldn't be touchy at a time like this. The baby's fine. Let me call J.J. and see if he's ready for you." She went back around the desk and hit the intercom button on her phone. "Korine's here. And the student affairs man from the university called with the information you asked for."

"Send Korine on back," J.J.'s gravely voice came through the line.

Korine could smell the peppermint before she got to J.J.'s office. He was trying to quit smoking and had taken to sucking on the candy instead of lighting up. From the irritated look on his face, it wasn't relieving his stress nearly as well as the nicotine would have done.

"Where is she?" Korine asked.

"Leon's with her, trying to find out what he can."

She frowned. "He's not harassing her, I hope."

"Old Man Franklin's with her, remember?"

"That's right."

Franklin wasn't Korine's favorite person, but he had the reputation of being a hard-nosed advocate for his clients. Perhaps Dora would listen to the attorney better than she listened to Korine.

"Can I see her?" she asked.

The stubble on J.J.'s neck showed what a hurry he'd been in when he left home that morning. Korine's heart pounded three times before he looked her in the eye. She thought she detected pity in his expression. "Not right now," he said. "I wish I could sit with you while you wait, but I've got this rash of burglaries going on. I'm so sorry you have to go through this."

Definitely pity.

Korine swallowed. "I understand."

J.J. picked up a piece of paper and waved it at her. "We

have a few leads, but Judge Carrolton's gone off some-where and I can't find anyone to grant a warrant."

Korine took the hint. "I'll wait up front."

"We'll get you when Leon's done with Mrs. McFaile." J.J. nodded once, then bent his head over his papers again.

Korine went back out to the hard plastic chair in front of Marlene's empty desk. A note on her keyboard informed the world that she'd gone to lunch.

Forty-five minutes later, Korine was still there. Nerves fraying even as she blindly turned the pages of what was surely a very good novel, Korine finally gave up.

The phone's shrill sound made her jump. After the second ring, Korine heard J.J. pick up in his office. With the low rumble of his voice in the background, Korine sank back in the chair to continue her morbid thoughts. Closing her book and putting it into her purse, she thought about Dora's delight the previous spring when the first robin arrived at the feeder. The woman used to be able to identify hundreds of birds by their sounds alone. No more.

Only recently, Dora had asked Korine what kind of bird was sitting in the driveway. It was one of the last chicka-dees of the season, stealing time for a quick snack before winging its way south for the winter. Dora hadn't even seemed bothered by the fact that she couldn't identify it.

J.J. left his office without a glance in Korine's direction. He headed down the hall and into the room where Dora was being questioned. Korine rose and looked expectantly after him. The door stayed closed. She began to count ceiling tiles to keep from going down and yanking open the door to see what was going on.

Leon came out of the room, closely followed by J.J. The

two men looked like a pair of bulldogs, neither one willing to give up and walk away from a fight. J.J. looked toward Korine and pursed his lips. He beckoned Leon into his office and shut the door. The sounds of anger coming from within weren't comforting.

Korine paced next to the chair. She couldn't have sat still if she'd wanted to.

Leon came out of J.J.'s office and slammed the door. Without looking in Korine's direction, he went back down the hall and into the room with Dora.

J.J. opened his door and came out. He turned first to look toward the room Leon had entered. Reaching up, he scratched his head, shrugged, and turned and walked toward Korine.

"You hanging in there?" J.J. didn't wait for her reply. "Something's going on I can't figure out. As you can probably tell, Leon and I have differing opinions on how to handle it."

She felt a surge of anger run through her when she noticed the difficulty J.J. had in meeting her eyes.

"Something about Dora?" she asked.

He passed a hand over his face, pushing his fingers against his eyebrows. His arm dropped to his side. "No. Unfortunately we have more than one situation here. We'll be done with her in a bit. I don't want to keep her here, and I don't think I have to."

"How long is a bit?" Korine asked.

"Not much longer. Franklin's about got Leon convinced he won't get anything more out of her this afternoon."

"Will you charge her?" Korine held her breath.

"We've got plenty of time to deal with that once the

magistrate looks things over and makes a decision. If I charge her now, I have to hold her. We don't have the facilities to take care of someone with her needs. She's not a threat to the community unless she gets back on the road again."

"She won't," Korine said with feeling.

"Jack Taggart's reaction may have something to do with which way we go with this, long term," J.J. cautioned her.

Korine's heart sank. Jack had gone to high school with Charlie. His disposition wasn't any better than Cal's. Had she really asked herself as she drove into town if things could get worse?

Leon came out of the room and started toward them. "Mrs. McFaile's doing all right, Mrs. McFaile," he said when he stopped next to J.J. "We won't be much longer."

"I'd like to see her," Korine said.

Leon sent an odd look to his boss, but J.J. didn't pick up whatever hint the younger man was tossing. He swallowed and looked at Korine. If he'd held a hat, he would have wrung it. "She doesn't want to see you. Franklin says since you don't hold power of attorney, we'll have to wait on her son to pick her up."

J.J.'s head whipped around to stare at Leon.

Leon shrugged, his what-can-I-do gesture not finding much play with Korine. He nodded sympathetically and turned to walk back down the hall.

"Was that what you were arguing about?" Korine asked.

"No," J.J. assured her. "As I said earlier, it's something else entirely. If I'd had a clue he was about to drop this bomb on you, I would have gone back there and talked to Mrs. McFaile first."

"So why are we all of a sudden relying on power of attorney?" Korine hadn't even tried to get her mother-in-law to sign a second one naming her. Dora had been too upset about signing the one Cal brought her several months earlier. He hadn't wanted to deal with the issues about his mother's care, but when it came to legal stuff, he was Johnny-on-the-spot.

"Franklin says we have to respect Cal's wishes."

Korine took a step back as if J.J. had struck her. "Cal's wishes? So he finally has wishes about his mother's care?" Her voice rose as her indignation got the better of her.

Behind Korine, something crashed through the entrance. She turned to see Cal standing there, one hand thrusting the door open. He glared at Korine and J.J. "What the hell have you done to my mother?" he demanded.

FOUR

J.J. STUDIED CAL. The man wore anger on his weathered face like a shield. What lay etched between the lines in those gaunt cheeks was something else again. J.J. was pretty sure that lonely trip on the road from Charlotte had spun worry into rage. If he had to guess again, he'd say that Cal's fury would eventually be self-directed. For now, it was far easier for the man to blame Korine.

"Cal," J.J. said, "I've got your mom in the back. I can tell her you're here, see if she's ready to see you."

Korine raised her palm to Cal, her eyes wide and angry. J.J. couldn't tell from her expression if she wanted to hit her brother-in-law or to ward him off.

"I want a lawyer in there with her," Cal said.

"She's got one," Korine snapped.

"Who'd you get? Chaz, on the phone?"

Cal had backed Korine up against the far wall. Her fists were balled up, although she'd dropped them rigidly to her sides. J.J. knew that Cal's treatment would have sent most women into hysterics. Korine, however, was so livid that tears were not an option. Even considering the contentious history between the two of them over Mrs. McFaile's care, J.J. couldn't fathom the depth of emotion he saw on their faces.

J.J. stepped between the pair. "I called someone local. Your mother was pretty agitated after the accident, so we've waited until now to talk with her." He faced Cal and waited for the information to sink in. As he watched, the man's expression downshifted.

"I want to see her now." Cal turned his head deliberately away from Korine.

"Leon," J.J. said to the officer, who had reappeared at the end of the hallway. "Tell Mrs. McFaile her son's here."

"Yes, sir," Leon said. He returned down the hall to the small room where he'd been talking with Mrs. McFaile and the attorney. He came out a moment later and beckoned Cal.

Korine started to move forward, but J.J. put out an arm and restrained her. "Let him go on in first."

She folded her arms across her chest.

"Take a deep breath," he said after Cal was out of earshot.

Korine's frame felt brittle under J.J.'s hands. For the first time he realized that she was more than a decade older than he was. Even more disturbing, she looked it. Her mouth was pinched right out to her ears, and there were frown lines he hadn't seen since her husband's funeral.

Korine saw his assessing glance and moved out of his grasp. She gathered her dignity together with an effort. "Don't pity me," she snapped. Her mouth trembled, easing the sharp lines. "Every time I think it can't get much worse…."

She turned away from him toward the wall. She put her hands over her mouth, as if reminding herself not to let go. Her shoulders told a different story, shaking with sobs.

J.J. turned Korine around. She clutched his uniform, and her head dropped forward. She cried, silently, into his shirt pocket. He stood there, feeling awkward as hell, with one arm around Korine's shaking shoulders.

"Well, well." An oily voice interrupted J.J.'s thoughts.

"Sylvester," J.J. said as Korine spun away and put one hand up to wipe her eyes. "So kind of you to stop in. Don't you know enough to stay put when you're an eyewitness?"

"I told Leon what I saw. Besides, I had some deliveries to make." Sylvester gave the station waiting area a once-over, as if assessing its move-in value.

J.J. got the uneasy feeling that Sylvester's deliveries had something to do with him. The man had been a fly buzzing around the police chief since he married Janey. Sylvester had been one of the more vocal townsfolk on the subject of mixed marriages. Despite the fact that his sallow skin and small, dark eyes were unattractive, he had a certain magnetism to him. He had put that to good use in his aborted campaign to run against J.J. for police chief a few years back. Fortunately for J.J., Sylvester was none too bright. Only after putting up a few signs around town announcing his candidacy had Sylvester learned the awful truth—the chief of police was an appointed position.

"You ready for me to take your statement?" J.J. asked the man.

"Like you're taking Korine's?"

"Oh, quit being stupid," Korine snapped. She blew her nose. For a minute, J.J. thought she'd throw the tissue in Sylvester's face, but she crammed it into the pocket of her jeans instead. "What are you doing here?" she said rudely.

"I'm an eyewitness," Sylvester said. He stood up straighter when he said it.

J.J. knew full well that despite his stated ambition of taking J.J.'s job, the man had never been inside a police station of any kind—unless he'd been too drunk to see straight. Sylvester's manner reminded him of Sarah Jane's.

Being this close to an incident not of his making was fueling old Sylvester Harris's self-importance no end. J.J. wasn't going to let that happen at Korine's expense. They'd been friends too long.

Korine leaned forward. "Where were you? Did you see how Dora came to hit that poor man?" Her questions flew fast and furious at the skinny man.

Sylvester held up his hand like a crossing guard. "Whoa, there, Korine," he said. "I don't know if that's any of your business. Unhealthy curiosity, if you ask me."

"Unhealthy curiosity?" Korine's voice rose.

J.J. let his hand settle on her shoulder and squeezed. "I'll call you later, Korine," he said.

She gave him a look as furious as the one she'd leveled at Cal earlier.

J.J. turned to Sylvester. "Leon's in with Mrs. McFaile and her son now, so if you'll go on down the hall to my office…. Second door on the left."

The suggestion to get out of there was phrased as politely as J.J. could make it, considering how he felt about Sylvester right then. He watched Korine carefully. Her face was as strained now as it had been earlier. Sylvester had interrupted just when Korine was starting to let go.

Korine lifted the small pink suitcase she'd brought in with her. "If Dora isn't being charged, she won't be needing this, will she?"

"No, she won't. In fact, it shouldn't be too much longer before she can leave."

"Will Cal bring her home?" Korine asked.

"I know it'll be difficult, but that's what Doc recommended for now. I think Cal will listen to reason once he sees she's all right. She needs both of you right now."

Korine nodded. She stood uneasily, canted under the weight of the piece of luggage. "Tell Cal I'll have a bed ready for him when he's done."

If that's not just like Korine, J.J. thought. *As angry as she is, she's all for turning down the guest room covers for him. She's amazing.* He checked behind him to see where Sylvester was before walking Korine out. The ratty heels of the sneering man's boots disappeared into J.J.'s office. *The idiot must have been hanging out to see what he could see.*

J.J. opened the front door for Korine. Letting the door close behind her, he picked up the extension on Marlene's desk. He punched in his home number. No answer. Briefly, he left a message asking Janey to call Korine when she got in. Trying not to worry about where his wife might be, he dragged his attention back into the police station.

His next call was to Amilou.

"I'm not buying anything," Amilou's soft drawl came over the wire.

"I'm not selling anything," J.J. replied. "Did you get my earlier message?"

"What message?" Amilou's voice sharpened with worry. "Janey's all right, isn't she?"

"Janey's fine, Korine's fine, but Mrs. McFaile took her car out and killed someone."

Amilou's breath whistled harshly over the phone. "Where's Korine?"

"She just left the station to go home. Cal's here with Mrs. McFaile."

"That's helpful of him." Amilou thought a moment. "I'll go on out to her house and see if she needs someone to hand her glassware to throw at him when he comes in the door." Some people called Amilou too frank for their tastes. J.J. liked her.

He hung up. At least he knew one of the women in his life was taken care of. Walking down the hall, J.J. stopped in the doorway of his office. "Get the hell out of my chair," he roared.

"Fine, fine," Sylvester said. "Just checking to see how it felt. Not very comfortable," he added, patting the worn oak arm of the chair as he slid out of J.J.'s place.

"The taxpayers don't pay me to sit in a cushy chair, they pay me to go out there and deal with troublemakers." He didn't add *like you,* but he might as well have.

Sylvester frowned and settled into the padded armchair on the visitor side of the desk. "I was standing in full view, you know," he said.

"So you saw everything that happened?"

"Damn straight. Taggart was over by the birdbath, like he always is, right before he…well, you know."

J.J. didn't. But he could find out. He nodded noncommittally.

"When Taggart saw Mrs. McFaile coming, he ran out toward her car. She stopped, rolled down the passenger-side window. They talked for maybe ten seconds, then he clutched his chest and went down. The old woman looked a little unhinged, you know what I mean? She floored the gas and took off."

J.J. motioned for Sylvester to continue.

"After she kethunked right on over Taggart, she looked even more confused—if that's possible. She stopped a few yards on because the car was going kinda bumpity, you know what I mean?"

The description made J.J.'s stomach feel like his intestines had been replaced by live eels. Reaching into his desk drawer for his last antacid, he waited for the man to go on.

"She got out. Took off crying and screaming when she saw what she'd done." Sylvester shifted in his seat. "She hightailed it right past me into the building. Maimie, at the desk, said Miz McFaile's first words were that she had to warn Taggart about something. *Somebody* should have warned him about *her*. She's just plain off her rocker." Sylvester's thin frame shivered dramatically.

J.J. watched the man's expression carefully. Like Sarah Jane, Sylvester tended to exaggerate.

"So," J.J. said, "the car was stopped when Taggart went under her wheels?"

"That's what I said, wasn't it? She looked straight at him, and when he fell, she peeled out like the devil was chasing her."

"Who else was around?" J.J. asked, making a note on his pad. His pencil lead broke, so he tugged open the metal desk drawer and pulled another one from the box he kept there.

"Sarah Jane was up in the parking lot next to her car. Rooting around in that big old purse of hers. Missed the whole thing. Screamed enough to make up for it, though, once the old lady ran practically right in front of her."

Sylvester wet his lips and then continued, "That new nurse of Doc James's, Colleen Taylor, was the first one to reach Taggart. She may be pretty, but she kept her head. Laid that man out straight and started thumping and pushing on his chest. Had on one of them short skirts they all wear. Quite interesting to watch her go to work." He caught J.J.'s stern look and changed what he'd been about to say next. "Didn't do any good though, did it? He's deader than a doornail."

"Where was Colleen when it happened?"

"Must have been out for a walk—or something." Sylvester winked. "She came racing out of the bushes by the side of the road when Taggart fell."

J.J. ignored the implication. Either he or Leon would talk with Colleen later to find out what she'd seen. She would probably be a better witness than Sylvester and Sarah Jane combined. "And no one else around?" he asked.

"That hour of the morning? Place was quiet as a church. Except for Sarah Jane. Do you know how loud she can scream?"

The two men exchanged a glance. J.J. realized that for the first time, he and Sylvester were sharing the same thought. Scared him to death.

"From what you say," J.J. said, "it sounds like a clear-cut case of accidental death."

Sylvester's eyes gleamed. The pink tip of his tongue flicked the corner of his mouth and disappeared. "Doc James is cuttin' on Taggart right now, isn't he. You ever been in on one of those autopsies?"

"Yes," J.J. replied. "It's not pretty." For a moment he considered telling Sylvester that the body had been sent to the state morgue for the autopsy, then figured he'd better not. If Sylvester ever tried to run him out of office again, the man's ignorance might come in handy.

J.J. typed up a summary of Sylvester's statements and had him sign it. Then he stood up and escorted him out to the door, if only to make certain he'd actually left the building. Back behind his desk, the slats on the back of the chair pressed against J.J.'s hips. Damn Sylvester for reminding him that the chair was uncomfortable.

The budget the mayor had given J.J. for the next year was tight. Too tight for a new chair, that was certain. The cruiser was badly in need of repair, if not outright replacement. No way J.J. was spending money on anything optional.

He rolled his tongue around in his mouth. Sure could use a cigarette. Hand on the bottom drawer before his mind could even register what he was reaching for, J.J. pried his hand off the metal pull and hauled open his middle drawer instead. The peppermints were running low. He'd have to stop by the grocery again soon.

Feeling virtuous, he reached over his notes and picked up the phone. First he called home, then tried Janey's cell phone again.

There was no answer either place.

The maddening beep of the unanswered ring nearly drove J.J. crazy with worry. Janey was never out of touch for this long. He hung up the phone thoughtfully and decided that most of the people he could call to ask if they'd seen Janey wouldn't understand why he felt it necessary to check up on his wife. A little over two years of marriage was too soon to be starting rumors. She was probably out shopping for her trip to Louisiana.

Walking down the hall, he found Cal, Franklin, and Leon arguing in the small room.

"She's coming home with me!" Cal said. The effort it took to keep his voice down so that he wouldn't disturb his mother, who seemed to be napping again in the corner of the room, only served to emphasize his anger.

"We're not keeping her," J.J. said evenly. "But for Mrs. McFaile's sake, she needs to stay here in town, preferably someplace where she can feel at home. I'm sure they've explained Doc's recommendation to you already. Take her to Korine's, which is familiar to her."

Cal's long face almost made J.J. laugh.

The lawyer nodded his approval. "Glad to know someone in this office is showing some signs of intelligence," Franklin said. Hefting the tattered leather briefcase he'd carried for the past thirty years, he took his leave. "Just let me know where you're staying," he said over his shoulder to Cal. He left, rigid back making it clear what he thought of his client's son.

J.J. turned to Cal. "I know you and Korine are at odds right now, but I hope you can figure out a way to get along, in order to do what's best for your mother."

Leon stopped at J.J.'s side before leaving. "Sorry," he said to both men before turning his attention to J.J. "You get that warrant yet?"

"Not yet. You have time to work on it some this afternoon? I still need to track down a few folks about Mrs. McFaile's accident. And talk to Jack when he gets into town."

"I'll go work on that warrant," the younger man said,

and he left, his large shoes making a racket as he walked down the hall.

J.J. turned back to Cal.

"I'd rather not go back to Korine's," Cal said. The man still had the mulish look on his face. He obviously thought his druthers won him the point, and he had no intention of being gracious about it.

J.J. wiped the smirk off Cal's face with his next words. "I don't blame you, after the way you two almost went at it in the hall like two alley cats. But think about it. If you sign your mother out, you're going to be the one responsible for her mental state. Any changes will upset her. Including, but not limited to, a change of location."

The men's eyes locked for a minute. Cal dropped his gaze first. "I understand what you're saying," he said.

"Korine's expecting you."

"Mom doesn't want to go back there." Cal made one last try.

"Your mother's upset. Understandably so. Once she gets home, she'll settle down some. If she doesn't, then you can revisit the idea of taking her someplace else. I don't, of course, have to tell you not to take her out of town? I'll need to talk with her again, I'm sure. But like I told Korine, some of that depends on the reaction of Mr. Taggart's son when he gets here."

Cal fiddled with the brown suede key ring he held in his hand. This time, he avoided J.J.'s gaze and, instead, concentrated on his mother's still-sleeping face.

"I suppose," he said finally, "you're going to tell me I should have listened to Korine?" For the first time, there was no fight in his words, only sorrow.

"I see no reason to tell you what you're already telling yourself," J.J. said.

Cal tilted his head and met J.J. face to face. "She's taken pretty good care of Mom," he said grudgingly. "But Korine should have told me things had gotten this bad."

J.J. pursed his lips before replying. Reminding Cal that Korine *had* tried to tell him would be a bad idea. The notion was tempting, though. Feeling nearly as virtuous as when he'd avoided the cigarette in his bottom drawer earlier, he said, "Your mother didn't get this bad until this morning. You knew as fast as Korine did. There was no way to anticipate that she would take the car."

Cal tightened his hand around the key ring. He turned and leaned over the sleeping woman. "Mom," he said softly, shaking her shoulder kindly. "Korine's expecting us home."

She lifted sleepy eyes to her son's face, and J.J. could see Cal's concerned expression reflected in the lenses of the woman's glasses. "You look nice," she said finally. "I don't live at home anymore," she said after Cal had helped her on with her lightweight wool jacket and gloves. "I live with her now. You have to lock the door." Her voice tone sharpened with worry on the last sentence.

"We'll keep you safe and sound, Mom," Cal said, ushering her out to his car, which was waiting in one of the guest spaces by the front door of the station.

J.J. watched through the glass door as Cal helped his mother up into the Ford SUV and buckled her seat belt. She laid a hand alongside his cheek. Cal pulled away and averted his face, stricken at whatever she had said. He shut the door slowly and stood staring at his mother through the tinted glass of the car window. The anger he'd earlier shown with Korine was gone, leaving only lines of pain carved into his face.

If he's worried about his mother, then it's about time, J.J. reminded himself before he could start to feel sorry for the man.

Cal shook his head as if to clear it and went around to get in the driver's side of the vehicle.

J.J. watched until the Ford turned onto the road to Korine's place. Then he went back down the hallway to his office. Leon had left a note that he would take care of the warrant and would execute it before he went off-shift. J.J. plucked his coat off the wooden coatrack in the corner behind the door and shrugged it on.

Once outside, he ran the engine on his cruiser a minute before putting the car into gear. There was a definite chill in the air. The clear sky above him starkly outlined the nearly bare limbs of the trees. Winter would arrive before they knew it. J.J. hit the heater button and pulled out onto the deserted road. He felt tired just thinking about Korine and Cal dealing with Mrs. McFaile—and with each other.

He shook off the feeling. Not his problem. Meeting with a grieving son was. Time to go to the Best Western on the highway and see if Jack Taggart had checked in. J.J. shoved his hat on his head and headed out to do his job.

FIVE

TWISTING HER WRIST SHARPLY, Korine tore the late-blooming dandelion out of the rose bed and tossed it onto a heap with the others. She'd badly neglected her weeding during the past season. Yanking them out wouldn't stop the weeds already sown during the last six months, but it felt indecently good to do violence to something that deserved it.

Was she responsible? With a slight catch in her breath, she wondered how Jack Taggart would feel. Would he blame her? Would he sue?

Korine leaned on her gloved hands and stared at the stone wall in front of her. She arched her back and stared upward, looking for answers, blind to the tendrils of ivy slipping delicately under the eaves. Shame bathed her as she tried to banish the thought of the potential pain and expense of a lawsuit. A man was dead. That was what mattered.

She shook her head and put one hand on her knee to rise. If she didn't stop worrying about things over which she had no control, she would go insane. She stood and pushed back the cuff of the leather gloves to check her watch. Two-thirty. J.J. had all but promised her that he would make Cal bring Dora home. They should have arrived by now. What was keeping them?

A vehicle pulled around the circle in the drive behind

the house. The late 1960s Chevy pickup belonged to Buster Klein.

"I heard," he said, hopping down from the cab. Kind brown eyes took in her disheveled state, and his bushy gray brows drew together. "What can I do?"

Korine raised her shoulders and let them drop. She couldn't even speak. There wasn't anything he could do to make this better.

He slammed the door to his truck. In a few quick strides, he was at her side. He pressed her damp face into the soft warmth of his flannel shirt. Buster was so tall that Korine's cheek fitted in right under his collarbone.

She could feel his chest rise and fall in slow waves of breath, comfort stealing over her with each beat of his heart. After a moment, she stepped away from his sanctuary. "Thank you," she said, slipping off her gardening gloves so that she could tuck a hand more comfortably around his waist.

"Why don't you come inside and make us some coffee," Buster said.

"Spoken like a true man," Korine laughed. "Give the little woman something to do in the kitchen, and she'll feel better. As it happens, there's some already in the pot."

She looked up into his kind face, and his anxious look eased when he saw that she was teasing him in return. The rush of gratitude for the friendship offered by this man warmed Korine. She couldn't pinpoint the exact time when she had allowed Charlie's memory to become just that, rather than a torch to be carried and brandished in the darkness to keep other people at bay. Her husband wouldn't have wanted her to be lonely after he passed away. It had taken her a long time to realize that.

"Let's go this way," Korine said, pulling Buster around to the front of the house. "I put some daffodils in that front bed, and I want to make sure the woodchuck hasn't gotten into them."

The bed was as she'd left it. No sign of damage yet, but she knew that the pest would make a try for it. She knew she ought to have someone come out and trap it, or shoot it, but she couldn't bring herself to make the call. She hoped entombing the bulbs under a sheet of chicken wire would do the trick this time.

Making a circuit of the house, she glanced up and thought she saw Dora's curtain move. She frowned. Surely Cal and Dora hadn't come in while she was around back.

They reached the corner of the house, and her cat shot out from under the southern magnolia. Rolling on her back in the gravel drive, Olmstead batted at Korine's hand when she bent down to pick her up. Righting herself, the calico ran off across the grass after a tumbling leaf. Korine glanced back up at Dora's room, but all she could see was the reflection of the trees swaying in the breeze.

A second car drove around the bend in the drive. From the expression on Amilou's face as she parked her battered Volvo by the rhododendrons, Korine knew she was in for a convention of concerned friends.

Coats hung neatly on hooks inside the back porch, the three of them entered the warmth of the kitchen. The large rug on the floor reflected the welcoming tones of the knotty pine cabinets. Against the far wall, a pair of porch rockers framed a small table above which hung an old cross-stitch sampler done by Korine's grandmother as a child. Since Dora moved in, Korine had found herself retreating more and more to the sanctuary this room provided her. Lately, nearly every evening after settling Dora down for the night, she would come down, fix herself a cup of tea, and relax behind the relative privacy that the closed door to the room provided.

Interesting that this was where Korine felt she could catch her breath from caring for her mother-in-law, considering that Dora was the one responsible for its current decor. The old cane-seated chairs and trestle table had gone to Knoxville with Korine's nephew Dennis and his wife, Katie Anne. Dora wanted her grandchildren to enjoy them. They'd wrestled the rockers in from the front porch to replace the other furniture, and now Korine couldn't imagine the room without them.

She crossed the kitchen and took out three blue earthenware mugs. The coffee that she'd put on to perk an hour before smelled sour, so she threw it out and began again.

Amilou straightened up from getting the milk out of the refrigerator and asked, "Where's Dora?"

"Back at the station with Cal," Korine replied. "J.J.'s trying to convince him to let her come back here." She sat down abruptly in the closest chair. The woven seat of the rocking chair groaned under the sudden weight. "He blames me."

Buster sat down beside her and took Korine's hand in his.

Amilou set the milk jug down on the counter with a snap. "No one can blame you for this!" she said. "If it's anyone's fault, it's Cal's. He has been spitefully unhelpful since Dora's gotten bad."

Korine brushed back a strand of her graying, curly hair. Her hand shook so that she dislodged the barrette she'd used to pin back the sides.

Buster retrieved it from the rag rug under the rockers and placed it on the small table. Reaching over, he took Korine's clammy hand and shook it gently. "It's no one's fault, Korine. It just is."

She closed her eyes. She was so tired that even though she felt like crying forever, no tears would come. Still, the darkness was welcome. Amilou came over and laid her hand on the tight spot between Korine's shoulder blades. The warmth of her friend's hand resting gently on her tense muscles gave Korine as much comfort as Buster's hug had earlier. Feeling lucky to have such good friends, she sighed as a little of the tension slipped away.

Amilou went to pour the coffee. Leaning back, Korine slowly rocked back and forth. Her hands relaxed, no longer talons gripping the smooth wooden arms of her rocker. After a moment, she opened her eyes.

"Feeling better?" Amilou asked.

"Yes," Korine replied, surprised to find that she felt better than she had in weeks. It was as if her friend's warm hands had siphoned enough of the worry that she could go on with things. She squeezed Amilou's fingers and favored Buster with a smile. "I'm so glad you two came over."

Amilou said, "J.J. called and asked me to swing by."

Friends are worth everything, thought Korine. "Well, I'll have to thank him, too."

Korine sniffed. The strong smell of smoke sent her flying across the room to check the coffee pot. It was fine. She frowned.

"I think it's coming from out here," Buster said, opening the back door and peering outside.

Korine shook her head. She'd completely forgotten. "The Tourneys said they'd be burning leaves this weekend. Must be pretty close to the fence line for it to smell all the way over here."

She picked up the pot and filled her mug. "Anyone else for a refill?"

A car door slammed, and moments later Cal stepped inside, closely followed by his mother. The elderly woman stood uncertainly in the doorway. Despite the fact that she had been living in Korine's house for six months, she hesitated coming over the threshold.

"Who's there?" Dora's sharp tone stabbed Korine. Her fear and anxiety were plain to all in the room.

Korine put the pot back and stepped forward. "It's just us," she said gently. "Korine, Amilou, and Buster from the hardware store. Cal brought you home."

Dora peered up into Korine's face. "Oh, it's you, is it, Missy? Burned something again, haven't you?"

Korine took this to mean that Dora recognized her. It had been the woman's stock comment every time she'd come to dinner at Korine and Charlie's during the early years of their marriage. "Not yet," she replied. She turned to face Cal and said, "I've put you in the room to the right of the stairs. I hope that's all right."

He didn't answer.

Korine stepped forward and put her arms around her mother-in-law. Surely those shoulder blades hadn't been that prominent the day before when Korine had bathed her.

She stepped back and studied Dora. The woman's posture was horrible. She looked like a question mark in clothing, all stick legs and curved back.

On the far side of Dora, Cal caught Korine's gaze with his own. As he spoke, a slight frown appeared between his eyes. "J.J. said I had to bring her back here," he said. "So I did."

Buster's jaw clenched, and Korine put one hand out and touched his arm. She shook her head in warning, then glanced at the door. He looked at her, his brown eyes warm and confused.

Korine reached out and took Buster's hand. "Thanks for coming. I'll call you later?"

His troubled look didn't ease up, but he did take a step toward the door. "Thank you. I want to hear how things went." His eyes cut to Cal's figure.

Cal looked up from helping Dora take off her coat and caught them holding hands. He turned to give Buster a careful examination.

The naked pain in Cal's eyes angered Korine. Obviously he felt that nearly a decade of mourning his brother was not enough. And this from a man who had left his first wife and children to move in with another woman.

Cal turned away and ushered his mother over to one of the rockers. His finger—brown, weathered, and slightly stained around the nails—traced a heart on Dora's powdered cheek. The gesture, a family tradition, shredded Korine's anger. No matter that she and Cal had never gotten along, despite all of her best efforts. No matter that she stood there holding the hand of another man. Charlie had done that to her cheek every morning before he left for work. For a moment, the ache of his loss was back.

Buster put his hand on the small of her back. Korine let out her breath. She hadn't even realized that she'd been holding it. The expression on his face was knowing, as though he'd read her mind.

"You sure you want me to go?" he asked softly.

Korine stretched up and brushed her lips against his cheek. "I'll be fine."

After one hard look at her, which seemed to reassure him that she would indeed be all right, Buster let himself out the back door.

Korine busied herself doctoring mugs of coffee for Cal and Dora. When she turned back, Amilou and Cal were laughing at something. Dora was looking at the ceiling, a fearful expression on her face.

"It's an old house," Korine gently reminded Dora.

The woman stared at her. Her blue eyes, sharper than usual, flew to inspect the closed kitchen door when a board sighed in the hallway. Dora's gaze sought Korine's again, then dismissed her with contempt.

Korine couldn't figure it out. The day before had gone so well. They'd had dinner and conversed almost like Dora was whole again. What had happened in the old woman's brain, overnight, to make her wake up and drive off in a car she hadn't shown the slightest interest in for over a month?

Cal reached over and took the mugs Korine offered him. He handed one to his mother and raised the other one to his lips. After a long sip, he put his down with a heartfelt sigh. Korine could see his shoulders relax like her own had under Amilou's hand.

"I could maybe put a few nails in your floorboards if you need me to while I'm here," he said. Cal's blue eyes, so like his mother's, met Korine's own gaze squarely. "Looks like I'd better stay a day or two to talk some things out."

Korine's shoulders tensed again. He hadn't apologized for how he overreacted at the police station, and now he wanted to talk? She caught an unfamiliar gleam in Cal's eyes. Could this be an olive branch? As difficult as it might seem with Olan Taggart lying cold, there might be a silver lining to the accident after all.

"I'm glad you're staying," Korine said. A little white lie never hurt anything. She stood up. "I'd better get a few things out for you upstairs."

"I'll take care of it," Amilou said. "Dora, do you want to walk up with me?"

Dora looked up at Amilou. "Fine, might as well, these two don't want me." With this unfair edict, she got up and followed Amilou through the swinging door to the hall. The sound of their footsteps on the wooden treads of the staircase echoed in the hallway. There was a pause, then a cry from Dora. Korine and Cal stood up at the same time and jostled one another in the doorway as they responded to the keening noise.

Upstairs, Dora clung to Amilou in the hallway outside her door. "You heard them," she hissed at Korine. "They've been in here again."

"It was just me," Korine said. "I had to get your things to pack in your suitcase."

Cal pushed past the group of women and shoved the door wide open. Dora's room lay in shadow. He flicked the light switch. No lights came on.

"Must have tripped a breaker," he said. "I'll go down and check it. Where's your breaker box?"

"Basement, to the right of the bottom of the steps." Korine put her arms around Dora. She was so frail, so thin. "Come on. We'll go into my room," she suggested.

In answer, Dora turned and moved back toward the steps. Stumbling a little, she allowed Korine to take one arm and redirect her into Korine's room. For all the fuss she'd made earlier, Dora seemed content enough now to lean on her daughter-in-law. After a moment, she allowed Korine to tuck her into the armchair by the window.

Amilou had gone down to the kitchen to fix a cup of hot sweet tea, which, when she returned and presented to Dora, seemed to calm her more than Korine's comforting arms had done.

"Short sips," Korine instructed as Dora raised the cup to her lips.

"I'm still here, you know," Dora said sharply. "I'm not crazy."

Taken aback by the venom in the woman's voice, Korine drew away sharply, dislodging a pressed-glass dish from the bedside table with her elbow. The dish hit the floor on one corner, shattering. Surrounded by the broken glass, Korine stared at her mother-in-law. As she looked into those overly bright blue eyes, she felt she could see through them to forever. Dora was right, she was still there. She was just so far away inside. Korine's hand stretched out, palm up, toward the woman. After a brief hesitation, Dora stretched out her own small hand and placed it in Korine's open palm.

"What is it?" Cal's voice came down the hallway. His rangy frame filled the doorway.

Korine bent to pick up a shard of glass. "I dropped this."

He came over and gathered up the rest of the sharp

pieces of glass from the wool hooked rug by the bed. "The breaker was tripped for Mom's room. It's fine now," he said, emptying his hand into the wastebasket.

As Cal stood, Dora cried out again. Bracing herself, Korine turned to see what had upset the woman this time. Dora scrambled out of the chair to pluck a tissue from the box next to the bed and press it to Cal's palm. Red showed through. He'd cut himself.

Fussing over her son, Dora took Cal into Korine's bathroom. Korine shook her head. She would never understand the way Dora's mind worked. Totally off one minute, then jumping back into herself the next. Cal had always been Dora's favorite.

Leaving the two of them, Korine went into Dora's room to see if anything else was out of place. Cal had put his mother's suitcase next to the bed. As he'd said, the lights worked fine now. Korine's gaze wandered the room, taking note of the spilled powder on the cherry dresser, and the books toppled from their perch on the chintz-covered footstool in front of the chair by the window. It was messier than she remembered, but not abnormally so. She had to admit to herself that she had been too upset to really pay attention to the state of the room earlier.

The acrid smell of smoke they'd noticed earlier downstairs was stronger in this room. Frowning, Korine followed the scent into the bathroom. There was a trace of ash on the floor by the toilet. Bending down, she used a piece of toilet tissue to sweep it up. Even as upset as she had been, surely she would have noticed the ashes if they had been there when she was packing for Dora earlier.

Opening the toilet to drop the tissue in, Korine was confronted with the sight of a soggy scrap of ash-laced paper. On the small portion left unburned, Korine recognized her handwriting.

She glanced over her shoulder at the sound of voices coming down the hall. Could Dora be right about people prowling the house? Korine shook her head to clear it. She was getting as paranoid as her mother-in-law. She closed the lid silently and stood. On the back of the toilet was a paper book of matches. She slipped them into her pocket; Dora had lit her last match.

Dora's voice filtered through the open door from the hall. She was apparently giving Cal the home tour. As Korine passed them, they seemed happy enough. Dora had led her son into her room and was touching things, putting them away. If they were lucky it wouldn't take too long to find them all again. Sticking her head in the door, Korine told them she was going downstairs to see about supper.

Cradling her coffee mug, Amilou was sitting in one of the chairs. Korine popped her mug into the microwave and sat down again.

"Is it always like this?" Amilou asked.

"Most days," Korine answered shortly. Then she giggled. "I mean, Dora hasn't actually killed anyone before, but…."

Amilou started laughing too. Appalled, Korine put both her hands over her mouth but couldn't stop shaking with laughter. The two women were giggling still when Cal walked into the room.

"You think this is funny?" he asked.

Korine looked up, sobering. "We're not laughing at Dora," she reassured Cal. She looked at Amilou, who began to smile broadly. "Oh, stop that," Korine told her friend, but she smiled back.

"I guess you've got to be able to find something to laugh at in all this," Cal said, "or it quickly becomes intolerable."

Was it Korine's imagination, or had Cal's sour face lightened?

"I know what you mean," he continued. "Kathleen used to do a fair job of putting a happy face on things."

Standing, Korine impulsively put a hand on Cal's arm. "I'd nearly forgotten about Kathleen, Cal. I'm sorry." His second wife had died some years before Charlie, during what Korine called Cal's decade of denial. After he'd left his first wife, he refused to speak to his brother. Sadly, the second marriage had been short-lived. He'd thrown his first family away for a relationship with the fun-loving Kathleen, then lost her to cancer in less than a year.

Korine removed her hand. She walked over to the refrigerator. Selecting things for a salad, she asked Cal if he'd mind a rabbit-food meal.

He didn't even crack a smile. "You have a hammer somewhere?" he asked. He was serious about fixing some of the loose floorboards upstairs.

Leaving Amilou to tear the lettuce, Korine led Cal out to the garage. She opened the doors to Charlie's tool cabinet. Cobwebs adorned the interior. Cal smoothed some of the worst of it out of the way, then reached in and grabbed the hammer off the pegboard. There wasn't a huge amount of rust on it, but the look Cal gave Korine said clearly enough what he thought about the state of the tools.

Korine couldn't care less what Cal thought of her housekeeping skills. If he could fix the floor and keep Dora happy, she'd *give* him the damn tools and buy new. With that unlikely thought, she smiled.

"I'm going to take Mom home with me as soon as J.J. lets me," Cal said.

"What?" Korine's smile faded.

"She's my mother." Cal seemed to think he'd said it all. He turned and walked out of the garage, closely trailed by a furious Korine.

"HE SAID THAT to you?" Amilou asked when Korine sat back down again.

"He's taking Dora back with him to Charlotte. No 'thank you very much for taking care of Mom for me while I was ignoring her problems.' No 'what do you think we should do with Mom.' Just 'I'm taking Mom back home with me.'"

"So he's short on manners. He's handy." Amilou glanced speculatively toward the stairs. "You don't suppose he's handy enough to come fix that kitchen faucet of mine, do you?"

"Amilou!" protested Korine. Amilou's standard joke lately was that she wouldn't date anyone who couldn't fix the leaky faucet in her kitchen first.

The irregular pounding on the floor overhead started an answering throbbing in Korine's head. "It doesn't matter how handy he is," she said. "How can you imagine going out with anyone like him?"

"I don't think I'll consider that loaded question right now, thank you. But you know—" Amilou's voice got lower—"he's not a bad looking sort of man, is he? Not enough to make up for that personality, though. Too bad."

Korine didn't dignify that with a response, instead gathering up the mugs and putting them into the dishwasher.

Amilou stood and picked up her purse. Pausing at the

door, she said, "Listen, I know this is the last thing on your mind right now, but I talked with Janey earlier. We sketched out some preliminary plans for Shady Acres. She leaves in the morning, remember?"

"I'd nearly forgotten she was going!"

"Understandably enough," Amilou said. "Maybe you and I can meet tomorrow and see what tweaking needs to be done. I know we promised Hazel we'd get back to her on Monday, but we all have more important things on our minds right now than landscaping plans. That said, it might be good to get your mind off this while Cal is in town. Call me and let me know if you're up to it."

"First thing in the morning." Korine shut the door behind Amilou, then hesitated, one hand on the smooth brass of the door handle. She lifted her hand and touched the lock on the door. The *why* of Dora's drive to Shady Acres continued to bother Korine. She shook her head. One flip of the wrist, and the door was locked. The toggle lock wouldn't keep Dora in, but it made Korine feel better anyway.

She turned to go upstairs. Hearing the whisper of voices overhead, she sighed. As with so many things connected to living with Dora these days, Korine's own disquiet didn't have to make sense. It just was.

SIX

J.J. TURNED IN TO the parking lot of the Best Western by the river. There were a lot of high-end vehicles in the lot. He was glad to see that the tourists had come chasing the autumn mountain color this year, same as last. Jack was lucky he'd gotten a room. J.J. pocketed his cell phone and walked across the parking lot. He stopped in front of number 59 and knocked.

"Minute," a deep voice called out from within.

Less than a minute later, the door opened. Even if the short, wiry man hadn't been holding his father's tartan plaid kilt, J.J. would have recognized Jack Taggart. Jack's face, like his father's, was built for laughter, although there was precious little of it there at the moment. Looking closer, J.J. could see that the lines etched into Jack's face were longstanding. Perhaps he wasn't as much like his father as J.J. had first thought.

"Sorry. You caught me going down memory lane," Jack said. He stood back. "Come on in."

J.J. took the two cement steps up into the hotel room from the porch. Jack closed the door behind him. Reruns of "Gilligan's Island" played on the TV set, without the sound. Jack's suitcase, a cheap faded roller bag, gaped open on the dresser. The clothes inside were faded shades of brown, neatly folded. Even the hotel linens looked beige. The colorful tartan Jack held fairly shouted "look at me" in that room.

One of the double beds was rumpled, the coverlet thrown back in a halfhearted attempt to disguise the fact that someone had been lying on it. The other one was covered with an odd assortment of items. Olan Taggart's disassembled bagpipe was scattered in pieces in the middle. A thin discount-store scrapbook rested on the pillow, pages open at a black-and-white wedding photo. Dumped in a pile at the foot of the bed were a few ill-matched items of clothing. So little left to describe a life.

J.J. raised his head and looked at Jack. The man looked back. Jack put his hand on his stomach as it made a rumbling sound. "Sorry," he said. "Didn't stop for lunch on the way here."

Making a quick decision, J.J. said, "You want to get a cup of coffee?"

"That sounds good." Jack folded the tartan and placed it on the bed next to the bagpipes.

The men walked silently side by side to the hotel lobby. Nodding at the hotel clerk as he passed by, J.J. led the way into the coffee shop. The red upholstery of the booths reminded him of the tartan so carefully folded on the bed across the way.

The pair settled into their seats, J.J. on the side facing the door. There were a few people sitting in the booths at the back, but no familiar faces. The waitress came over and took their orders, decaf coffee for J.J. and the BLT special for Jack.

"I'm sorry for your loss," J.J. began formally.

The lines cutting around Jack's mouth tightened. He looked J.J. square in the eye. "I lost my father years ago. Once I had to haul him into court and prove his incompetence, he cut me off. I had to take Dad and his most treasured possessions to Shady Acres. Cleared the rest out of the house and sold it. Haven't seen him much since then."

J.J. stayed quiet, not at all sure how to react. First Cal and now Jack. This was the second man in as many hours that J.J. had confronted who seemed composed of pure anger.

Jack grimaced. "Sounds bad, I know. Not my choice. I'd come up for those support group meetings, and Dad would go off his rocker when he saw me. I couldn't take it anymore. Talked to Hazel and asked her if we could do the care-plan conferences by phone. I wrote the checks and mailed them. I would have moved him down to the city with me, but she convinced me that keeping him here was better for him."

"It must have been hard on you, not seeing your father like that," J.J. said.

"Not seeing him was hard. But, in a way, he kind of did me a favor." Jack laughed bitterly at J.J.'s startled reaction. "You really have no idea, do you? Watching the man who taught me how to pitch, who embarrassed the hell out of me all through adolescence, and who stood up for me at my wedding as my best man, just fade away. It's like he was walking down a long hall to nowhere, without even looking back. He left, and there's this crazy old man inside his body."

Jack's bitterness was making J.J. even more uncomfortable. He wished now that he hadn't brought the man to the coffee shop.

"...and then there was the expense," Jack was saying.

J.J. tuned back in. "I thought Medicare paid for nursing home costs."

Jack laughed out loud. "Aren't you funny," he said bitterly. "Not even close. I sent a $1500 check every month for the privilege of having my father piss in the marble halls of Shady Acres. And that doesn't count the doctor bills."

"So for over two years you've—"

"Mortgaged my home, paid out half of my retirement money, and lost my father all at the same time."

"Your dad had life insurance, right?" J.J. asked.

"Yeah. According to the agent down at Tri-Mutual, I'll get the money back I paid for his care, with interest. His policy had a double payout if he died accidentally."

J.J.'s eyebrows rose. "Is that so," he said neutrally.

"I've been thinking about what you asked me last night," Jack said, switching the subject. "I don't want to press charges against either Mrs. McFaile or her family. I asked around, and it sounds like Korine's been trying to do the right thing by her mother-in-law." He stared at his plate for a minute, his lips pressed firmly together. Then he looked up. "Doesn't mean I don't wish she hadn't done a better job of taking away that woman's keys."

Their glances held for a minute, long enough for J.J. to measure and fully comprehend that anger would probably always outweigh the pain of grief in this man's mind. His words sounded noble enough, but the fine print on his brow said that he was mad as hell about the way his father had died. Jack broke eye contact and signaled the waitress for the check.

"I'll walk you back," J.J. said.

Jack threw his napkin on the table and rose. "Sure."

On the way back, Jack said, "I talked with Reverend Richardson. I guess I'd better ask when we can plan on holding the service."

"If you want a full-fledged funeral," J.J. said, "then I'd hold off a bit. The state may not release the body for a few days."

Jack reached his right hand into his pocket and started fiddling with his change. "Let me know as soon as the funeral home can pick him up." He paused and got an odd expression on his face. Looking sideways at the police chief, he smiled, giving J.J. a glimpse of the man he was before his father's illness. "Makes it seem like we're taking him on a vacation, doesn't it? Pick him up." Jack's face crumpled. He wiped his eyes and reached into his shirt pocket and pulled out his room keycard. Sniffing, he opened the door and they went inside.

The slanting late afternoon rays of the sun picked out the bright red of the kilt on the bed. Jack looked at it and swallowed hard. "Just let me know, okay?" he said, head still averted.

"I'll keep you up to date as best I can." J.J. settled his hat on his head and let himself out the door.

Climbing back into his car, he wondered if the insurance really would pay off all of Taggart's bills. J.J. stared at the door to room 59 and picked up his phone. Using the tip of one finger, he traced the numbers from his notebook for Colleen's apartment. He called. No answer. He'd swing by on the way home, just in case. She was the only witness he hadn't yet interviewed.

J.J. HAD ASKED EVERYONE he could think of about Colleen. No one would admit to seeing her since that morning. He sat in his cruiser outside her apartment, weighing his final options for finding the woman, when she parked her Mustang convertible in front of her steps about five o'clock. She got out of the car and fumbled her purse to her shoulder. She was crying.

He stepped out of his cruiser and caught up to her before she got inside. "I've been trying to find you all day."

She put her head down as she fished in her purse for a tissue. "I went and got that medicine Doc ordered for Mrs. McFaile. By the time I got it filled and got back to Shady Acres, you were gone." She fit her key in the lock. She still hadn't met J.J.'s eyes.

"Didn't Leon tell you I wanted to talk with you?" J.J. knew he had. He wasn't going to cut Colleen any slack. She had to understand how important this was.

"Yes," she whispered to the sisal mat at her feet.

"Shall we go in out of the wind?" J.J. suggested, indicating the half-open door.

She stepped inside. J.J. followed her and shut the door behind him. Shrugging off his jacket, he looked for a logical place to put it. Nearly every available surface was covered with books. Medical texts, for the most part.

Colleen took J.J.'s coat and draped it over the back of a gray card-table chair. Pulling a stack of basic science books off the only upholstered piece in the room, she indicated he could sit in the La-Z-Boy. The broken-down seat yawned under J.J. like a bottomless pit. He'd be lucky if he ever stood again. The girl tossed her own coat on top of the kitchen counter and folded herself into a compact position on the floor.

He tried to get comfortable. "Why don't you start by telling me why I had to look all over town for you."

"I freaked out. Here I am, studying to get into med school—maybe the biggest mistake of my life—and the first dead person I see sends me out of control." Colleen wiped her palms on her thighs. "After I ran that errand for Doc, I got in my car and drove to Asheville. There's this place I like to go when I'm upset. Took me the better part of the day to settle down enough that I could face coming back."

J.J. assessed the young woman. She looked pretty calm to him. Then he noticed that she held a small black river rock in her left hand, turning it over and over again.

He leaned forward and rested his forearms on his knees. "You ought to be proud of the fact that you were able to keep your head enough to pull the man out and try to save him. Not many could have done that much."

Colleen's eyes widened. Then she ducked her head. Her fair, straight hair fell over her face, closing her off from J.J.'s view. "Thanks," she said. The stone still turned in her hand, but more slowly. She looked up, smoothing her hair back behind her ear with her free hand. "Mrs. McFaile came in the driveway. I knew she wasn't supposed to be driving. I started up the hill so I could call her daughter-in-law. Then, when I saw Mr. Taggart heading toward her, it was like I knew what was going to happen. I never got to the phone. I ran to him instead."

J.J. regarded the woman. "Why did you run?"

"What kind of question is that?" Colleen asked, startled. "She ran over that man."

"Tell me exactly what you saw."

"I don't understand." Her lips looked scarlet against the pallor of her skin.

"Tell me exactly what you saw," he repeated. "Who was there. Where Mrs. McFaile was driving. Where Mr. Taggart was when her car struck him."

"Mrs. McFaile drove up the driveway. Mr. Taggart came out from behind the bushes along the driveway going up toward the building. Mrs. McFaile slowed down, then her car went behind the bushes. When she came out from the other side, Mr. Taggart was under her wheels."

Obviously he was going to have to go back out to the place and do some careful looking around. Even though Colleen and Sylvester had been standing in wildly divergent locations, the only thing even close to the same about their stories was the damn shrubbery. Either someone was lying, or there were a lot of bushes placed in strategic positions. He sighed and asked, "Did you see Mrs. McFaile strike Mr. Taggart?"

"Not actually hit him, no. I got there as soon as I could." Colleen stopped. Her knuckles showed white as she gripped the stone in her hand. Her head dropped forward, hair swinging down to obscure her averted face.

"You tried," J.J. said gently.

Colleen moved her head once, more a sigh than a nod. "For all the good it did him," she said bitterly.

J.J. changed the subject. "What were you doing out at Shady Acres that early on a Saturday?"

"I do temp work on the weekends. Some nights too. Saving up for tuition for med school—if I get in. I had Mrs. Grant out in her wheelchair. She likes to go early to hear the birds."

"So what did you do with Mrs. Grant after the accident?"

Colleen glared at J.J. "I left her sitting there in her wheelchair. One of the staff took her in while I was working on Mr. Taggart." The stone hit the floor with a muffled thud. She massaged the hand which had held the stone, wringing it down to the tips of her fingers and starting over again.

Why was she so nervous? Was it just losing someone she'd worked on? He didn't know of any immediate tie-in between the young woman and the old man. In fact, no one he'd talked with about Colleen knew much other than the obvious. Leon was the only one J.J. had talked to so far who knew her well at all, and he didn't much like her. Something to think on.

"You told me about Mrs. McFaile and Mr. Taggart. Who else was out that morning?"

For the first time since she'd come home, Colleen stopped fidgeting. "Well," she said, holding up a hand to tick off fingers. "There was me. Mrs. Grant in her wheelchair. Somebody on the front steps. I suppose a couple of people in the parking lot—it was close to change of shift."

"You were walking down by the driveway?"

"On it, until Mrs. McFaile came in. We cleared out of the way pretty fast then."

"And no one else was out walking?"

Colleen hesitated, wrinkling her nose. "No, we were the only ones out at that hour of the morning."

"Was Mrs. McFaile the only person you saw drive in?"

"Well, like I said, it was change of shift. A couple of the nurses, the administrator, and the lady who runs the kitchen all came up earlier. No one after. They couldn't have gotten in, anyway."

J.J. wrote everything down and asked, "You moved here about six months ago, didn't you?"

"More like five, but yeah, I've been here a while."

He didn't respond. *A while* meant something different in Pine Grove than in the city. "Move here from
Asheville?"

Colleen searched his face before answering. Personal
questions seemed to bother her. "Charlotte. I graduated
from nursing school there. Worked a while and decided I
wanted a quieter place to live."

"But you'll go leave Pine Grove if you get into med
school?"

She grimaced. "Yes, I'll go to Chapel Hill if I make it
in. If I even apply after all this." She reached over to the
textbook in front of her and flipped it shut with a thud.

J.J. glanced down at the pad of paper in front of him.
"If you've been at Shady Acres doing this temp work with
the patients, you must be well versed in dementia?"

"As much as anyone, I guess." Colleen reached down
and took the stone in her hand again.

J.J. longed to reach out and take it away from her to get
her to concentrate on the matter at hand. "Mrs. McFaile has
been very paranoid recently," he said. "Keeps complaining
that people are in her house, moving things around. I find it
fascinating that she and Taggart shared this same delusion."

"I think that's pretty common," she said. She stood up,
smoothing her skirt down. "Would you like something to
drink? I think, after today, I'm entitled to a beer."

"No thanks," J.J. said, struggling to haul himself up
from the depths of the chair. "Will you come in to the station tomorrow morning to talk with me further?"

"What about?" Colleen's voice broke. She looked suspiciously like she was going to start crying again.

"Your memory may come up with something between now and tomorrow."

Her face cleared. "I'll stop by."

"Good, I'll see you tomorrow then." J.J. let himself out of the apartment and walked down the short flight of concrete steps to his car. His watch said nearly six, so he decided to go on home. Plenty of time to finish his reports after dinner. Sometimes talking things over with Janey produced a fresh perspective. He hoped this was one of those times.

SEVEN

An hour later, J.J. stood in front of the open refrigerator, trying to see why Janey felt the need to drive all the way to the Super Wal-Mart in Pickles to get something for dinner. He would have understood it if she'd said she was going over to Korine's to see how her friend was, under the circumstances. When he'd talked to Janey earlier that afternoon, he'd told her about Taggart. As he'd expected, the news had upset her, but her focus was more on Korine's problems than her own hopes for reconciliation with her grandmother.

He glanced again at the yellow scrap of paper she'd left on the kitchen table. It didn't tell him any more than it had when he'd walked into the house and found it pinned down on one corner by the honey jar. He shut the door to the fridge, plunked the package of sliced turkey onto the counter, pulled two pieces of bread out of the wrapper, then commenced making his supper.

Halfway through the sandwich, J.J. heard the sound of Janey's car as it pulled into the drive. He got up and went outside to meet her. The snap of the storm door hitting the jamb was more forceful than he intended. The cold settled into his knee as he walked down the steps to the garage. Ignoring it, he opened his wife's car door for her.

"Sorry," Janey said as she got out.

She was wearing the jeans and sneakers she'd worn that morning, and she had added one of J.J.'s rag-wool sweaters over her T-shirt. He didn't care what she had on. With her features painted with shades of gray by the dusk, she looked like an old picture he'd once seen of Lena Horne. Beautiful.

"I got your note," J.J. said. He headed around to the trunk to help her carry the groceries. Handling three plastic sacks per hand, he followed Janey to the back door. "What's with all the food?" he asked.

"I'm stocking up for you, remember? I'm leaving in the morning for Memaw's."

Up until now, Memaw had indicated that hell would freeze over—although she would never, ever use such foul language to describe her feelings—before she visited Janey's home while J.J. was there. He didn't take it personally, because Memaw had made the same stipulation when Janey was married to Raynell.

In fact, in all the time that Janey had lived in Pine Grove, the woman who had raised her had never even been for a visit. After divorcing Raynell, Janey had gone home to Louisiana every few months or so to check on her grandmother. But since her marriage to J.J., she had been only once.

It hadn't gone well.

Yet, when Memaw had called on Wednesday and asked her to come home, Janey didn't hesitate. Like Korine putting Cal up, these women did the right thing. Janey might resent how her grandmother felt about her marriage, but Memaw was family.

J.J. knew how that went. His family hadn't been too

keen on their marriage either. They'd come to the wedding, but they hadn't been very communicative since then. He'd still stand by them if they called for help.

Thinking about Memaw's attitude made him think about Sylvester. Several of the good townsfolk of Pine Grove felt the same way Memaw did about J.J.'s marriage to a woman of color. "Should have stuck with your own kind," was one of the nicer things he'd heard from those who disapproved. He'd expected it from people like Sylvester. J.J. was ashamed to admit that it had stung harder coming from Janey's kin.

"Your grandmother give you a reason she wants you home yet?" he asked.

"She still won't say." Janey put the jug of milk into the refrigerator, then turned to face her husband. She stood, looking down at the linoleum between them, hands hugging her elbows.

"And you're scared?" J.J. put his arms around her.

"Yeah."

Silence stretched between them. For the first time that he could remember with Janey, he felt uncomfortable. "You want me to come with you?" he asked, not sure what he'd do if she said yes.

"No!" she blurted. There was a searing pain in her brown eyes when she looked up at him. "You know how strongly she feels about…this." Janey waved one hand between the two of them.

J.J. pulled her in closer to his chest. He wanted so badly to shelter her. He knew how hard Janey had fought to attain the calm and thoughtful way with which she now dealt with life. The abuse she'd suffered at the hands of her first husband was far worse than most people knew. It was a tribute to her strength that she had lived through it at all. While it had been more than a year since his wife's last panic attack, J.J. couldn't erase the memory of how devastated she was whenever one hit her. He didn't want her to find herself alone and needful without him there to help.

Janey squeezed him slightly, then pulled away. Nodding at the sandwich on the table, she said lightly, "Couldn't wait for me?"

"Lunch," he said truthfully.

"Let's get this put away, and I'll have supper while you finish your lunch."

After the groceries were tucked into the pantry, Janey pulled the tea out of the refrigerator and poured two glasses. She opened the freezer and put a couple of ice cubes in before setting them down on the table. J.J. had slapped together another turkey and cheese sandwich and put it down at her place. They sat.

Reaching over, J.J. clasped Janey's hand in his. "Are you sure you want to go?" he asked.

"Despite the way things have been the last few years, she loves me. I've got to go."

"It'll be hard."

Old ghosts chased across Janey's fine features. "Memaw gave me a good childhood. I owe her this trip. Besides," she said. "I still love her, even if she can't accept you."

Janey pulled her hand out from under J.J.'s and looked searchingly at him when he didn't respond right away.

He forced a smile. "You going to drive straight through?" His voice sounded dead, instead of the concerned tone he had been striving for. He wanted Janey to feel comfortable going, but he couldn't seem to squash his own fears long enough to hide them from her.

She finished the bite of her sandwich before replying. "If I start out by six, I ought to make it."

J.J. got up and rinsed his plate at the sink. The chip on the rim had started a crack across the surface. Pretty soon they'd have to throw it out and replace it. Not yet, he thought. Still some use in it. Carefully, he put it in the white rack on the drain board.

He pulled the trash bin out from under the sink. The smell of rotting food rose and filled the room. "I'd better go ahead and take this out."

"Great idea," Janey said, wrinkling her nose. "Do you mind if I go make sure I've got everything packed?" she asked.

"Sure," J.J. answered, tying a knot in the top of the bag.

Janey went upstairs as J.J. pushed open the back door with his knee. As he dropped the bag into the trash can outside, he wondered if Janey regretted her marriage to him. This was the first time since they got married that they hadn't sat down together for dinner and stayed there talking for a while afterward. As he opened the back door, J.J. pushed away the thought that his wife might not return with the same feelings for him as when she left. Everything would be fine. Nothing would change.

Then he entered the bedroom and saw all the things Janey had out on the bed to pack. Dora McFaile didn't have the paranoia market covered. Not by a long shot.

WHEN THE TELEPHONE RANG an hour later, J.J. was glad to answer it. Janey's packed bag sat by the back door, and he was sitting alone at the kitchen table. He should have been in bed, holding his wife, instead of doodling notes to himself about Taggart on a piece of scrap paper. He couldn't stop thinking about what-ifs. It made him restless.

"Hello?" he said.

"It's Jett."

"What's up?" J.J. was instantly alert.

"You asked me to call you as soon as I heard something about the autopsy report."

J.J. leaned forward in his chair.

"I called down, they can't get to him until later tonight. Still want me to call you when it comes in?"

J.J. rolled his wrist over so that he could check his watch. "Plenty of time for that in the morning." Thoughtfully, he set the receiver back in its cradle on the table by his side. Morning wasn't that far off.

He looked up at the sound of a floorboard creaking under the weight of Janey's feet. Probably getting up to see who called. He hauled himself out of the chair and went to greet his wife as she came down the stairs. Meeting the question in her eyes with a smile, a sudden urge came over him. Better she should have something sweet to remember him by when she went down home. Something that would call her back to Pine Grove. He stepped in close, swept Janey off her feet, then carried her up the stairs.

EIGHT

KORINE PRIED HER EYES OPEN. Rolling over, she forced her mind into focus as she judged the morning light beginning to show outside the filmy curtains at the windows. Probably six or so. Much closer to her usual than the day before.

Taking into account how little sleep she'd had and what they'd been through, she felt pretty darn good. Dora had had a lot of trouble settling in the night before, until Korine had offered to stay in the woman's room with her. She slid carefully out of bed so that she wouldn't wake her still-sleeping mother-in-law.

The old woman lay curled on her side, small wrinkled hands folded together under her chin like a child in prayer. The light green flannel nightgown she wore rose and fell gently with the rhythm of her soft snores.

Korine pulled on her royal blue velour robe, slid her feet into the worn terry scuffs, and let herself out of the room. Pulling the door closed, she jumped about a mile when something cold and wet nudged her ankle. She looked down and found the stray cat sitting at her feet, purring like a motorboat. Korine put her hands on her hips and regarded him. It was one thing to have the stray hanging about outside; it was another entirely to have him inside the house. Her calico, Olmstead, was about as much as she could handle. No more cats. She reached down to pick up the ginger tom. Oozing between her hands, he eluded her grasp, then walked haughtily down the hall toward the steps. She followed hard on his heels, wondering how the animal had gotten in.

The answer to her question stood in his bare feet in the kitchen, pouring coffee from the pot. Cal handed her the steaming mug and opened the cabinet door for another one, as if he owned the place. The cat butted his head against Cal's calf, then looked at Korine as if she were the intruder there instead of Cal. Korine tried not to mind.

"Does Mom always cry out at night?" he asked.

Korine sat down and pulled the top section of the paper off the counter. "Yes and no."

At the impatient sound Cal made, Korine explained. "She does this about once a week or so, but never as long or as loud as she did last night. She usually settles down once I go in and reassure her."

"Do you think it's Taggart?"

"Probably." Korine hadn't slept well after the previous day's upset; Dora had even more reason to be restless.

"You up to talking yet this morning?" Cal asked.

Korine thought about it. She knew how Dora felt about nursing homes, yet the past twenty-four hours proved that Korine simply couldn't provide what her mother-in-law needed. Shady Acres was about the only way the old woman could stay in Pine Grove. Would that really be better than going to Charlotte to live with her son? Korine still thought so. One look at Cal told her that he didn't feel the same.

"Put that cat outside and then we can talk," she said. She

really didn't have the strength to argue, but she had to try, for Dora's sake.

The lines around Cal's eyes and the dark smudges underneath showed that he had also been up most of the night. He picked up the purring cat, opened the back door, and deposited him on the porch. Cal came over and took the rocker next to Korine's. Turning to face her, he laid his arms carefully along the arms of the chair, tracing the weathered tip of it with his rough fingers.

"I'd like to take her home with me." At least Cal had the grace to sound like he wanted Korine's blessing this time.

"Cal, think about this," she urged.

His brows drew together and he began to look more like the disagreeable brother-in-law that she knew so well.

"Dora made Charlie promise never to put her in a home," Korine said. "And I'm betting she did the same thing to you. I've kept her here longer than is good for her out of respect for that promise. She needs more than either one of us can give. Do you honestly think it's fair to your mother to take her to your place, which is unfamiliar, and far from her friends?"

"She's stayed with me before," Cal protested.

"Stayed. Not lived. Every change that she has to adjust to makes her lose ground. I saw it when she moved in here."

Cal seized on that statement. "She's not happy living here! She'll settle in fine with me."

Korine spread her hands out in front of her. "You're right. Dora's not happy. How could she be? She knows what's happening and is scared silly by it. Moving her isn't going to make her any happier." She looked at Cal to see if he understood her. From the mulish look on his face, he wasn't even close.

"I've already hired someone to come take care of her when I'm at work." Cal's bold statement pierced Korine.

"What?" she said, breathless.

"I hired her a few weeks ago. She's been keeping an eye on things here for me."

"What?!" Korine said again, this time with the dawn of anger in her voice.

"I had to. Mom called me and told me about what was going on, and I had to find out what you were doing to her."

"Doing to her? Don't you mean doing *for* her? I've given up quite a bit the last six months to keep her independent."

"I know about the money trouble with that business of yours. You've systematically been bleeding Mom dry. She hasn't seen a cent of her income for months. Griff down at the bank says you even took Mom off her own checking account."

Korine took several deep breaths to steady herself. He was obviously referring to Dora's delusions. He had no idea how paranoid his mother could be. Surely once he understood how things were, he would do the right thing for her.

"Cal, your mother can't keep track of what she had for breakfast, much less her own money." Korine tried to curb her impatience. "She was answering any and all solicitations with checks, like they were bills. She had overdrawn her account for six months straight and couldn't pay her health insurance. I paid for it out of my own pocket. Did Griff tell you that?"

From the look on Cal's face, Griff had mentioned it, but evidently it didn't fit Cal's notion of what was going on.

He'd only listened to what he wanted to hear. Korine had purposefully left out the fact that she'd tried to talk to Cal about it and he'd responded by not returning her phone calls. It had been easier to just pay the bill and leave her brother-in-law alone.

"I thought that the latest medication would have helped with Dora's delusions. It hasn't." Korine pressed her point. "You've got to face facts. The woman who raised you was a levelheaded woman. Can you see her behaving the way she did yesterday if she was in a normal state of mind?"

Cal shoved out of the chair, the wooden back striking the wall behind it. He threw his coffee mug into the sink so hard that shards of it showered upward and fell on the floor. He flung himself out the back door, giving the outer door a slight shove to emphasize his anger. The windows rattled in their frames.

That had not gone well. Korine heard Dora call out from upstairs, frightened.

A man with a temper like that has no business taking care of someone as fragile as Dora, Korine thought. She looked at the sink and felt like throwing a little temper tantrum of her own. Instead, she left her mug cooling next to her chair and went up to reassure her mother-in-law.

"KORINE?" LORRAINE'S WELCOME frame filled the doorway from the back porch.

Korine stumbled over the hem of her robe as she straightened. She left the dustpan, half filled with mug fragments, on the floor where it lay. Lorraine was a regular at church on Sunday mornings. For her to be here was a miracle. With Lorraine visiting, Korine wouldn't have to face the day alone.

A quick surge of familiar guilt shot its flush up her neck. Lorraine had more to do with her life than watch Dora for Korine. There was her new grandbaby, born in the wee hours of Saturday morning, for one. She pulled the collar of her robe tighter to cover her embarrassment. "How's the baby?" she said quickly.

"Only the cutest, most intelligent girl ever born," Lorraine replied. "How are y'all doing here?" Her deep-set brown eyes hadn't missed a beat of Korine's reactions. The woman reached out and patted Korine's arm. "It'll be all right. Your friends are going to see you through all this."

"I still can't believe that she found her keys. People are going to think...." Korine couldn't finish her sentence.

"There isn't a body in town who doesn't understand." Lorraine paused to reconsider her remarks. "Well, except for that old Sylvester Harris."

Korine couldn't help but laugh. "Well, if Sylvester was on our side, we'd know we were wrong."

"Sure enough." Lorraine went over and opened the refrigerator. "I brought you a coffeecake from Mrs. Hawkins. After I talked to you yesterday, I thought it might be good for there to be some food in the house for Mr. Cal that you didn't cook."

"I'm sure he'll enjoy it if there's any left by the time he comes back." Korine couldn't keep the bitterness out of her voice.

Lorraine shut the door to the fridge, hiding the coffeecake from view. "This his doing—or yours?" She picked up the broom and swept up the rest of the mess on the floor.

"It's not as bad as all that," Korine said.

Lorraine eyed her. Korine had never been good at lying.

"Jake's mother is over there today. Jelzie's her grandbaby too. Can't grudge her this one. How 'bout I stay with Miz Dora this morning to keep me busy so I don't think about going over there anyway?"

Dora usually got herself up and dressed. Took half a day sometimes, but she did it. The house was already clean— Lorraine had seen to that while watching Dora the week before.

"I hate to ask you to do that," Korine said, "but after yesterday, I'd love it if you could stay a few hours. How about a cup of coffee?" She crossed the floor and picked up the insulated pot. "It's still pretty fresh, if you're willing to take a chance on it."

There was a small crash from Dora's room, then the sound of her voice calling out, "Who's there?"

The pot hit the counter with a crack as Korine started to her mother-in-law's aid. A puddle of coffee spread around the base of the pot. Trembling, Korine stared at the spreading stain on the counter, then at the door to the hall, and back again. Dora's voice rose. Korine let go of the pot's handle to head for the door.

Lorraine's hand fastened on her arm, stopping Korine in her tracks. "You're in no shape to comfort her. I'll go up. She knows me. You take care of this. I'll bring her down in a minute."

Guilt again raised its ugly voice, shouting loudly in Korine's ears. Lorraine stood her ground. Finally, Korine nodded her agreement. The other woman tightened her grip briefly on Korine's wrist, then walked through the doorway to the hall, stopping to nudge the iron doorstop out of the way and letting the door swing shut behind her.

Korine reached over the sink to get the yellow dish sponge. Using short strokes, she pushed the spreading puddle back from the edge of the Formica. She wiped up the last of the spill and squeezed the sponge over and over under the running tap to clean it. As the murky liquid turned to clear, she found she could think again.

It was only a matter of time until Dora disappeared entirely down the solitary lane of memory loss. Until the day before, Korine had resolutely focused on the woman's memories and strengths that remained, not those that were lost. Dora still knew who belonged to her and how much they cared. Most of the time, anyway.

The question that had been worrying Korine still begged for an answer: What could have caused Dora to forget herself so completely that she had killed a man?

After giving the sponge one last squeeze, Korine tossed it back in the stoneware dish at the back of the sink. After tidying up a few things on the counter—the sugar still out from refilling the bowl the night before, the box of mint tea she'd tried the other night—she went over and dropped into the closest chair to think. She'd checked out Shady Acres. She'd planned on looking at another facility a few miles away— sometime. Talking with Hazel, Korine had thought she was looking far into the future to be doing even that much.

Hearing sounds behind her in the hall, Korine turned her head to watch the doorway. Dora came in, closely followed by Lorraine.

"How are you this morning?" Korine asked.

"Fine, considering you hid my hairbrush."

Korine thought back to the bag she'd packed for Dora the night before. "It's in the—"

"Pink bag," Lorraine finished. "We found it."

"Sorry," Korine said. What an inadequate statement. Sorry she'd packed Dora's things and not unpacked them. Sorry she'd not hidden Dora's keys better. Sorry she hadn't gotten rid of the damn car in the first place.

Korine picked up her mug from the table between the two chairs. She took a sip, then put it down quickly. Bitter and cold, it served up no comfort. Lining up the mug with the squares, she considered Dora. "Why don't you sit," she said to her mother-in-law. "We need to talk."

Lorraine bent over and took the mug out from under Korine's fiddling hand and, muttering under her breath, walked to the sink and plunged the mug in the hot water, then made a show of being busy.

Dora sat.

"You promised me you wouldn't drive anymore," Korine said.

"I know that, but…."

Korine felt her face tighten with the effort of waiting for the frail woman sitting next to her to catch up with her thoughts. "Why did you need to go over there?" Her tone of voice was sharper than intended.

Lorraine's hands stilled in the dishwater. The clock ticked off the seconds as Dora's expression congealed to anger.

"You told me to!" the woman accused.

Korine couldn't believe her ears. "I did no such thing!"

"You left me a note. You told me to go over to Shady Acres."

"I did not. The only note I left about Shady Acres was to Lorraine, on Friday, telling her how to reach me out there."

Eyes clear, Dora's hands gripped the arms of her chair. She drew herself up and glared at Korine. "I may not be able to find my hairbrush when you hide it from me, but I am still here. You left a note on the kitchen table. With a map."

Korine struggled to keep calm. "Do you still have the note? I'd like to see it."

"I put it in my purse before I left." Dora paused. "The map is in the car."

"Dora," Korine began, feeling helpless.

The woman exploded. "I tell you it's true. You won't change the locks on the doors. You don't believe me about the people being in the house. You don't believe me when I tell you I'm so afraid, I can't sleep at night. You don't believe anything I say that's the truth. All you'll listen to is lies, lies, and more lies. *That* you have no trouble swallowing."

Dora pushed herself up from the chair. She moved with a speed that surprised *Korine*—past Lorraine, who backed up to the sink as the diminutive fury stalked across the kitchen floor. Dora plucked an old cardigan off the peg by the door. Twisting the glass knob, she pulled the door open so hard it hit the wall behind it. She took a step out, then turned back. Face bitter, as if she'd eaten nothing but turnips for weeks, she said, "No wonder I'm losing my mind. Don't come with me. I can't take the car, now can I, it's…." Her eyes lost focus, as if the word she was searching for was just out of reach.

Dora snapped, "You know what I mean. I'm going to go sweep the walk. Somebody's got to keep an eye out for things here. Heaven knows you don't."

With this parting shot, she let the door slam behind her.

The porch door swung shut with an echoing snap a second later.

Lorraine recovered first. She patted her hands dry on the dish towel and carefully folded it and placed it on the counter next to the sink. She undid her apron strings and folded it, too, and put it on the counter next to the towel. "I'll go out with her," she said.

"I'm going to go up and check to see if I can find the note in her purse."

Lorraine nodded and finished fastening her jacket.

Korine watched through the window as Lorraine caught up with Dora. The older woman shook off Lorraine's hand, gentle on her shoulder. From what Korine could see, Dora was giving Lorraine as much hell as she'd just given Korine. Korine walked out into the hall and up the steps.

Dora's room was just as it always was. Korine could see the things from the suitcase shoved hastily here and there. She smoothed the quilt on the bed and picked up the hairbrush from where Dora had left it on the nightstand. Korine walked over and placed it on the dresser where it belonged.

She had to do some digging before finally finding Dora's purse, which had somehow found its way into the lingerie drawer. As Korine had suspected, there was no note inside. As long as she was upstairs, she decided to put the room back to rights. If she didn't, Dora would be back up within the hour, going on about how someone had moved her things around in her room.

It wasn't until she was almost back downstairs that Korine made the mental connection to the burned paper in Dora's toilet the night before. Dora must have misinterpreted the note Korine left for Lorraine. Had she then burned it? If so, why?

As she leaned heavily on the railing, the fatigue of the previous few months felt like a knife between Korine's shoulder blades. She drew a deep breath, forcing her head back up and tightening her grip on her emotions. There was no way anyone could predict how Dora's mind would work on any given day.

Back down in the kitchen, Korine shoved the curtains away from the window to let some natural light inside. It was past nine, so J.J. ought to be at work by now. She picked up the phone and punched in the number for the police station.

Marlene answered. J.J. was out talking with Doc. She assured Korine that he'd make it to her house before lunch.

Returning the phone to the receiver, Korine glanced around. She had no shortage of things to keep her busy while waiting on J.J. The landscaping plans Amilou had left curling on the dining room table called to her.

Amilou had offered to draw up the proposal for Hazel so that Korine could concentrate on Dora. Korine had demurred, knowing that what Janey had said about work taking her mind off things would help her through the day.

She got a fresh cup of coffee and sat down at the table. With Lorraine willing to stay, she could lose herself in the possibilities offered by the plans they'd sketched out the day before. Sure beat spending the morning worrying.

Korine turned her head as she caught the *brush, brush* of Dora's broom against the porch outside the window. She smoothed her hand over the garden areas that Amilou and Janey had outlined. Dora would love this when it was finished. If Cal would let her enjoy it.

One good thing. Korine was pretty sure it would come

in within the budget Hazel had given them. She reached for a fresh sheet of paper and picked up a pen. At least something in her life was working out the way it was supposed to.

NINE

JETT MERRIWEATHER AND Leon Winters were sitting in the spare office in the station when J.J. got there Sunday morning. There were two mugs on the table. Leon's was missing a chip in the top, which cut off part of the last word on the marquee running around the rim of the mug. WORLD'S GREATEST OVER didn't have quite the same ring to it as the original. Considering how frequently Leon changed dating partners, it could be considered a case of truth in advertising. Jett's was equally battered, but it had the attractive advantage of steam rising from the surface of its murky depths.

J.J. picked up his own University of Texas mug and poured a slug of thick liquid from the pot. Sitting down, he waited for his officers to report. Jett had come a long way in the two years since he'd arrived in Pine Grove from the Atlanta department. He still lacked common sense, but his organizational skills had improved considerably. Leon hadn't started his career until after Jett, yet he showed an aptitude for police work that the other man simply didn't have. Bringing along a young officer like Leon wasn't bad for a small department in the middle of nowhere.

"Any news on the autopsy?" J.J. started the ball rolling.

Jett and Leon exchanged glances.

"Actually," Jett said, pulling a sheet of paper off the top of the stack in front of him. "It did come in."

"And…," J.J. prompted when Jett didn't hand it over.

"And Taggart was already dead when Mrs. McFaile ran over him."

"What the hell?" J.J. said, reaching his hand out.

Jett surrendered it.

J.J. scanned the paper. Lots of complicated jargon, but the upshot was that the cause of death was overdose of Depacote, not the injuries that Taggart's body had sustained. J.J. wondered how the lab had known to test for this particular drug. He scanned the autopsy again and saw a faint note that must have been penciled in the margin by the lab tech to notify Darryl James with the results of the test.

He swore again. "Doc know about this yet?"

"Marlene said he was out on a house call," Leon said. "He'll be in his office around nine or ten."

"I'll talk to him." J.J. looked down at the sheet of paper again and frowned. This case was getting weirder by the second. "Leon, you go back out and talk to Hazel again. Find out how much of this drug Taggart was on and when his last dose was."

J.J. turned to Jett and asked, "You talk to anybody down at Shady Acres after this report came in?"

"Yeah, I called. Dr. Randle said that looking at the blood level, he wouldn't put any money on a simple medical error."

"That's what I was thinking," J.J. said as he placed the paper on the table. He needed time to think about how best to pursue the investigation. "Anything else unusual happen last night?"

Jett shrugged. "The Grinsteads were fighting again. Had to go over and pull him off of her."

The couple lived in the same apartment building as Colleen. The police got so many calls out there, they'd all but given up trying to remain objective. More than once, J.J. had handed Mrs. Grinstead the phone number to the women's shelter in Charlotte. She hadn't used it yet.

"Any new burglaries?"

"Sorry," Jett answered. "One. The Kohls. Older couple over on Greer Dairy Road. The only other thing last night was a suspicious character behind the Tastee-Freez, around midnight. Didn't catch up with him, but I did scare him off."

J.J. doodled on the piece of paper in front of him. "Any connection to the kids we arrested last week for the street-sign thefts?"

"I don't think so," Jett answered. "Looked too old to be out at the college. Report's on your desk."

Jett looked across the table at Leon. The two men seemed to be struggling with something.

"Out with it," J.J. said, putting his elbows on the table and lacing his fingers round the solid comfort of his mug.

Leon and Jett both turned to look at J.J. If he hadn't been in such a rotten mood, their identical expressions of dismay would have amused him.

Jett broke the silence. "We were thinking...." He paused and threw Leon a get-me-out-of-this-mess glance.

Leon picked up the ball. "It's been a while since you've done job-performance reviews."

"You want a raise?" J.J. asked, thinking of the conversation he'd had the previous day with Hank. Sometimes, having the mayor as a friend meant he wasn't taken as seriously as he'd like. A clear picture came to mind of the duct tape he'd used to put the steering wheel back on his cruiser three days before, not to mention the still-broken radio he'd hoped to have repaired.

"Well," Leon continued, "we were thinking...you know how we're working these twelve-hour shifts? Well, we would rather have you go all out and hire somebody so we could go back to having some kind of regular life. Still do the rotation of shifts and all—" He spluttered to a halt at the look on J.J.'s face.

"I'll look into it." Judging from the men's expressions, J.J. figured he'd better kiss that new cruiser good-bye and concentrate on getting funding for a new officer instead. "Meanwhile, we've got this burglary to investigate. And there's the Taggart case to wrap up."

"How'd Taggart's son take the news?" Leon asked, evidently willing to let things go for the time being. "He coming to town?"

Jett didn't look as willing, but he kept his mouth shut anyway.

"Came in last night," J.J. replied. Talking to folks who have suffered a loss like Taggart's was hard enough the first time. Thinking of the autopsy report, J.J. sighed. He was not looking forward to telling Jack that his father had been murdered. "I'll talk to him later this morning, after I catch up with Doc."

Leaving it to the two men to finish dissecting the events of the night before, J.J. went back to his office to call the mayor. When Hank's machine answered, J.J. left a message asking him to call.

Pulling open his desk drawer, J.J. picked up the paper

bag nestled inside. He tipped it gently onto the pile of papers on his desk. A small glass paperweight spilled out onto the Taggart file folder. A little gift for no good reason—he'd meant to slip it into Janey's suitcase. In all the excitement, he had forgotten to take it home with him the night before.

Janey had been ready to go, bags in the car, before the sun was even up that morning. Their good-byes had been awkward. J.J. hadn't been able to tell her how afraid he was.

His wife had sensed something, though, before she left. She had reached through the car window to pull him down to her. Giving him a kiss that nearly welded his steel-toed boots to the ground, she had finished up by patting his cheek like a little boy. Her brown eyes had promised him all sorts of things when she returned. Then she'd driven away.

The bright flowers in the center of the glass seemed to be wilting. J.J. balled the paperweight back up into the bag and replaced it in the drawer. This was not getting the job done.

Jett had put three reports on his desk: the suspicious activity at the Tastee-Freez, the domestic disturbance at the Grinsteads, and the burglary. He picked it up first. The Kohls had been fixtures in Pine Grove all their lives. Now in their seventies, they had lived in the house just outside of town for fifty-two years. They'd reported finding their back door open. The jewelry box on Harriet Kohl's dresser had been overturned and a necklace stolen.

Tapping his fingers on the desktop, J.J. looked up when there was an answering tap at the door. Marlene stood there.

"Don't tell me," J.J. said, "you want a raise." He smiled as he said it to rob the words of any sting, but his tone came out whip-sharp.

She tilted her head to one side. "That's quite generous of you. I'll have to consider it. A dollar an hour raise would come in pretty handy right now. Thanks. Not what I came in for, but I'm delighted to hear you're thinking ahead, before it becomes an issue. I actually needed to let you know that I have a doctor's appointment Monday afternoon. The service'll pick up from noon on."

J.J. didn't feel up to tackling the sticky issue of the raise. He'd put his foot in it in a big way this time. "Everything all right?" he inquired instead.

Marlene raised one of her carefully manicured eyebrows. J.J. hated how easily she could make him feel that he'd crossed that line from concerned employer to overly familiar pig. Sometimes he wished she'd stayed away on permanent maternity leave. Most times he recognized how she bullied everyone into being well-organized. That attitude was good for something.

"Never mind," he said. "We'll miss you, but you do what you need to do."

"Thank you."

J.J. flipped the worn Rolodex cards to the P's. He had an inside contact in the state crime lab. He'd first talked with her during Greg Whittier's murder investigation, and she had been helpful in expediting cases for him ever since. He picked up the phone and cradled it between his cheek and shoulder as he punched in the number on the card.

An unfamiliar voice answered.

"Is Esther there?" J.J. asked.

"Honey, Esther Patton's retired now. This is Dolores Perkins. How can I help you?" She didn't sound real sincere about her wish to be helpful, but J.J. gave her all the pertinent information on Taggart and asked if she had any information she could send him about Depacote. Therapeutic levels, how long it took to act, that sort of thing.

Dolores promised to look and to fax him something as soon as she found out. J.J. had to trust her on that one. If she came through, he'd send her candy like he'd done with Esther.

A few minutes later the fax machine hummed. Surprised, J.J. smiled broadly. Looked like Dolores was going to get a special delivery. He flipped back through the cards until he came to the C's. Chocolates With Love, 201-825-0128. Korine's sister lived in New Jersey and had brought some of their lemon and raspberry crèmes the last time she came for a visit. Kendra said her "buds" had voted it the best chocolate around. J.J.'s mouth watered just remembering how good they tasted.

A minute later he stood in the doorway of the room where he'd left Jett and Leon. He handed Jett the sheet Dolores had faxed over. "Definitely murder."

Leon took the sheet from Jett's hand. "This is good news for the McFailes, right?" He sounded hopeful.

"I wouldn't go that far," J.J. said. "A man's still dead. And we have our work cut out for us."

Jett stood up. "In that case, I'd better go home and get some sleep."

"You do that," Leon said. "There'll still be plenty of work when you come back on duty tonight."

After Jett left, Leon and J.J. discussed a few other things still pending. They agreed to meet back at the station to compare notes sometime in the early afternoon.

Leon stood up and collected both his mug and Jett's,

which the man had left in the middle of the table. J.J. shook his head. Jett's mother must have picked up after him a little too much as a child. From the expression on Leon's face, it was a good thing Jett had already left the building. His frown looked anything but motherly.

J.J. went back to his office and spent the next half hour trying to clear some room on top of his desk. It was still too early on a Sunday morning to knock on people's doors. By the time he had pecked out a report of his talk the night before with Colleen, it was only eight o'clock.

The phone rang. J.J. picked up.

"You must think I work pretty quick," Hank said, evidently having gotten J.J.'s message.

"I'm changing my request."

"What now?" Hank's voice echoed with reservations.

"Meet me for lunch?"

"I was planning on the Penny Whistle after church. That good for you?"

"Works for me," J.J. agreed.

After hanging up with Hank, he picked up the phone again, then set it down. He decided to take a short walk to clear his head. If he stayed inside, he was going to wind up lighting up. Janey would be disappointed that he hadn't lasted through her first day away before he started back smoking.

He stood and lifted his hat off the bentwood hat stand by the door. Leon had already gone, and Marlene was on the phone when he went by. He floated the reports he'd filled out into her "in" box and left before she could tell him they were late.

The crisp scent of burning leaves assaulted J.J. when he

got outside. Mr. Younger, no doubt, ignoring the no-burn law within the city limits. J.J. ambled down the road a minute and looked over the back fence. Sure enough, Corey Younger stood holding his rake next to a metal trash can. The crackle of flame issued from within.

"Don't look at me like that, young man," Younger started in. "Can't afford not to do this, you know. It would cost me a fortune to have these leaves hauled away. Besides, I'm being careful."

"Yes, but—"

"I've heard it all before. 'It's against the law.'" Younger's voice deepened, accent parodying J.J.'s east Texas drawl. His wrinkled face twisted, and a rain of tobacco juice splattered on the pile of leaves at the old man's feet. "I've been burning leaves for longer than you've been drawing breath, and I'm not going to let them pile up in my yard to suit you."

"You still have to put it out." J.J. held his ground.

After a few more minutes of blustering. J.J. offered to call the fire department and have them come by and put it out.

Younger got the hose and soaked the contents of his trash can.

"You know I still have to send you a ticket," J.J. said wearily. They had this argument every year.

"Cheaper than a ticket to the Policemen's Ball," Younger called after him as J.J. walked away.

J.J. glanced back at the old man over his shoulder with a frown. Even for Younger, that was an odd comment. The man seemed satisfied. He sure didn't deserve to, looking at a fine of upwards of a hundred dollars and piles of unburned leaves, to boot. J.J. felt his forehead start to pucker.

Then the sight of a man standing, hands on his hips, in the driveway of the house behind Younger came into focus. J.J. turned back around quickly so that Younger wouldn't see the grin that threatened to split his face. The man was the very city councilman who had been responsible for the in-town burning fine going up so high that year. He'd declared war after Younger's leaf burning had gotten out of hand and torched a century-old hickory tree in the councilman's backyard. Younger wouldn't be so cheerful when his fine came flying through the mail slot of his front door.

J.J. waved to the councilman, who was now smiling as J.J. passed him. With luck, this might count in J.J.'s favor when it came time to vote on budget items.

TEN

DOC'S WAITING ROOM was deserted. J.J. had walked on over after dealing with Corey Younger. The door was unlocked, so he knew Doc was back from his house call. Old issues of *Time* magazine littered the chairs, interspersed with *Woman's Day* and *Field & Stream*. J.J. would have expected to see the waiting area neater than this on a Sunday morning.

"Doc?" he called.

"Office is closed," Doc's impatient voice came from behind the frosted glass window of the receptionist's desk.

"It's J.J."

The glass slid back. "So I see," Doc said. He closed the glass. The door separating the waiting area from the office proper opened, and he ushered J.J. in.

Doc was a tall man with an enviable shock of blond hair. His beard had a reddish tinge to it. His broody, dark eyes, hidden slightly by his wire-rim glasses, seemed out of place in his fair complexion. He stood frowning down at some lab results he held in his left hand.

"I've got a question for you about Jack Taggart," J.J. said.

"Yes?" Doc put the paper down in a stack of other results on the counter. "You get the autopsy report in? I have to tell you, I am so glad that's the state's job and not mine. I prefer my patients breathing."

"I do, too," J.J. agreed. He cleared his throat. "So, what do you know about Depacote?"

Doc's mouth pinched in at the corners. "It really was an overdose?" He sat down on the rolling stool by his side. "If I'd known this was going to become a trend, I would've mentioned something sooner."

"Mentioned what?" J.J.'s attention was riveted on Doc, who in turn didn't seem to be able to look the police chief in the eye. J.J. pulled out his notebook and flipped it open.

Doc shook his head. "I'm probably just reading too much into these cases. There aren't that many people around here with age-related dementia, but more than I like to think on. I had a patient a few months ago who suffered an overdose of Depacote."

J.J. felt a stir of anger. "A few months ago? And you're just now mentioning it?"

Doc looked up from the folder he'd pulled out of the cabinet in front of him. "She recovered after we pumped her stomach. It happened about four months ago. Colleen was helping out the family at home at the time, and she can assure you that it was indeed an accident. One family member gave the dose. Then another person came along and didn't know the first one had given Mom the pills—you get the picture."

"And you're bringing this up now because?" J.J. asked.

"Maris Falkirk was on Depacote too."

"I thought she froze to death."

"She did, but it happened two weeks after I put her on the Depacote. I didn't drug-test at the time, but I'd lay odds now that her blood levels were high."

"Shit."

"Yes, Sherlock."

"Cut it out," J.J. said. "This is serious. If you're surprised that the blood level is so high for Taggart, then why did you ask the lab to run the test in the first place?"

"Because one of the aides at Shady Acres, Lyndsey Babbitt, told me that Maris Falkirk had acted just like Taggart did right before he died. She wandered off and died from hypothermia; he fell under Dora's car."

"Did the aide think to tell Leon about her suspicions?"

"According to Lyndsey, Hazel told her she'd fire her if she told anyone. She only told me because she's more scared of me than she is of Hazel."

J.J.'s lips twisted. That didn't sound like the Hazel he'd had contact with so far. Just one more thing to check out.

"What is Depacote, anyway?" he asked.

"A sedative. Alzheimer's patients often have paranoia, makes them very combative. The drug calms them down. Gives the caretaker a chance of being able to keep up with the patient."

"And Taggart was taking it too?"

"Called in his prescription about two weeks ago."

J.J. rested his hand on the counter in front of him. He reminded himself that he did not believe in conspiracies. Then he told Doc what Taggart's blood level was and asked, "Do you think someone out at Shady Acres was careless with the medications?"

"That's way too high for an accidental overdose," Doc said, confirming J.J.'s fear. "Besides," he added, "what if Maris was given an overdose on purpose too?" He took off his glasses, leaving his eyes naked and pleading without their protection.

"That's pretty far-fetched," J.J. responded.

"I know, but we've got a lot of families in a support group together. They all knew about that first incident. I'm wondering if one of them didn't think letting the people out of their misery wasn't a good idea—and then figured out how to make it work."

J.J. thought for a moment. His eyes traveled the rows of manila folders, bright with colored stickers indicating the last names of Doc's patients. How many of the town's secrets were hidden there?

"Maris Falkirk," J.J. said finally. "What can you tell me about her?"

"She wasn't as far along the road as Taggart. Frankly, at the time, I thought the family was putting her into care prematurely." Doc shrugged. "Only the family can make that determination. They were exhausted. In hindsight, I think they were right. Maris had gotten combative, so we'd started giving her Depacote to try and control some of her outbursts."

"And this support group," J.J. said. "Who's in it?"

"Well, Jack Taggart was one of the first ones to join, along with Maris's daughter and a couple of the other family members of folks up at Shady Acres. After that first meeting, more folks joined who were doing care at home. Colleen helped out with the group; it's something near and dear to her heart."

Colleen again. She was beginning to sound like a paragon. Or something quite the opposite. J.J. scuffed his hat against the side of his pant leg. "So, are you saying that these families decided to do away with their loved ones because of that one first incident?"

Doc wiped his glasses on his bandanna. "I would hate to think so. These were my patients we're talking about. However, looking at all the possible facts makes it sure seem that way."

"*Possible facts* is an oxymoron," J.J. said automatically. He hated even the thought that Taggart had been murdered, much less the prospect that there was a murderous string of deaths going on. He snapped his notebook shut.

"You going to need medical records?" Doc asked.

"I'll get back to you with the necessary paperwork."

Doc slid his glasses back in place on his face. His eyes receded behind the thick lenses. "Since Maris's death, Hazel's had the medicine locked up tighter than Dick's hatband. Despite the Babbitt girl's story, I trust Hazel. As much as I hate to say this, my bet's on murder."

"Don't think I'll take that bet," J.J. said.

"No," Doc replied. His dark eyes sad, he opened the office door for J.J. "Let me know if I can help you any more."

"I think you've helped quite enough," J.J. grumbled, but the look he gave Doc was pure gratitude. He didn't relish having another murder in Pine Grove, but he couldn't deny that he would hate even more for a killer to go free.

"By the way," he said, "I'd appreciate it if you didn't tell anyone about this development for a few days. I want to talk to the families—ask a few pertinent questions—before we go public."

"Sure," Doc said. "Whatever you say."

J.J. let himself out the front door and went back to his car. Looked like he would have time to get to the Penny Whistle to meet Hank. After that, he'd go back to the police station and check out a few things. He wanted to make sure of his facts before he said anything to Jack Taggart and the McFailes.

THE NEWEST INCARNATION of the café on Main Street was Penny Whistle. The owner, Juanita June Osborne, liked to change the name to reflect the decorating scheme. Or vice versa—J.J. was never sure which one came first. It had been green. It had been blue. It had even, for a mercifully short time, been orange.

The day after the orange paint went up, one of her regulars put a jar out on the counter to collect for a redecorating fund. Since the jar filled up mostly with pennies, Juanita June had a brilliant idea. She decided to plaster the place with the contributions. Personally, on sunny days, J.J. found that the effect assaulted his senses like a disco ball. Still, even a University of Texas grad knew that just about anything beat orange walls.

The minute J.J. walked in the door of the café, he knew he was in trouble. Juanita June came up to him and planted her fists on her hips—a sure sign of feminine displeasure. She jerked her head in the direction of the kitchen as an indication for him to follow. He walked meekly past her, through the swinging door she held for him, into the gleaming world of stainless steel ruled over by Juanita June's mother, Mrs. Hawkins.

"What is the meaning of this?" Mrs. Hawkins hissed at J.J. The petite woman, her snow-white hair neatly pinned into a coil at the base of her neck and secured with a hair net, wore her usual work uniform: floral housedress, large white cotton apron, and fuzzy purple slippers. She stepped up to J.J. and thrust a piece of yellow paper under his nose.

He put out his hands to defend himself and found his fingers clasping the paper. He read the bold headline, which announced the First Annual Policemen's Ball. "What the hell is this?" he asked.

Juanita June and her mother stood side by side, equal looks of anger on their faces. "That's what we're asking you," Mrs. Hawkins said.

J.J. took a step back. "This is the first I've heard about it," he said.

Mrs. Hawkins reached out and snatched the paper away from J.J., ripping one corner in the process. "It says right here," she said, jabbing her nail on the page, "to send the money for our tickets to you, at this post office box." She shook the paper in the air under his nose again. "How could you go and hire a caterer from out of town without at least letting us know? We would have given you a really good deal."

Enlightenment dawned. At least J.J. knew the real reason for the women's anger, even if he had no idea where the flyer came from.

"I can tell you that if I had planned such a thing, you and you alone would be catering it," J.J. assured the pair truthfully. He gingerly eased the flyer out of Mrs. Hawkins's hands so he could examine it.

"Good," Juanita June said. She threw her mother an I-told-you-so glance. "The Pine Grove police force isn't large enough to constitute much of a ball, anyway."

J.J. looked at Juanita June. "You mind if I keep this?" he asked.

"It's mine," Mrs. Hawkins said. "And yes, you may have it," she graciously added, handing him a plastic bag into which J.J. placed the flyer. A bit late to keep anyone else's prints from being on the paper, but it would keep the coffee off it while he talked with Hank.

"Where did it come from?" J.J. asked.

"It was taped up in the window. Half the town was in here yesterday. I thought you'd done it. Was mad as fire when I saw it was being catered by that poor excuse for a restaurant over in Pickles."

"This the only copy?" J.J. asked.

Juanita June looked at her mother, who shrugged. "You might as well tell him," Juanita June said.

"We've had customers in here all morning asking about it," Mrs. Hawkins said, "not all of them happy."

He took a moment to look the flyer over more carefully. "Five thousand dollars to sit at my table?" J.J. couldn't help it. He started to laugh. The laughter dissolved into a wracking cough. He got his breath back after Juanita June handed him a glass of water and he swallowed half of it in one gulp.

"You better find out who put it up—advertising that sleazy place in our window." Mrs. Hawkins turned away, house shoes shuffling along the spotless floor back to the stove. "Some people's children," she muttered under her breath, expertly flipping an omelet.

J.J. backed away, taking the opportunity to run while he had the chance. He wasn't out of the doghouse with her yet.

"Somebody's got himself a great sense of humor." Hank stood on the opposite side of the door, scowl firmly affixed to his face.

"You saw the flyer too?" J.J. said. "I can't believe any-one had the nerve to put something up with my name on it."

Hank's face relaxed some, but not enough to suit J.J. "Sarah Jane was going to call Marlene this afternoon to RSVP to this shindig."

"There is no shindig!" J.J. said. Several people turned in their seats to stare. J.J. made apologetic motions and led the way back to their habitual booth in the back corner and slid in. Hank followed and slid into his spot on the other side of the booth. They liked it because it was the one place in the café where they could sit and both see the door.

"I gathered that," Hank said. "She said, by the way, that she'd see me in hell before she let someone else get that head table."

"Sarah Jane used profanity?" J.J. was impressed in spite of himself.

Hank's smile appeared briefly. "You know she didn't."

The full meaning of Hank's words hit J.J. a second later. "You'd actually pay that much to have dinner with me?"

"I'd pay that much to make Sarah Jane happy," Hank corrected. "You've been harping on me to ask the council for money for quite a while now. I thought maybe some-body had convinced you to have a fund-raiser."

"So who would actually go to the trouble of doing some-thing this…unbelievable?" J.J. asked.

"Sylvester," Juanita June said. She slapped a pair of paper place mats on the table in front of the men, then filled their glasses with tea. Setting one on the upper right-hand corner of each man's place mat, she raised an eyebrow at J.J. "His favorite spot to sit is right by the window where we found the flyer. And he's sneaky enough to have done it, too."

"He stiff you a tip this morning?" Hank asked.

Either Juanita June was still riled about the flyer, or something else had set her off. Her flaming red hair fairly crackled with suppressed energy. But then, it usually did.

The difference this afternoon was the militant set to her mouth. Lips pressing together so tightly that a white line had formed around her pink lipstick, Juanita June slapped her hand on the side of the plastic pitcher. "I've had about enough of his needling folks. He started in on Mother this morning. Didn't like that she had her house shoes on while working. Does he think he's the taste police? Her ankles swell too much to wear shoes."

J.J. relaxed. "Don't mind him. If your mother's feet hurt, there's nothing to say she can't wear what she wants on her feet."

"I'm sick and damn tired of him coming in here and pinching my butt. And may I remind you that he used my café window to advertise this scheme of his? Just because you shrug it off doesn't mean it's all right. Some folks are simple enough to listen to Sylvester and believe his wild stories." She whirled around and marched off.

J.J. stared after her. Instead of the usual swing in her hips, her back was stiff and straight. Juanita June threw open the door into the kitchen and disappeared.

"You called this morning," Hank said, bringing J.J.'s attention back to the table.

"Yeah. Leon and Jett sat me down and told me they'd both quit if I didn't hire another officer."

"And you're asking me to get the money for you, in addition to what you've already requested?" Hank shook his head. He picked up his glass and took a sip of tea. He was one of those men who appeared calm, no matter what.

J.J. thought it was the effect of living for over twenty-five years with Sarah Jane. He had to be unflappable to put up with her. The only time J.J. had ever seen Hank riled was when he lost that big bass on Glory Lake. J.J. felt his lips twitch, just remembering.

Hank raised an eyebrow.

J.J. shook his head, deciding that reviving that particular memory wouldn't help his cause. He cleared his throat and outlined the situation with his men. "I think they're serious about quitting." When Hank looked less than convinced, he added, "They're worked to death. And that was before we had murder to contend with."

Hank picked up his napkin and dabbed at the spilled tea on his polo shirt. "Excuse me?" he said. "You charging Dora McFaile with murdering Olan Taggart? Or is there another death out there I haven't heard about yet?"

J.J. considered what he should say next. Hank was all right, but if he leaked a word to Sarah Jane before J.J. had a chance to tell the McFailes, J.J. might lose a friend.

"Actually," he said slowly, coming to a decision, "you're wrong and right. Taggart died of an overdose. We're looking into how that got into his system." J.J. sketched out the results of the autopsy report. He kept the conversation he'd just had with Doc under his hat.

"Don't worry." Hank had seen J.J.'s hesitation. "I'll keep this news from Sarah Jane. She was upset enough, seeing Taggart die. I sure hope it wasn't a medication error. There's been enough trouble out at Shady Acres, as it is."

"Such as?"

"Nothing medical that I know of. Just the usual: the place being too hot, too cold, the food's horrible, they don't do things right, the wallpaper's ugly."

"Sarah Jane's mother?" J.J. asked.

"Yep."

Was J.J. mistaken, or did Hank's hand tremble as he raised the glass to his lips. Not a good sign. "How's she doing?"

"Getting worse in a hurry," Hank said. "Part of the reason Sarah Jane was so rattled about what happened out there."

"I'm sorry she had to see that yesterday. It would upset anyone."

"Frankly, it's hard to tell which upsets Sarah Jane more: Taggart's death or her mother's failing health."

J.J. raised his eyebrows and waited for Hank to continue.

"At least the delusions have gotten better. For a while before we put her in there, she thought people were getting in the house and moving her things."

J.J. frowned. Doc had mentioned that a fear of people coming in and moving things was a common theme among his older patients. Korine had said her mother-in-law recently began complaining of the same fear. Could there really be a conspiracy afoot?

"She on any medications that could cause this?" J.J. asked.

"The only medicine she ever took in her life was a vitamin. Now she's in there and takes so many pills, I can't even count them all. I'll say this, though. She's calmer, and she seems happy. Well, as happy as she'll ever be. I only wish that it didn't tear Sarah Jane up so much to have put her mother away."

"Too bad she and Korine don't get along better. They could probably help each other with this burden."

Hank grunted and looked out the window. Obviously he took Sarah Jane's side. As he should, J.J. thought. J.J. might not like Sarah Jane, but he thought more highly of Hank because he stood by his wife—when he wasn't able to talk her out of the more outlandish of her ideas.

"Not to switch hobbyhorses in mid-stride," J.J. said, "but what do you think our chances might be of getting the council to approve hiring another man?"

Hank tossed his sodden napkin on the table. "I don't know," he said. "I'll try. Where we'll get the money is another issue." He stared down J.J.'s protest. "I said I'd try. I know better than to promise you the moon and only be able to come up with blue cheese." He gave J.J. a stern look.

Smiling, J.J. conceded the point. "I better get going. I have a few other things to check on this afternoon." He drained the rest of his tea, then stood up and awkwardly put one hand on Hank's shoulder. "I appreciate anything you can do to convince the Powers That Be to approve the funding. Talk to you later."

He paid for a to-go sandwich and his tea at the cash register. After he slid into the cruiser out in the parking lot, he carefully placed the flyer in a real evidence bag and marked it. He decided to deal with Sylvester later. Before he went out to Shady Acres, he might give that nurse's aide a call himself and see what she had to say about Hazel.

ELEVEN

WHEN LORRAINE HAD no longer been able to stay away from the new baby, finally leaving around eleven, Korine abandoned her work littering the dining room table and lured her mother-in-law back inside with a piece of Mrs. Hawkins's cake. After that, they went upstairs to brush Dora's teeth.

Leaving the woman to her task in the bathroom, Korine straightened the bedroom. As she smoothed the floral coverlet into place under the pillows on Dora's bed, she heard the sound of a car coming up the drive. Hoping it was Cal returning home, she twitched the curtain aside. J.J. pulled his police cruiser in by the back door.

Korine poked her head in the bathroom doorway. Dora hadn't made much progress. In fact, she was still trying to get the toothpaste on the brush. On bad days, activities like this one played out in an endless loop.

As Korine sighed, Dora squeezed an exact amount of toothpaste onto her brush and, watching herself in the mirror, popped the brush into her mouth. Starting on the upper right-hand portion of her gums, she moved her hand up and down in a steady rhythm. She startled as she caught sight of Korine in the mirror, apparently only then realizing that someone had been standing behind her. Crying out, she dropped her toothbrush into the sink.

Korine put one hand on the woman's shoulder until she stopped shaking. "J.J.'s downstairs," she said. "I need to talk with him. Will you be all right?"

Rhetorical question that it was, Dora didn't answer. She tore her gaze from Korine's image in the glass and looked down at the toothbrush sitting in the sink in front of her. Slowly, she picked it up and regarded it. Nodding her head, Dora frowned in concentration. She stuck the brush under the running water in the sink and rinsed it thoroughly. She picked up the toothpaste and began her ritual again.

The knocking on the back door was getting louder. Dora would be fine on her own, Korine reasoned. There was nothing that she could hurt herself with that wasn't locked up or unplugged already.

Korine backed out of the bathroom and ran down the steps. It was too late to do anything about the circles under her eyes or the dark stain on her white cotton shirt. The remains of the morning paper lay discarded on the counter; the coffee had dried in the bottom of the pot. She knew that letting things go like this didn't constitute failure on her part, but the feeling remained. Telling herself to calm down, she opened the back door and let J.J. in.

"Sorry I'm running so late," he said.

"We're not going anywhere," Korine said. "Janey get off all right?"

"She said she'd call me from her grandmother's this evening."

Korine frowned. "That's a long drive. She really going all the way to Louisiana in one day?"

"She promised to drive carefully." Clearly, his wife wasn't going to be careful enough to suit him. If Janey really planned on making her grandmother's house in one day, she wouldn't be driving carefully enough to suit any of them.

"How is Memaw?"

"Can't say. Like I told you earlier, she wouldn't tell Janey what this trip was all about."

"You look like hell," Korine said, then wished she could take it back.

J.J. passed a hand over his chin, then smiled gently down at her. "I suppose I'm entitled. Starting with that phone call from Janey's grandmother, then with all this.... It's been a hell of a week." He sobered. "You're not looking any better."

So he'd noticed. At least she'd cleaned up the pottery shards from Cal's smashed mug. Korine agreed with J.J.'s assessment. It was hell.

It wasn't going to get any better. Cal hadn't been seen or heard from since he'd stormed out earlier that morning. Korine could shoot the man for being so much like himself in a moment of crisis. She wished with all her heart that it had been his good qualities that came to the fore when times got rough, but it wasn't to be. Truth be told, Cal was probably wishing the same thing about her.

Korine turned her head toward the dining room. As inappropriate as it felt, the unfinished work on the table in the next room kept calling her name. Hardly surprising, it would be far easier to deal with than either Dora or Cal. Still, it was one more thing to carry around with her that she hadn't taken care of properly.

Korine smoothed her hair back behind her ears and took a deep breath. "You here to talk with Dora?" She wondered if she should call Franklin to come out while her mother-in-law talked with J.J. Or was an attorney really necessary?

"Where is she?" J.J. looked beyond Korine, out into the hallway.

"Upstairs, brushing her teeth. Could be a while. You want lunch while you wait?"

"Thanks, I'm taken care of," he said. "I wanted to talk to you first, anyway." He shifted his weight.

"What?" Korine's tone was sharp.

J.J. took a step forward, his face coming out of the shadow. He started to speak, then hesitated.

Surely it couldn't be any worse than what they'd already been through, Korine thought. The floor overhead creaked under Dora's weight as she moved from bathroom to bedroom. Korine felt like every nerve ending was on call for action. She stiffened and gave J.J. her full attention.

His face twisted. "I have to tell you something important. The autopsy report came back. Taggart was already dead when Mrs. McFaile hit him."

"What?" Korine couldn't take it in.

"Mrs. McFaile didn't kill Taggart."

Korine felt her knees give out. She reached behind her, blindly catching the counter with one hand. The metal strip on the edge bit into her fingers, but she held on for dear life. "How do you run a man over and not kill him?"

"He was already dead when she hit him," he repeated.

Korine couldn't stop the bark of laughter that ripped through her. "I can't believe this."

J.J. looked at her strangely. Evidently he didn't like what he saw, because he took her elbow and escorted her to the closest chair.

"You are serious," she said, looking at her friend's face.

J.J.'s lips twisted into a ghost of his wry grin. The tight band around Korine's heart eased slightly—hope, sneaking in to give her some breathing room from the shock.

"Yes," he answered. "But Mrs. McFaile still needs to give up driving."

"Already done!" Korine said fervently. She had the staggering sensation of living in two worlds: one in which her worst nightmare had occurred, and the new one in which a reprieve had come. The awful feeling of responsibility for Olan Taggart's death remained firmly ensconced in her stomach, but she couldn't deny that her mood had lifted.

She put one hand to her chest to still the hammering dance of her heart. Korine felt ashamed of her joy at hearing the news. In the end, fault would hardly matter. The man was still dead and mourned by his family. That was reality.

J.J. took the chair next to Korine. "Hazel said you talked to her about placing Mrs. McFaile at Shady Acres," he said.

"Yes, I thought I'd do some investigating so when the time came that Dora needed more care, I'd be ready with a plan." She rolled her eyes. "I didn't expect to need that plan the very next day."

"Do you know yet why she went over there?" J.J. asked.

"You're not going to believe this either," Korine said. "Dora said I left a note telling her to go over to Shady Acres and find Olan Taggart, along with a map so she wouldn't get lost on the way. She said she left the map in the car. I don't suppose you found one?"

J.J. shook his head.

Korine tried to explain. "She thinks people are after her. Sometimes she thinks those people are me. I told Lorraine and Dora that I was going over to the home to discuss landscaping. Dora knew it was business. Or she did when I left. Somehow, in her mind, she twisted it all around. Hence the note, supposedly from me, telling her to go to Shady Acres."

Korine raised her eyebrows meaningfully at J.J. He gazed blankly back at her. She spread her hands and said, "All I can say is that it's the most coherent hallucination she's had yet, and you know how she had me believing all kinds of things before we figured out what was going on with her. She was so frantic that I actually looked for a note."

"What did you find?"

"Nothing, of course." Honesty pricked Korine. "I take that back," she said slowly. "Last night, I did find something. A burned piece of paper in Dora's toilet—with my handwriting on it."

J.J. frowned. He crossed his arms and shifted his weight. Once again, the floor commanded his complete attention. Nodding once, as if answering an internal question, he refocused and bore down on Korine. "You leave any notes around the house about Shady Acres?"

She nodded. "For Lorraine, with the phone number."

"I see."

"The funny thing is that we noticed a burning smell soon after I got back home, and I found that note in her toilet after that. We put it down to the neighbors, but it might have been the smell from the note." Korine frowned. "I didn't really think about this earlier. But the timing's all wrong for that. There was no hint of smoke when I packed that bag for Dora when she was down at the police station. We smelled it after I got home—and before Dora and Cal got in."

J.J. held up his hands and shook his head. "Stop right there. In my experience, the easy answer is the one that's truthful. Don't go inventing conspiracies to explain something that's probably all in your mother-in-law's mind." He looked thoughtful just the same.

"What?" Korine asked.

"Nothing," J.J. said.

Korine knew that look. It was the same one her nephew Dennis had worn just before he was busted for drug possession as a teenager. J.J. was lying.

"Whatever you're not telling me," she said, "it's not something to do with Dora, is it?"

"I'm not withholding anything from you that you need to know." J.J. held his hands out, palms up, as if showing her that he had nothing to hide. His circuitous words confirmed Korine's fears. He was concealing something to do with Taggart's death.

She swallowed her anger. It wouldn't do either of them a bit of good if she lost her temper now. Korine cleared her throat and changed the subject. "Did you know that Cal has had somebody up here watching me for two weeks?"

"Cal did what?" J.J.'s hands fell to his side.

"He hired someone to check into things up here," she repeated grimly. "Dora told him I was stealing her blind. The missing jewelry. She thinks my theft extends to her bank accounts too."

"Missing jewelry?" J.J.'s voice sharpened.

"One day we won't be able to find her favorite necklace.

The next morning it's back on the dresser. You would not believe how many things go walking off one day, only to find their way back to where they belong by the following morning."

"I see," J.J. said slowly. Abruptly, he asked, "What medicine is Mrs. McFaile taking?"

Korine tried to read his expression. "Baby aspirin, something for blood pressure, and her Alzheimer's medicine."

"Depacote?"

Korine felt a shiver go down her spine. Doc had put Dora on that medication after she'd hit Lorraine the week before. She stared at J.J. for a minute before answering. "Yes. Why?"

"Something Doc said to me earlier this morning." J.J. pulled back the sleeve of his shirt and glanced at his watch. "Would you mind going up and seeing if Mrs. McFaile is ready to talk with me yet? I'm going to need to get going, and I still need to know if she saw anything that would help me figure out what happened to Mr. Taggart."

"I'll go get her." Korine stood up. "Have you told Cal?" she asked.

"Not yet. Isn't he here?" J.J. looked around, as if he expected to find the man standing behind him.

"He lost his temper and took off first thing this morning. Hasn't been back. Hasn't called. Probably doesn't care if we're worried. And he wants me to let him take Dora down to Charlotte with him? I don't think so."

"Korine, are you sure? He is her son. Maybe it would work out all right."

Korine was sure. She'd never been more so. "I know he wants to do for her. But I don't think it's the right thing for

Dora. He can't give her any more right now than I can. The fact is that she needs more than either of us can give, and she ought to stay here where she can see her friends. Cal and I can go visit her at Shady Acres easily enough."

Korine turned around at the gasp from behind her.

Dora, hands hanging limply at her sides, stood in the doorway. "You're going to put me away?"

Korine crossed the room in two strides. "Not put you away. Get some help taking care of you so that you're safe."

Dora's eyes closed for a beat, then opened. Looking past Korine to where J.J. stood next to the sink, she said, "After yesterday, you think that place is safe?" The derision in her voice was plain.

J.J. made a motion of denial with his hands.

Korine stepped toward Dora and slowly put one arm around her mother-in-law. "J.J. has some good news."

"Olan?" the old woman said. Her body shivered as she said her friend's name. The hope on Dora's face was painful to see.

J.J. moved forward and took her hand in his. "Why don't we sit down for a minute, Mrs. McFaile, and I'll try to explain."

Dora looked at Korine.

"Go ahead," Korine said. "I'll get some tea for you if you want something to drink while you two talk."

"Yes, please," Dora said, like a little girl on her best behavior. Then her voice turned sharp. "It's not sweet, is it?"

"Of course not. You don't like it sweet." Korine smiled at her. Bending down, she tucked a silver pin curl back into the crown of hair on the woman's head.

"No, I don't." Dora sat back in her chair, gently rocking herself.

The rush seat sighed as J.J. settled his big frame into the old wooden rocker. Korine pulled a slender depression-glass tumbler out of the cabinet and quietly poured it half full of unsweetened tea.

When Charlie had brought Korine home as a young bride, following a romantic elopement, Dora made it clear that Korine didn't measure up. Cal, still in high school at the time, took his tone from his mother, using Korine as another round of ammunition in the never-ending sibling rivalry between the brothers.

Then Charlie was diagnosed with cancer, and the two women closed forces against the common foe. That they'd lost the fight on Charlie's behalf hadn't stopped their belated friendship from blossoming. Cal, however, had never bothered to give up the old grudge.

After Dora had started to forget things, her newfound friendship with Korine was one of the first things she lost. Interesting that she'd looked to her daughter-in-law for approval when she sat down to talk with the police chief. Korine shook her head and tried to pay attention to what J.J. was saying to the woman.

"Mrs. McFaile, I'm sorry to have to bring this up again with you. I wanted to let you know that you had nothing to do with your friend's death."

Korine's eyes traced the furrow in Dora's brow, willing it to ease. If anything, it deepened with J.J.'s news.

"They did get him," Dora whispered.

"What?" J.J. said, abandoning his soothing monotone.

Korine went over and knelt in front of the old woman. "It was a horrible accident, but you're not responsible."

Dora bent her head and shook it from side to side, knitting her hands together in her lap like a student of etiquette. She looked up and blasted Korine with a stare from icy blue eyes that were all too aware. Korine hadn't given Dora enough credit; this was one of her good times. She fully comprehended what they were telling her, and it was scaring the woman to death.

"You're not going to listen to me, are you?" Dora said. "Just like you won't ever lock the doors."

Korine searched Dora's face. If it hadn't been for all the odd things happening in the previous few days, Korine would put this down to another one of Dora's apparently lucid paranoid fantasies, but now, she wasn't sure.

"Who are 'they'?" Korine asked.

"They told me not to tell. 'He removeth away the speech of the trusty, and taketh away the understanding of the aged,'" Dora quoted. Just that quickly, she was gone. She had retreated deep inside herself. If past experience was any guide, they had no way of knowing if the old woman would remain like this for seconds or hours.

Korine stood.

"What is she talking about?" J.J. asked.

"Do I look like I know?" Korine answered. "You just gave her great news, and she's falling apart. I don't understand it."

J.J. put one of his large, weathered hands over Dora's trembling one. She regarded him as if he were a writhing snake, but she didn't pull away.

He patted her hand and said, "I'm so sorry you had to go through all that yesterday. The fear and frustration of trying to make us understand."

"They killed my friend," Dora said suddenly. Her voice

was high-pitched, her pupils dilated, eyes so wide open that she looked like a feral animal.

"Who did?" J.J.'s voice was gentle.

Dora snatched her hand out from under J.J.'s. She muttered something under her breath about silly young men.

J.J. looked up and caught Korine's eye. His brows were nearly touching, his frown was so deep. He took a slow, deep breath and tried a different tack. "I realize that this is a shock to you, but we need to try to find some answers to a few questions."

Korine listened for any signs of impending disaster. None came.

"No," Dora said. She sounded more than ever like a small child.

"I won't ask about the accident, then," J.J. promised. "Are other questions all right to answer?"

Dora nodded reluctantly. She sent a brief look of supplication to Korine that nearly broke her heart. The frail woman looked back toward J.J.

"Why did you go out yesterday?" he asked.

Dora looked at J.J. a full minute before replying. "She left me a note telling me to go over to that place."

"So you found your keys...."

"They were on the note," Dora said. Her withering glance scorched Korine again.

J.J. nodded at Dora as if that were logical. Which it wasn't. Korine had not left a note, much less the keys to her car. This had to be one of Dora's nightmarish notions, yet she was so consistent about it.

He tried again. "You drove over to Shady Acres. Who did you see as you went up the driveway?"

She sat up in her chair as the floor overhead settled. She darted a glance behind her at the doorway to the hall, then folded her arms across her thin chest. "I can't remember." Dora's voice was barely above a whisper. She was no longer making eye contact. Her upper lip had curled slightly, like a dog warning off something threatening.

Korine gave J.J. a sharp look. Dora was clearly close to the edge. If he pushed anymore right now, she'd retreat entirely.

He leaned forward. Dora glanced at him, then away, her gaze skittering over the familiar objects in the room as if seeking a place to hide.

The old woman's head whipped around as she heard a car coming up the drive. She listened intently. Then, when the engine cut off outside the kitchen door, she struggled to rise. "They told me not to tell about Olan, and I won't. Ever!"

She shoved past Korine and fled through the front hall to the staircase. Korine, about to follow the sharp clatter of the woman's heels against the wooden steps, heard Amilou's raised voice outside. She'd promised Amilou that she would call her that morning and had completely forgotten. Dora wasn't the only one with memory problems.

TWELVE

THE CRUISER TOOK the left turn from Korine's driveway onto the highway without the usual groan from under the hood. Despite Dora McFaile's dramatics, J.J. had been worrying about Janey instead of focusing on the case at hand. Maybe the absence of car trouble was a sign that putting his personal problems first had been the right thing to do. He wondered what the "Car Talk" commentators on NPR would make of that. Not that he'd ever know what the Tappet brothers thought. The radio hadn't worked for so long, the memories of listening to the wisecracking show had dimmed in J.J.'s mind.

He tightened his hands on the steering wheel, remembering how upset his wife had been the night before. She had known that Memaw wasn't in great shape or the woman wouldn't have called her home. What Janey hadn't anticipated was how hard it would be to try to mend fences while trying to convince her grandmother that she had no business living alone.

J.J. shook off the wish to drop everything and run down to Louisiana. Not only was it irresponsible to even think of doing such a thing, it wouldn't do anyone a bit of good. Janey said she could handle it. She deserved the chance.

He adjusted his rearview mirror, then glanced down at

the phone nestled on the seat beside him. He'd expected to hear from Leon about his interviews at Shady Acres before now. Frowning, he brought his gaze back to the road in time to miss hitting a bicyclist. It was hard to tell who was more startled when J.J. swerved past him, the slim man clad in black stretch shorts, or the police chief.

Waving his hand in apology, J.J. pressed the accelerator and followed the road down toward the river. The highway back into town was all but deserted. No wonder the man thought he was safe to ride out on the open road.

J.J. rolled down his window and stuck his hand out, palm up, letting the cool air wash over his skin. Turning his hand over in the breeze, he closed his fingers into a fist. Korine was right, Dora was far more than any one person could handle. That business about "them" was enough all by itself to make such a judgment. But if Doc was right and the overdoses were deliberate, then Dora might be telling the truth.

With that scary thought, J.J. pulled his hand back inside the car and rolled up the window. A breeze ruffled the tops of the maples along the fence line by the Careys' farm. Scarlet leaves showered the cruiser as he passed. The discarded finery danced in his wake like a horde of demented devils.

Climbing the hill on the town side of the river, J.J. slowed as he neared the exit from the highway. He glanced over at the new apartment building by the side of the road and thought he had time, before his meeting with Hank, to see if there were any corpses littering the parking lot. Jett's report on the Grinsteads' Saturday-night domestic disturbance sounded like the violence in that home was escalating. J.J. hoped she'd have the sense to get out before it was too late. His sister Georgia hadn't.

Shutting the door firmly on that thought, J.J. steered between two oversized pickup trucks. The parking lot was empty of Grinsteads, dead or alive. But there was definitely something of interest.

J.J.'s eyes narrowed. Cal McFaile stood on the bottom step of one of the ground-floor apartments. Behind him, arms crossed loosely, and looking pretty disheveled, was Colleen Taylor.

J.J. went on by and parked about three spaces down. Colleen again. His fingers tapped the gray duct tape on the steering wheel while he thought that one over. He pushed open the car door and got out. The couple on the steps were too busy frowning at each other to notice the police chief until he was nearly next to Cal.

"Morning," J.J. greeted the pair. "I was just out at Korine's."

Cal raised one hand in a wary greeting.

"Your mother's having a rough time of it. I was surprised you'd left her." J.J. could have kicked himself as soon as the words were out of his mouth. Cal needed careful handling at the best of times. Antagonizing him was counterproductive.

Cal had the grace to look ashamed. "Korine and I…."

"She told me."

"It's not Cal's fault," Colleen said.

"Never said it was," J.J. replied, holding eye contact with Cal.

Colleen flushed and pulled her robe closer around her body.

J.J. watched Colleen out of the corner of his eye while he asked Cal his next question. "Korine said you'd hired someone to check up on how she was doing with Mrs. McFaile. Is that true?"

"That's my right," Cal protested.

"Yes, it is." J.J. cut his eyes toward Colleen, and her flush deepened.

"I didn't know what to believe," Cal said, giving Colleen an angry look.

In return, her eyes lingered on the way the wind ruffled Cal's hair. J.J. saw Colleen's fingers twitch, but she mastered the urge to reach out and touch the older man. Here she was, messed up in every aspect of this case, but she looked head-over-heels in love with him. J.J. could see her spying on Korine for Cal, but sending Mrs. McFaile out in a car on public roads? Hard to figure this one.

J.J. said, "I just got back from telling your mother and Korine how Taggart died."

"Was there any question?" Cal said harshly.

"Not until the autopsy report came back this morning. He died of an overdose of Depacote."

J.J. caught Colleen's quick intake of breath and watched her. She'd lost the flush and now looked alarmingly pale. She touched her lips with her tongue and winced, as if something bitter lingered there. J.J. waited out the pause.

Colleen focused in on his face. Her head tilted a little to one side as she looked up at him. "He would have died no matter what I did?"

"That's right." For a minute, J.J. felt sorry for Colleen. She had tried to save the man's life, after all.

Cal was so thrown by the news that he wasn't paying a

bit of attention to Colleen's reactions. He took a step toward J.J., fingers curled into fists at his side. "Someone
killed that man and tried to make it look like my mother
did it, didn't they?" he said.

"Why would someone want to do that?" J.J. asked.

Colleen glanced at Cal, then looked down at the ground.

"How should I know?" Cal replied with his usual anger.
He thought for a moment, then asked, "This means I can
take Mom on to Charlotte now, can't I?"

"I don't know about that," J.J. replied. "She won't have
to worry about jail, but I can't say she's not involved. She's
a witness."

Cal nodded. "I suppose so."

J.J. turned back to Colleen. "When did you first see
Taggart that morning?"

"Like I told you last night, I didn't see him until he
came out of those bushes and headed down toward Mrs.
McFaile's car."

At the mention of his mother's name, Cal took a step
closer to Colleen. She reached out toward him but then let
her hand fall when he took no notice of her gesture. J.J. resisted the urge to shake Cal. No matter how personally sat-
isfying such an action might be, it wouldn't instill any
sensitivity in the man.

"Wait a minute," Colleen said. She put one hand up to
shade her eyes as she met J.J.'s gaze directly for the first
time. "I picked up a prescription for Mr. Taggart from the
grocery Friday night. Doc had sent me over for a couple
of refills. We do that when I know in advance that I'm
going to be up at Shady Acres doing private duty. I drop
them off, then pick them up once I'm done with my shop-

ping. The pharmacist handed me one for Mr. Taggart, along with the others. Said it had been called in for him."

The girl's pupils were huge, darkening her pretty eyes. "It was for Depacote. This is horrible. Mr. Taggart died just like Mrs. Falkirk."

J.J. regarded Colleen. "Maris Falkirk died of exposure. What makes you put her death together with Taggart's?"

She stammered, "Doc said." She looked at Cal, as if expecting him to help her out. "Doc said she died right after he put her on Depacote. As though someone knew Mrs. Falkirk's quality of life was near its end, and they put her out of her misery."

J.J.'s eyes narrowed. That was not the way Doc had told it. "Who did you give the prescriptions to when you got there?"

Colleen shrugged. "Most likely the evening charge nurse, who probably handed them to someone who was holding the keys to the medication room, who may have handed them to someone else. That's the way it usually works."

Cal had relapsed into his own deep thoughts. He hadn't noticed that Colleen was on the verge of tears. She solved that by putting her arms around him and burying her head in his chest. Startled, he responded by putting his arms around her and patting her awkwardly.

"Call Korine," J.J. told Cal, "so that she and Dora don't worry about you any more than they have to."

Cal nodded, then walked Colleen back to her apartment.

J.J. returned to his car. He would definitely have to do a lot of hard thinking about Colleen. She was in way too many places to ignore. He'd put Jett onto checking out her background. Leon couldn't possibly be objective where Colleen was concerned.

J.J. unlocked the cruiser and got in. Cal had left Colleen at the door of her apartment. Watching the man climb into the SUV next to him, J.J. snagged the cell phone off the seat and pressed the speed-dial button for the station.

Marlene answered, for once without a complaint. She put him right through to Leon.

"Yeah, I broke the news to the folks out at the nursing home." Leon summed up the situation. "Hazel is some kind of upset."

"I would hope she's not the only one," J.J. responded.

"Jack Taggart drove in as I was leaving. First words out of his mouth, when he heard how his father died, were about lawyers and large sums of money. And that was after the owner had been tearing Hazel apart for 'letting' Taggart die while at Shady Acres."

"The owner would have been fine with it if Taggart had died someplace else?"

"That's about how she described the conversation. Taggart's son was also on a tear about some family heirloom that's missing. A pin his father used to wear on his kilt— evidently quite valuable."

J.J. was silent. Taggart had a piece of jewelry missing too? He thought about the recent burglaries and the story Korine had told him about Mrs. McFaile's missing jewelry.

He relayed those thoughts to Leon. Leon's reaction was pretty close to J.J.'s, something of a cross between *oh shit* and *no way*.

"Did you tell Jack how high the drug level was?"

"No," Leon answered, "but I did ask him where he was

the morning his father died, and I have the stripes off my hide to prove it. He wasn't happy, but he finally told me that he was home from work, sick. His boss called him at home about the time that Taggart would have gotten the overdose."

After writing down the business number that Leon read off to him, J.J. said, "I just left Colleen's apartment. She says she picked up a new prescription for Depacote for Taggart Friday night."

"Well, that's interesting," Leon said. "The nurses out at Shady Acres showed me the half-full bottle of pills they had locked up for him in their medicine cart. I dug around in the Dumpster outside and found an empty bottle with Taggart's name on it." He swore. "If I didn't know better—"

"You know a good reason Colleen would want Mr. Taggart dead?"

"How'd you know I was going to say something about Colleen?" Leon's voice was annoyed.

"So who were you going to say something about?"

"Colleen, of course. I've been working for you for too long if you can read my mind."

"You haven't worked in Pine Grove long enough. And I didn't read your mind at all; it's plainly obvious that she would be the first suspect. That said, you really don't like her, do you?"

"No." Leon's tone was rigid with disapproval.

"I'd go ask her if she wanted him dead, but I think I'll run up to Shady Acres instead."

"You want me to come over and talk to Colleen about why she might slip patients extra doses of pills, then push them under cars?" Leon offered.

"No, I don't think that will be necessary. Anyone remember seeing the empty bottle before you showed it to them?"

"I asked everyone who worked days, and no one saw it. Evening shift comes on about four. Jett or I will go back out later when they come back on duty. Those ladies work almost as many hours a week as we do."

"Subtle, Leon, subtle. I talked to Hank. We're trying. I'll wait and go to Shady Acres around change-of-shift time and talk with the night crew once they get there."

"Good luck."

"Thanks." J.J. hit the end button and punched in the number Leon had just given him for Jack's work.

"Hello?" A tinny voice answered the call.

Not a professional answer. Most businesses told you who they were when they answered the phone. "Is this Betty's Laundry Service?" J.J. asked.

"I'm the only one here."

He thought the soft voice on the other end of the line was a man. J.J. hoped that he wasn't the brains behind the business. "I need to leave a message for Betty," he said.

"She's not here," the man answered.

"Can I leave a message?" J.J. repeated.

This was obviously something new. After directions from J.J. and much searching, there was a remote possibility that Betty might someday receive a message from J.J. Bascom. It might also wind up in the trash. Sundays were not the most efficient time to try to conduct an investigation.

J.J. twisted his key and put the car in gear. Lifting his foot off the brake, he refocused on the scene around him. Most of the cars had left the lot, taking advantage of the crisp, clear day. As he pulled out onto the road and headed back for the center of town, he thought about Olan Taggart.

Colleen popped up pretty damn near everywhere a guilty party would be, but Jack was an obvious choice as Taggart's murderer. Despite the son's palpable grief, J.J. would have to consider him carefully. He'd call Betty again in the morning. He'd also have to check with the insurance company to see how much money was involved.

Not that the amount would be a deciding factor. It was the amount of perceived gain people murdered for, not always the concrete, count-the-bills type of gain. Although, J.J. conceded to himself, thinking of the story out of Atlanta about the man who'd killed not one but three wives—all for the insurance payouts—sometimes there was that too.

He pulled into the Texaco station on the corner. When he finished filling up the tank, he went inside and got a cup of coffee. The aroma of the fresh brew rose through the sipping hole in the plastic lid. J.J. closed his eyes and took a big whiff. Even though it was decaf, it smelled like the real thing. Close enough. Janey would kill him if he had a heart attack because he overcaffeinated himself while she was gone.

Back out in the car, he considered his options. It was still early to try to time his visit to Shady Acres with the evening shift coming on. He pulled the car forward, away from the gas pumps, and parked it, letting the engine idle. He took out his notebook and turned to the page about Jack Taggart. There was the note he'd just made to himself to check with the insurance company. Sunday afternoon wasn't the best time to try to reach them, so he put that call on hold until Monday morning.

He thought about it for a minute, then decided to go and

talk to the Kohls about their burglary the night before. He shifted the car into gear and negotiated his way back out onto the road. Greer Dairy Road was out of town, but it was in the direction of Shady Acres. A good use of his time. He picked up the phone and let Marlene know where he was headed.

THE OUTSIDE of the small whitewashed wooden farmhouse was in good repair, but the yard had been neglected shamefully. Beds full of late-blooming mums had been ransacked by invaders. The orange and yellow of the flowers peeked out from behind the tangle of triple-leaved vines. Poison ivy.

Being heavily allergic, J.J. went around back.

There was a young woman he didn't know coming out the back door. They looked warily at each other.

J.J. identified himself, and she introduced herself as Trudy, a home-health aide with the Visiting Nurses Association. At least she wasn't Colleen.

"They doing all right?" J.J. asked.

"As well as can be expected. Mr. Kohl is pretty agitated. Mrs. Kohl's going to have her hands full today."

"You work here often?" J.J. asked.

"Four days a week. They're pretty self-sufficient." She plucked a set of car keys from her open purse and nodded at J.J. "Hope you can find who took that necklace. Mrs. Kohl's pretty shook up about having somebody in the house."

J.J. watched her go, then he turned back to the house, raised his hand, and knocked on the back door.

The raw-boned woman who answered didn't look like a senior citizen. Her blue eyes wide with perpetual surprise, cheeks smooth, she smelled of nutmeg and cinnamon. The only thing old about her was the gray of her neatly plaited hair. J.J. made an amendment to his list when her sleeve fell back as she reached up to unlock the door. Her arm bore a road map of fine white scars crisscrossing her tissue-paper skin.

She noticed his gaze and pulled her sweater back down over her wrist self-consciously.

J.J. took off his hat and introduced himself.

"Please come in," Mrs. Kohl said. She sounded like there was nothing else in the world that she would like better than to have J.J. visit a while. "Sit down," she urged, indicating the empty chair at the kitchen table. "If you have a minute?" She checked to get his nod of assurance. "Thank you. I'm just pulling some schnecken out of the oven. Let me get Mr. Kohl fixed up, then I'll show you about the necklace."

Wondering what the heck schnecken was, even while his mouth watered at the heavenly smell, J.J. remained standing. He didn't want to sit down in the only available chair while she bustled around. He stayed next to the wall, if only to keep out of the way of a woman who clearly needed no help in the kitchen. Mr. Kohl, propped up inelegantly by the wall next to him, didn't appear to match the woman behind him. As she pulled on a pair of black oven mitts to take the baking pan out of the oven, Mrs. Kohl cast a worried glance at her husband.

She looked over at J.J. and noticed that he was looking at a Shady Acres brochure, which peeped out from under the desk calendar on the counter.

"My children dropped that off," she said, reaching over

and shoving the brochure into a drawer. "I won't abandon him that way."

"Mrs. Kohl, I completely understand. I have a good friend going through the same thing right now."

"He's my husband, not a wool coat I can put into storage. They want me to put him away so I can live my life. Living with him is my life." Her blue eyes turned cold and hard.

"Each person has to make their own choice. No one else knows what you can do, or what your husband can still enjoy," J.J. said carefully.

Mrs. Kohl seemed only slightly mollified as she pulled out a tray of perfectly browned cinnamon rolls.

"How long has he been like this?" J.J. asked.

"He's not 'like this,'" Mrs. Kohl said sharply. "It's not him, it's the disease."

Okay, J.J. thought. *So she isn't as sweet and cheerful as she seemed when she opened the door.* Reminded him, in a way, of Jack Taggart's mental state during their conversation back at the hotel. "Does Mr. Kohl sleep often?" he asked.

"Lately," Mrs. Kohl said. Her eyes lingered on her husband while she shoved a spatula under the rolls on the cookie sheet. Her face softened. "It's better than when he was walking all the time. I'd never know who was going to call me to come get him."

"You have good help?"

"Ever since George fell, I can't handle him alone."

"I'm so sorry," J.J. said. He saw now what age and responsibility had done to her. When she wasn't consciously holding herself erect and forcing a smile, her bowed shoulders told the true story. Her children were probably suggesting Shady Acres in a vain attempt to make sure that their mother didn't collapse.

"It can't be helped," she said.

"Has Doc James changed Mr. Kohl's medicines recently?" J.J. asked.

She put a plate down in front of her husband. The steam rose from the schnecken, and Mr. Kohl opened one eye. His nose quivered slightly as he inhaled the yeasty scent. He looked up at his wife, then put his hand out. He overshot, hitting the edge of the plate and knocking two of the rolls onto the floor beside him.

Mrs. Kohl picked the rolls up, hesitated, then dropped one on the plate. The other she broke in two and placed one half in her husband's hand. She absently took a bite of the piece she still held. "No. We don't see Doc James anymore. Switched to the neurologist over in Pickles about two months ago."

"Is that right?"

"I just…." She paused, eyeing J.J. to see if he was censuring her choice. "I know it seems odd, but that new office nurse of his just plain old got on my nerves. Every time we went to the doctor's office, she would tell me how my husband was too much for me and tell me to call her anytime. I was doing fine, although he was getting to be a handful." She unconsciously rubbed her arms, exposing those fine scars again. "So I took George over to Pickles."

"I understand completely," J.J. said neutrally.

Mrs. Kohl gave J.J. a sharp look, as if she'd picked up on how he felt about Colleen. He'd have to watch it with this woman.

She walked over to the counter and shoved a spatula under the remaining rolls on the cookie sheet. She lifted them one by one onto a plate. J.J. looked wistfully at them. Mrs. Kohl made a *tsk* sound and apologized, handing him the plate. Three tiny cinnamon rolls lay nestled there. He picked one up and broke it in two as Mrs. Kohl had done. Placing the roll in his mouth, he felt it melt, leaving raisins and nuts and the memory of cinnamon.

"Don't let Mrs. Hawkins know about these," he said between bites. "She won't rest until she has the recipe."

"She's been trying to get me to give it to her for years. If that was what had disappeared, I'd know who broke in last night."

J.J. swallowed the last of the schnecken from his plate. "Speaking of which," he began.

"I know what you're going to say," Mrs. Kohl said, "and neither of us could have misplaced it."

J.J. wiped his mouth with a napkin. He pulled his notebook out and jotted their names, address, and phone number down. He added Colleen's name below theirs, with a note that the Kohls had switched doctors because of her.

He asked, "You wouldn't happen to have a picture of the missing necklace?"

"No," she said. Her hand touched the sagging lines under her throat, then dropped away, empty. "It was George's mother's. Not particularly valuable, but I'd planned on giving it to my granddaughter when she turns thirteen later this month. Leah was named for her."

"Where was it?" J.J. asked.

"Let me show you."

Mrs. Kohl led him through the small hallway and took

a left. The staircase hugged the wall. The carpet was loose on a step about halfway up. A few steps higher, J.J. noticed a rip in the black flocked wallpaper, as if someone had stumbled on the carpet and knocked against the wall.

"This new?" he asked.

Mrs. Kohl glanced back. "No, that happened when George fell." Her hand tightened on the rail as she turned and climbed the rest of the steps. At the top, she crossed the landing to the door straight ahead. She twisted the knob and led the way into a pink and green bedroom.

A soft chair in one corner had a chenille throw on one arm that looked as if someone had just pushed it aside. On top of it was a tattered paperback romance novel by Meg Chittenden. The dresser stood opposite the still-unmade bed. Lying on its side on the dresser was an old-fashioned child's jewelry box like the one J.J. had given his sister for her tenth birthday. The ballerina was motionless, guarding the jewelry that spilled from its small interior.

"It was like this when I woke up this morning."

"Have you touched anything?" J.J. asked.

"Well," she said, looking sheepish, "I did push things around. I wouldn't have known the necklace was missing if I hadn't."

"If you can, don't touch anything else until my officer gets by to check for fingerprints."

"Certainly," she answered, but she didn't look happy about it.

"I understand that the back door was open when you got downstairs this morning?"

"Wide open." Mrs. Kohl's expression deepened into embarrassment. "I may have forgotten to lock it last night."

That was entirely possible. Most break-ins happened because the house was easy to get into.

J.J. followed her back down the steps and into the kitchen, where George slumped against the wall. Mrs. Kohl sat down in the chair next to her husband.

She put her hand on his shoulder and shook it gently. "George?"

He roused slightly. The woman placed another roll in her husband's hand. She then reached over and held his arm and guided it closer to his mouth. Once he'd taken a bite, his muscles remembered what to do and he quickly finished what he had in his hand.

"Has this happened before?" J.J. asked.

"The necklace? No."

"How about other things?"

"Yes, but they were always George's things. Mostly his tools. He'd pick them up, forget he had them in his hand. He'd go somewhere else in the house and put them down. I found his jigsaw in the freezer one day. That's when I knew something was really wrong with him."

"You mentioned he walked a lot?" J.J. asked. If the man had gotten up during the night, he might have taken the necklace and put it somewhere else in the house.

"I said he used to," she corrected. "He can't get up without help. If Trudy hadn't come by this morning to help me, he'd still be in bed."

"How did you get him downstairs?"

"He sleeps in the living room." She turned and fed her husband another piece of roll, saving J.J. from getting caught with embarrassment written large on his face.

"And you didn't hear anything?"

"I took a sleeping pill," she replied. "It's the only way I can sleep through his nightmares."

J.J. didn't know how to react. She had someone this dependent on her care and yet she took a sleeping pill so strong that she slept through a burglary in the very room in which she slept. Her blue eyes took in his expression. She sighed deeply, the sound like dry leaves blowing in the wind.

"George gets something too," she added. "It's not like he's in physical danger. As I said, he can't get up on his own. That's no longer part of his memory. Which is why I know he didn't move the jewelry box and hide the necklace."

"I'm sorry. I had to ask."

"I know," Mrs. Kohl said. "I know. That's what my son said too, when he called. Why everyone thinks I've lost my mind along with George is beyond me." Her expression softened as she leaned over and straightened her husband's slumped figure.

J.J. followed her gaze and wondered how she endured caring for someone who was obviously oblivious to everything but his own basic needs. George was once again leaning against the wall. And unless J.J.'s nose was leading him astray, the man had soiled himself too.

Mrs. Kohl laid a gentle hand on her husband's shoulder and shook him. He roused and took another bite.

J.J. thanked her and let himself out. He thought about the difference between the way Mrs. Kohl handled the slow, cruel loss of her husband and the way Jack Taggart was so quick to vent his frustration at Shady Acres. It wasn't hard to tell which one was the better of the two; what J.J. needed to ask himself now was whether or not Jack's anger had led him down the path to murder.

THIRTEEN

NO ONE COULD HAVE GUESSED that the tranquil vista meeting J.J.'s eyes as he entered Shady Acres had been such a grisly scene the day before. The willow by the gates waved its saffron-yellow leaves over the car as he passed. An oak gleamed chestnut brown against the vivid colors of the hills behind the building. There were even ducks bobbing on the small pond on the left as J.J. drove slowly up the hill. The long stain on the drive was still evident, but even it seemed to have faded.

As J.J. passed the spot where Olan Taggart's body had rested, he wondered how the man's son had felt driving over the same ground where his father had died. J.J. flashed back to the drawn look of Jack's face in the uncertain light of his room at the Best Western. The way his eyes had hollowed into his face. J.J. thought of Janey and wondered if she'd found her grandmother slipping in her golden years. He couldn't bear to think of her experiencing the kind of pain that Jack, Korine, and countless others had endured.

He picked up the phone and thought about calling her, then decided to follow Korine's advice. Janey did have sense. She'd call him when she needed him.

J.J. RAPPED ON the door to Hazel's office. Hearing her call for him to enter, he turned the knob and found Jack Taggart sitting across from Hazel.

His lean face averted, Jack fiddled with one of his father's pipes. "Thank you for all your help," he said to Hazel. His mouth twisted on the words. They must lay sour on his tongue.

Hazel had the good sense to leave Jack's sarcasm alone. "I wish I could do more," she said. "We'll keep a weather eye out for your dad's pin." Her lips puckered. No love lost between these two.

J.J. cleared his throat. Hazel nodded at him, her gaze shifting from his face to the hat he held in his right hand. Jack looked up at J.J., then glared across the desk at Hazel.

"You looking for Leon?" Hazel asked. "He left a little while ago."

"I talked to him," J.J. replied. "Jack, Leon said you were here. I figured I'd come up and fill you in on what we've found so far."

Jack settled back. He pulled a Wal-Mart sack off the chair next to him and dropped it on the floor at his feet. He turned slightly so that he could look at J.J. without craning his neck. There was a fresh cut under Jack's jaw. He hadn't been as careful with his razor as he might have been. Grief did things like that to a person.

"Leon told you about the medicine bottle he found?" J.J. asked.

"Yes," Jack said. "Sounds to me like someone made a fatal medical error."

Hazel opened her mouth in protest, then shut it firmly. White lines bled around her lips as she pressed them together. She gave Jack a telling look and glanced longingly at a Waterford letter opener on the edge of her desk in front of J.J.

He reached over and picked up the letter opener. Not that he really thought Hazel would give in to her impulse. "Actually," he said, "we think the dose that killed your father was brought in from outside."

"How?" Hazel and Jack asked together. They glanced at each other, clearly startled to be in unison on anything.

"Colleen Taylor picked it up from the pharmacy. Somebody called in a refill."

"It wasn't my staff," Hazel said firmly, her look at Jack defying him to contradict her.

"It wasn't Doc," J.J. said. His next words were interrupted by the ring of a cell phone. He checked his pocket, but the phone wasn't vibrating, so it wasn't his.

Jack reached into his shirt pocket and pulled out a small phone. He flipped it open. "Hello?" he said. "Who is this? Hang on a minute." His eyes cut toward J.J. "Sorry," he mouthed. "Work, gotta take it." Holding the phone close to his chest, he inched past J.J. and down the hall to take the call in private.

After the man left, J.J. handed Hazel the letter opener. "Pretty thing," he said. "I guess it ought to be locked up around here."

Some of the tension went out of Hazel's face as her eyes relaxed in a slight smile. She reached out and took the opener and placed it in her desk drawer. "You never know where it might wind up," she agreed.

J.J. turned his hat over in his hand, while he gave Hazel a good look. "You doing all right?" he asked.

"Sure," she said shortly. She picked up the file folder in front of her and tapped it on the desk, shifting the papers inside to precise alignment. She placed it carefully on the desktop and took a form filled out with harsh black strokes and tucked it inside. Closing the file, she turned and slid it into a file box on the credenza behind her.

"That Taggart's file?" J.J. asked.

She nodded. "Complete with death certificate, autopsy showing a possible medical error that cost our patient his life, and official complaint from the closest relative about missing items. I didn't fill out an incident report about how Jack verbally threatened me. Seemed like overkill."

"Ah," J.J. meagerly replied. He leaned forward. "Colleen said she turned the Depacote in to a staff member during report between the day and evening nurses. If you don't mind, I'd like to talk with the evening folks about that. See if they remember anything."

Hazel slid open her drawer and took out a bottle. Shaking out a pair of capsules, she popped them into her mouth. Following those with a swallow of Coke from the open can on her desk, she said, "Sure. Between you and Jack, it'll be a regular party back there."

J.J. looked at her more closely. Her neat hairstyle of the day before had fallen into a barely combed bob. Her hands shook as she placed them on top of her desk. When Hazel caught him looking at them, she folded them down in her lap.

"Yes," she snapped, "I'm a mess. Wouldn't you be?"

"Those weren't Tylenol you took this time."

Her green eyes sparkled with tears. "No, but don't think for one minute I've been pilfering from the patient medicine stores. Doc gave me a prescription for something stronger so I could go on here until my replacement arrives."

"They've told you they're replacing you?"

"I figure I have about three days before they make a decision. By Wednesday, they'll send someone to confiscate my keys and escort me to the door. Quite frankly, I'm surprised they haven't done it already."

She sat back, smoothing her dark hair behind her ears, and said, "Change of shift is in about fifteen minutes. You can catch both sets of nurses and aides if you go back there now. It might help if you're there when Jack asks about that pin of his dad's."

"Is he really getting threatening?" J.J. asked.

Hazel wrinkled her nose. "Only with me up to this point, but that's because I'm not letting him back on the unit without a supervisor. So far, that has been me. I asked the on-call administrator to stay on that unit tonight just in case."

"I can't do damage control for you," J.J. said.

"I'm not asking you to," Hazel snapped. "I'm afraid he might try to intimidate some of the night shift. They're not quite as experienced as the day shift in dealing with families, and I can't afford to lose good staff."

J.J. gave Hazel the benefit of the doubt. She wasn't usually this snappy, but then he doubted she'd ever faced a situation like this before, either. "I'll go on back then."

"Thanks." Hazel smiled.

Her face relaxed some, and J.J. knew he'd been right not to take her tone personally. As he let himself out of the room, Hazel lifted the phone and punched in a number. She smiled at him as he closed the door behind him.

J.J. nodded to the few people he knew as he walked toward the unit on which Taggart had lived during his last days. He keyed in the combination which opened the magnetically locked door. He dodged one man who had made a beeline for the opening, running into the door just as it closed firmly behind J.J.

"I have to get to work," the burly man said.

One of the nurses came up and stood next to the man. "Mr. Lange? There's a phone call for you back this way."

The man allowed her to take his arm and steer him away from the door.

J.J. looked around as he walked behind the pair. The furniture was nice. It looked clean enough. But there was a sour note in the perfumed air. Shady Acres was gussied up, but it was still a nursing home.

A small group of uniformed women stood talking together at the end of the hall. One of them waved. Carly Fontenot, one of Janey's friends from church. Hazel must not know her staff very well; Carly could hold her own with anyone.

J.J. looked back as he heard the door open. Jack pushed through. The door shut firmly behind him.

"Everything all right?" J.J. asked, inquiring about the phone call Jack had taken in Hazel's office.

"My boss is hoping I can get back to work soon. She has some things I need to take care of for her."

They reached the nurse's station, where most of the women seemed to have become suddenly busy. There was only one large woman left at the desk.

She stood, arms folded across her ample chest like a sumo wrestler ready to do battle. "What can I do for you?" she asked Jack.

"Carly, you know I don't think badly of you, but somebody slipped my dad an overdose."

J.J. cleared his throat. "I wouldn't accuse hardworking women of anything. You never know when they might call an attorney and try to sue for defamation of character."

Jack's face turned a slow shade of tomato red. "Might have known," he muttered. He turned back to the nurse. "You find Dad's pin yet?" he asked. "Can't deny that's missing, can you?"

"Can't deny it, no. Can't find it, either. Your dad was wearing it the night before he died. Maybe it went with him when they took him away after the accident."

"I never got it if it did."

"So you have another place to look for it instead of here," Carly said. "We got work to do here. People to care for. Do you mind if we get on with things?"

Jack stalked back down the hallway and out the door. If the hydraulic closer on the door would have allowed, he'd have slammed it, for sure.

"He's hurting," Carly said. "I know that. But we took good care of his dad. He ought to be polite about things."

"You get that kind of thing often?" J.J. asked.

"Sure," Carly answered. "Families have to have someone to be angry with. Can't be mad at themselves, can't be mad at their family. We're convenient."

"Tough."

"Sure is," she said. "Now, what can we do for you?"

"Colleen Taylor. Tell me about her."

Carly's dark face seemed to slip a subtle mask into place. "Good worker. Little bit flighty when a man's around."

"You don't like her?"

"I didn't say that."

"Say what you mean, then," J.J. said.

Carly stared at him a minute, black eyes expressionless. "I wouldn't want her taking care of my mother," she said. "Not that she isn't kindness itself to the patient, but things wander when she's here."

"And you get blamed for it," J.J. said, jerking his thumb back over his shoulder in the direction Jack had left.

"Yeah. We be black women. She be white." Carly exaggerated the urban-speak to drive home her point.

"Gotcha. Tell me about Lyndsey Babbitt."

"What you want with Lyndsey?"

"I need to talk with her. She here?"

"She's off today." Carly assessed J.J.'s face. Evidently she didn't find anything there to keep her from divulging the information J.J. needed. "She's good with our people. I don't know anything against her except that I had to send her in to talk with the nursing supervisor about that mouth on her."

J.J. raised his eyebrows.

"Cursed in front of a patient," Carly explained. "I don't let that go on here."

A woman wandered down the hallway, wearing the most wrinkled birthday suit J.J. had ever seen. The only thing covering her body was a large purple diaper which swaddled her middle.

"Mrs. Grant, you need help getting those clothes back on, don't you?" Carly went over to the woman and put her jacket on her. "See you later," she said to J.J. as they passed him.

He spent a few minutes talking to the other evening shift staff. They all said that Carly had taken the pharmacy bag from Colleen, put it on the medicine cart in the locked utility room, and put all the bottles away after change of shift.

By the time the staff finished telling their side of the story, Carly was back, having settled Mrs. Grant. She had little to add to the story except that there hadn't been anything in the bag for Mr. Taggart. If the bottle disappeared, it had done so before Colleen dropped the medications off at Shady Acres.

"You saying that you think Colleen took the bottle?" J.J. pressed.

"I'm only saying that we never saw it here."

J.J. wrote that down in his book, several question marks next to it. Typical that he would finish up an interview with more questions than he had coming in.

A short, lively looking woman with expressive brown eyes came down the hall and stopped next to the desk. "Now I know why Jack Taggart wasn't ever allowed on the unit to visit with his daddy," she said. "He's enough to make anyone crazy. How about all of us look for this pin of his so he'll get off our backs." The aides moved off down the hallway, splitting up as they got to the doorway of the first set of rooms.

J.J. slipped the scrap of paper Carly handed him with Babbitt's phone number on it in his notebook and put it in his pocket. He stopped in Hazel's office to let her know he was leaving and that Jack had walked out earlier. She left the paperwork she was working with on her desk and went back to talk with the staff as J.J. went on out to his car.

"I DON'T CARE if you're a Royal Mountie in full uniform, you woke me up!"

The young woman on the other end of the line was trying to refuse to talk with J.J. "Miss Babbitt?" he said.

"What?" she asked.

At least she hadn't hung up.

"I need to talk to you about Maris Falkirk and Olan Taggart."

"I didn't mean anything." The girl sounded scared. "I was just talkin' to the wind, if you know what I mean. Doc just happened to be standing there and heard me."

"Suppose you tell me what you noticed about their behavior that inspired you to talk to the wind." He resisted asking Babbitt to think of his voice as a gentle breeze. For one thing, J.J. didn't think he could pull it off with his gravely bass voice. For another, she sounded intelligent enough to resent that sort of remark.

"They both died."

J.J. could almost hear her lift her hand and start to tick off fingers. It was a certainty that she started with the middle one.

"They both were more disoriented than usual for about a day before they died. Well, with Miss Maris it was before she got herself locked out, you know what I mean?"

J.J. made a noncommittal noise.

"And they both lost things important to them a month or so before they died."

"What things?" J.J. asked.

"Well, Miss Maris's family was looking for a necklace she'd lost for a week. Finally found it in her drawer, buried under her socks. We think whoever took it got scared because of the fuss and brought it back. But it made her real crazy while it was gone. We had to change her medicines around a little to calm her down."

"And Taggart?"

"He had some pin he was making a fuss about. But it turned back up again just before he died."

"And you treated him the same way, changed his medicines?"

"Yep, both of them put on Depacote. Don't know what we'd do at night without it. Sundowners is a real thing, you know?"

"I see." J.J. was beginning to see quite a lot he didn't like.

"There going to be a reward for this?" Babbitt asked. "Because I might be losing my job, talking to you this way."

"I don't think you'll have to worry about that. It would be illegal for you to lose your job for cooperating with the police."

"Oh."

J.J. smiled. Her young voice sounded disappointed.

"It would also be illegal for you to withhold evidence," he added.

"Well, I can't be accused of that, now can I?" she said.

"What you've told me isn't enough to actually arrest anyone, but it is enough that I'm going to have to ask some nursing home folks to take a pretty close look at how Shady Acres is run."

"Oh." This time her voice was small. "I don't want them to close."

"I hope it won't come to that. You just keep on working. If you wouldn't mind, let me know if anyone else misses anything and gets wild enough to change their medications around."

"Sure. I'll keep your number by my bed," she said.

Sure you will. J.J. made a mental note to call her back. "Thank you," he replied. He hung up the phone, his mind already on the state nursing home commission. This was not going to be fun.

FOURTEEN

AMILOU LOOKED UP from the paper and sighed. "I think we're done."

Korine looked over her shoulder and nodded. "I can see it now," she said enthusiastically. Surrounded by Amilou's colored pencils—and a heavy sprinkling of eraser dust—lay the finished landscaping plan for Shady Acres. Korine had totted up all the numbers and estimated that it would be within Hazel's proposed budget.

All they had to do now was get Hazel to approve the plan. Then they could start digging. It was more ambitious than any of the women had intended it to be. But one good idea had led to another, until the final plan seemed meant. Amilou and Janey had done a wonderful job with the initial planning Saturday afternoon. All Korine and Amilou had had to do was fine-tune the plan to get it picture-perfect. Far from shutting Korine down, the horrible situation with her mother-in-law had served to spur her imagination to produce idea after idea that would please Dora.

"The pergola with the swings inside was an inspiration," Korine said. "I'm so glad Janey took the time to stop and call us with that idea."

Amilou's expression dimmed. "Do you think she's going to be all right going back down there alone?"

"You're starting to sound like J.J. Her memaw's not a demon. Janey's a big girl and can handle herself fine." Korine tried not to show the exasperation she felt over the coddling everyone gave Janey, but she knew she'd failed.

Amilou pushed back her chair from the dining room table, stood up, and stretched. Her fine hair, still the same shade of golden blonde it had been when the two women met so many years before, shone in the late afternoon sun filtering in the windows of the dining room.

Like the mature forty-year-old woman she was, Amilou stuck her tongue out at Korine. "Worrying over her doesn't do Janey any harm," she said.

"No, but treating her like a child does," Korine snapped. She was immediately sorry.

"Aren't you thinking of Dora?" Amilou asked pointedly. "She's the one who's being treated like a child. For goodness' sake, you even had to put her down for a nap to be able to get anything done with me this afternoon."

"I've had about enough of people telling me how I've mishandled my mother-in-law," Korine said, her voice rising.

Overhead, the floor creaked, then they heard slow footsteps leading out into the hall. Korine could feel the muscles between her shoulder blades tense. Dora should have slept another hour. The rest of the afternoon would probably be worse than the morning had been, if that could be possible. And Cal still hadn't returned.

Amilou dropped her pencil onto the cherry table and put her arms around Korine. After a quick hug, she pulled back and said, "I was not telling you that at all." Her brown eyes searched Korine's. "We're simply worried about you."

"I'm just so tired," Korine said as Amilou's face swam in her suddenly foggy vision.

"I'm going to go find that Cal McFaile and let him have a piece of my mind."

"Don't bother," Korine said. "It won't do you a bit of good. But I feel better knowing somebody's on my side."

"Where's Mom?" Cal stood in the kitchen doorway. He smiled at Amilou and tipped his gimme cap to Korine.

Apparently he didn't remember slamming out of the house that morning.

Korine stood there. She knew her mouth was open, but she couldn't seem to recover fast enough to say all the things he had coming to him.

Amilou heeded Korine's wish that she not rip Cal to shreds. Smiling a bit grimly, she indulged herself enough to say, "We were beginning to get worried about you."

Cal held up two Winn-Dixie bags. "I forgot a few things when I packed to come up here," he said. "What's for dinner?"

Either the man was being deliberately provocative or he was dumb as a post. Korine would have voted for the second, but she knew better. She'd seen the assessing glance he'd shot her way. He hadn't forgotten their fight that morning, after all.

Amilou opened her mouth. Korine put out a hand to stop her, but the words rolled out uninhibited, "If you're hungry, please feel free to try that new restaurant over in Pickles. Or maybe you'd prefer the inn across the state line. Korine's been spending too much time taking care of your mother to plan meals for you like you were company." She paused to draw breath.

Cal remained in the doorway, as if turned to stone.

Korine stepped over and took her friend's hand. "I can handle this." She squeezed hard and gave Amilou a look that cut off what she had been about to say.

"Today's been worse than usual for Dora," Korine said, "and by extension the rest of us who were around to help her. You say you want to take her home with you, yet you run out the first time your temper gets the better of you. You cannot do that if you decide you're going to participate in your mother's care." She paused to let the emphasis sink in.

Cal opened his mouth to speak, but Korine was on a roll. "She's been asking about you all day," she said. "Why don't you go up and see how she is, and I'll see about ordering some dinner from the Chinese restaurant. I'll even go and get it." This last was no hardship at all; she would be out of the house, and Cal would begin to figure out what taking care of his mother really entailed.

Korine would give Cal this, he had the grace to look embarrassed. He looked her over, then dipped his head once.

"You're right," he said. "It's not surprising that Mom had a bad day today, and I should have been here for her. I owe you both an apology." He slid a look over Amilou that obviously did not include her in his apology. Despite that, the man actually sounded contrite. "The reason I asked was because I have a chicken and salad I picked up at the grocery. I was trying to be funny. Any way we could start over?"

Amilou mumbled something inarticulate and turned to the table to roll up the plans.

Korine was appalled at her behavior. "I'm sorry. I'm as

guilty of judging you as—" Korine stopped. She would be damned if she likened herself to him in this way. Even if he'd brought home dinner, he'd still left them alone all day. "Dora should be down any minute. I heard her get up a minute ago."

"You wanted to talk. How about I put the chicken in the oven to warm it up and we can have that talk while we make the salad?" he suggested. The smile looked out of place on his rugged face, as if he'd gotten it new for this occasion.

Amilou spoke up. "You want me to stay, Korine?"

"Not unless you want dinner."

"I've got something tonight, but nothing I can't reschedule if you want more company." She shot a potent look toward Cal.

"No," Korine said, looking at her brother-in-law. It might be best to have this out alone. "You go on. We'll be fine."

Amilou eyed her but continued packing up her drawing materials. "Are you sure?" she asked when Cal went back into the kitchen.

"Really," Korine assured her. "I won't kill him."

"I'm almost as worried about him killing you. But I don't suppose we ought to even joke about it, after Mr. Taggart." She switched the plans to her other hand, picked up her purse, and juggled her way out the back door.

With mixed emotions, Korine watched Amilou go. On the one hand, it would be wonderful to have someone there to back her up when she put her plan to Cal. On the other hand, as much as she loved her friend, Amilou's quick temper would probably not help soothe Korine's already frayed nerves. She'd need all the calm she could muster to talk Cal into doing the right thing by his mother.

Korine picked up the wooden broom Dora had abandoned on the front porch earlier in the day. Amilou's car lights faded down the drive, leaving the yard painted a uniform shade of black, with a stark outline of the light spilling out the kitchen window in the back of the house. Korine glanced up at the night sky. It was supposed to be clear with a full moon. The weatherman had missed the boat on his forecast. No moonlight would find its way down through that cloud cover.

Korine closed the front door and snapped the deadbolt in place. She jumped at a sound at the top of the stairs. She chastised herself and leaned the broom against the front door. She'd put it up later. Placing one hand on the newel post, she called up the steps, "Dora?"

No answer. The woman had probably gotten up, gone to the bathroom, then gone back to bed.

Hesitating, unable to decide if she should go up to check on her mother-in-law or wait to beard the lion in her kitchen, Korine found the decision made for her when Cal poked his head out of the kitchen door at the other end of the hall.

"Is your friend gone? I got the stuff hot enough to eat while we talk." He disappeared back into the room.

Korine took her hand off the banister and pushed through the still-swinging door into the kitchen where her brother-in-law lay in wait. He'd turned on the old glass lamp on the counter that Korine usually used as a night light. The soft light was soothing. She walked over to the fridge and pulled out the bottle of wine she'd opened a few days before. Eyeing it, she judged there was enough left for the two of them.

She held it up toward Cal. "Can I pour a glass for you?"

"No, thanks." He hesitated, then, watching for her reaction, added, "I've quit drinking."

And to think she'd assumed Cal had taken his drink once Korine and Dora were safely tucked in the night before. She gave him a mental apology and decided she'd better wait to see if he was serious or not before she made a verbal one. If he could make the effort, then she could support him in it.

Korine put the bottle back on the shelf and closed the refrigerator door. "Water, milk, or tea?" she asked.

"Water, please." His sidelong glance of gratitude was quick.

Once they had food on their plates and were sitting side by side in the rockers, Korine looked over her glass at Cal. His face wore his habitual frown, which could be accounted for by any number of things, not all of them bad. As Korine took another bite of chicken, Cal shot a look at the ceiling. There had been no movement from upstairs, and, it seemed, they were reasonably well content to sit and talk things through like adults.

Cal put his empty plate on the table and picked up his glass of water. "I stopped by and looked over the information that my detective collected. I owe you an apology."

This was a different man from the one who had thrown things and left, swearing, that morning. Korine took another sip of her water, not trusting herself to speak.

"I said I'm sorry," Cal said, sounding peeved. He looked put out that Korine hadn't automatically forgiven him and moved on, the way his mother always had.

"I accept your apology. But I am still angry enough with you to wring your neck," Korine said. "Sometimes sorry isn't enough. Sometimes you ought to examine what you say and do, ahead of time. Charlie used to make excuses for you, but I won't. Your automatic discounting of everything I say about Dora has cost her. And I'll freely admit that it's cost me too. But to go and hire a detective to investigate me is beyond anything I even imagined you would do."

"I understand that your feelings are hurt," he began.

"My feelings are not the point. The point is that you decided, without having all the facts, that I wasn't taking care of your mother. Instead of coming here yourself and talking to me, you sent someone to spy on us. You have a history of getting other people to do your dirty work, don't you?"

The color drained from Cal's face. Korine almost thought she'd gone too far, but she didn't care anymore. His willful ignorance had interfered with Dora's care, just as his neglect had caused his son's problems not so long ago. Korine hardened her resolve. It didn't matter to her anymore how much he loved the people he hurt. They were still hurt at the end of the day.

He shoved himself out of the chair like he had that morning. But this time he turned on Korine. "Do you have any idea what it's like to know what I allowed Dennis and the other boys to go through?" he said.

Korine swallowed and tried to look away. She couldn't. The man actually had tears in his eyes.

"I knew I'd lost Dennis to you. Even hiring professionals to try to help him didn't work. I had to get sober to do that, and both his mother and I were too far gone to do that for him. How ironic is that? I just got it together enough to try to build some kind of relationship with my children, and my mother loses her mind so that she can't watch me make things better." Cal whirled and paced the kitchen floor. He tripped on one corner of the rag rug spanning the linoleum. Catching himself on the counter, he bowed his head and stood, shoulders shaking.

Korine's indignation fled. She forced herself out of the chair and walked over to him. "I guess it's my turn to say I'm sorry. I know it isn't easy for you. And I know you don't mean to hurt those people you love. It's just—"

"I know," he said bitterly. "They're still hurt, no matter how hard I try to do the right thing."

Korine put out a hand hesitantly. She didn't know if she and Cal were ready to mend any of the larger fences in their lives. There was so much history of animosity between them. Starting with the sibling rivalry between Cal and his older brother, through his neglect of his sons, and ending with this latest incident. For Dora's sake, for her own sake, she had to try to ignore the hurt and concentrate on what needed to be done.

The muscles under Cal's flannel shirt vibrated like a bowstring when she placed her hand on his arm. She lifted the hand quickly.

He turned his head, still leaning on the counter for support. "I know. We still have to talk." His voice was hollow, which made him sound as tired as Korine felt.

"Let's sit down and talk, then."

Once they were seated, the chairs gradually synchronized their rocking until Korine felt like part of an old married couple. She smiled.

"What?" Cal demanded.

Korine indicated the chairs.

His lips curved up at the corners, erasing the white lines in his tanned hide. "Days like today, I could start back up again."

"When did you quit drinking?" Korine asked, then realized she probably shouldn't bring up any more controversial subjects.

"I was talking about smoking. But I joined AA in June."

After their last fight, then. "Congratulations," Korine said. "I know it's hard to quit both those things."

They rocked a bit more, and Cal said, "I went by to see Doc James this afternoon, after J.J. talked to me about Taggart. Doc told me that people like Mom don't take change well. He said that moving her to Charlotte would make things worse pretty fast."

"Did he tell you that moving her to someplace like Shady Acres would do the same thing?" Korine asked. She kept her eyes trained on the kitchen clock, as if it would tick out the answer she wanted.

"As a matter of fact, I did ask him about that. He said it would cause her some trouble too."

"So we're left with trying to decide what's best for Dora, but with no real good choices."

"That's about how I see it, Korine." Cal swung around to face her. "I don't want Mom to go someplace like Shady Acres without me to visit her regularly. I can't get up here but every couple of weeks. I could get to someplace in Charlotte several times a week."

Tears sprang to Korine's eyes. "I promised her," she said.

"Tell me how that promise is any more binding than the

one she made me give her not to put her in a nursing home at all. She's changed. She's not even a shadow of the woman who raised me. Seeing her last night brought that home to me with a vengeance. Knowing that she could have killed a man because I didn't step in…."

Cal put his fingers together in a steeple over his nose and blew a deep breath out through the arch of his hands. "I'd give a pretty penny to know how Mom just *happened* to be there when Taggart died."

"She says it's my fault," Korine said.

"*Your* fault?" Cal's eyes narrowed. "How's that?"

"Well, thank you for your trust," she said. She described the note story to him. She finished, then frowned as Felix the clock let them know it was seven o'clock.

"Does Mom usually go to sleep this early?"

"Actually, she hasn't had dinner yet. I heard her earlier, remember, but this has evolved into the longest afternoon nap on record. She didn't sleep well last night, and it looked like tonight was going to be more of the same."

Cal stood. "I'll go get her up. As you said, if I'm going to take responsibility for her, I might as well figure out what's involved in her care."

"We didn't decide anything," Korine said quickly.

"Not yet, but we can talk again tomorrow. I'm going to be here for a week. Took my vacation early to try to sort this thing out." He started toward the stairs.

"I'll put a plate together for her," Korine said as Cal went upstairs. She walked to the sink and rinsed their dinner dishes, then put them in the dishwasher.

"Korine!"

She heard his cry as she took a plate out of the cupboard.

Putting it down on the counter, she rolled her eyes. He couldn't even get Dora out of bed without help. She took the steps and arrived to find Cal looking wild-eyed by his mother's bed.

"I can't wake her," he said. He held Dora's bottle of Depacote, empty, in his hand.

Korine whirled and ran into her bedroom. She fumbled the phone to her ear and called 911.

Korine's hand shook. She had locked up Dora's medicines. She knew she had. Hadn't she?

FIFTEEN

J.J.'S CELL PHONE RANG AGAIN at ten-thirty Sunday night. He clicked it on immediately, hoping of course that it would be Janey calling from Louisiana. Jett's voice put that attractive notion to rest.

"Chief, I've got some good news and some bad news."

"Good news first."

"Colleen has a record."

"Is that so?"

"A Grady Francis took out a restraining order against her for stalking. She'd been helping him take care of his elderly mother in Asheville last spring. Seems she decided she'd like to become a permanent part of the family. It made the local papers, and she was fired from her day job at the hospital. That's when she came to Pine Grove."

"Does Doc know anything about this?"

"I doubt it. Said he hired her right out of school."

"You asked him about her history already?" J.J. was impressed with Jett's initiative.

There was a pause. "Actually, I talked to Doc right after she came to town. I wanted her phone number. Leon got there first."

J.J. sighed. If things went along the way they had been going, and the case went to trial, he sure hoped that the judge wouldn't ask his officers what kind of relationship they had with Colleen.

"Can you contact the man who took out the restraining order?" J.J. asked. "Ask him if she's contacted him at all since then. And find out exactly how she harassed him."

"Will do, Chief."

"You mentioned bad news?"

"I lost a bet with Leon about whether or not Colleen was involved in all this."

Typical.

The phone beeped, indicating an incoming call. J.J. hung up with Jett and answered the new call. It was Doc James. Dora McFaile was in the hospital with a probable overdose.

J.J. opened his desk drawer and stuffed some peppermints into his pocket. The burning sensation in his stomach warranted Tums, but he didn't have any more of them. The peppermints would have to do.

APPROACHING THE ENTRANCE to the emergency room, J.J. could see Cal and Korine conferring with Doc. Colleen stood next to Cal, her hand possessively on his arm. Their features swam green behind the thick glass of the sliding doors. Their expressions were anxious, but not devastated. J.J. took a moment to catch his breath.

He searched each face in turn. The thick glass caused enough of a distortion that J.J. fancied he was offered a heightened perception of each of their personalities. Cal stood back, his lip curled, brow furrowed, eyes dark with worry. Korine's posture stooped under the fatigue that she had been less and less able to hide over the past month. The pinched set to her lips betrayed her anxiety. Doc, rock solid, nevertheless showed signs of having caught some of Korine's anxiety. Colleen, though she stood next to Cal, seemed outside the group.

The doors whooshed open to let a patient enter, and only the impression of concern remained. There was an urgency to Doc's voice belied by his posture. Mrs. McFaile was in a bad way, after all.

Those twenty feet across the tiled floor took ages. J.J. walked over and stood behind Korine.

"I don't know how she got them." Korine's voice was hoarse and pleading, as if she'd repeated it a hundred times until it became a prayer. "They are always locked up."

"Just like you always hid her keys?" Cal said.

He might as well have struck Korine. J.J. placed his hand in the small of her back to keep her from falling. She jumped at the touch.

After a brief startled glance at J.J., she turned back and threw her words at Cal. "Like you lifted a finger to stop her from driving at all?"

Doc put a hand on Cal's shoulder and held him back, probably saving Korine from occupying the next gurney.

"Look, you two," Doc barked. "Dora may be comatose, but I can assure you she hears more than you'd think. She needs both of you ready to do what needs to be done, not at each other's throats like a pair of petty playground bullies. Besides," he went on, "as J.J. can tell you, it likely isn't the fault of either of you that Dora's where she is right now."

Korine swayed. J.J. pushed her into the nearest seat, a rickety roller stool that wouldn't catch her if she fell, but at least she'd be closer to the ground.

"You really think she can hear us?" she said.

"What are you talking about?" Cal demanded of J.J. at the same time.

"Is there a family room where we can take this discussion?" J.J. asked Doc.

Doc turned and led the way down the hall to an unoccupied room, scarcely larger than a closet. There was a small wooden table, propped up under one side by a smashed aluminum can and surrounded by five of the same kind of yellow plastic chairs that graced the waiting room of the police station. The waiting room outside was first class. Must be a staff break room. At least it was private.

"First of all," J.J. said to Doc after they were seated, "how is Mrs. McFaile?"

"We won't know for a while. She got a whopping big dose of Depacote. We've pumped her stomach."

"As much as Olan Taggart got?" J.J. asked.

Korine inhaled sharply. "You think someone tried to kill Dora?"

J.J. and Doc both nodded.

Cal stood up. "Of all the stupid things to say about my mother!" He hit the table with his open hand. "Why would anyone want to hurt her?"

"That is the question of the hour," J.J. said dryly.

"You're going to be cute at a time like this?" Cal said.

"No, I don't think it's cute that someone has poisoned your mother." J.J. looked across the table at Cal, taking in the tremor in his hands and the slightly dilated pupils. "I tend to get sarcastic when I'm angry. I would think you'd be pretty angry too. Instead of sniping at each other, why don't we work together to find out what happened—and keep it from happening again."

J.J. turned to Korine. "Who was in the house today?"

Korine still looked dazed. She thought a minute before answering. "Cal, me, Amilou, Lorraine, you, Dora. I locked her medicine cabinet after lunch, but when I checked it before we left, it was unlocked."

"You're absolutely sure you locked it?"

"After everything else going on, you'd better believe I've been double and triple checking. It was locked." Korine's posture had improved while she talked. Her hand was in her pocket, fiddling with something. "I heard someone moving around upstairs right around the time that Cal came home. I assumed it was Dora."

"Assumed?" J.J. asked. "You didn't check?"

"It never occurred to me it could be anyone else. When Dora didn't come right down, Cal and I used that opportunity to talk."

J.J. could just imagine that conversation.

Cal took up the narrative. "We'd had a bite of supper, and I went to wake Mom from her nap so she could eat too. I found a bottle of pills by her bed. I thought she'd stopped breathing." He drew a long breath that rasped over his dry lips. "She was so still."

All four of them jumped when Colleen spoke. "Cal, honey, can I see that bottle?"

Interestingly enough, Cal Honey didn't seem too happy to remember that Colleen was there. He pulled a brown medicine bottle out of his shirt pocket.

"Don't," J.J. said, intercepting the bottle with his handkerchief. "If you don't mind, I'd like as few people as possible to touch this."

J.J. saw sudden understanding ignite in Korine's eyes.

Fists balled under the table, she did what she did best: buttoned her lip and kept her own counsel. J.J. was glad she did. They could have hung wash on the tension strung out in the room.

"You haven't happened to pick up a prescription for Mrs. McFaile, have you?" J.J. asked Colleen.

"What's that supposed to mean?" she asked. Lip quivering, she looked the picture of outraged justice.

J.J. waited long enough for the lip to settle down and for her outrage to turn to something else. He couldn't quite read what.

"Just that one I ran out to Shady Acres for her after Mr. Taggart died," Colleen finally said, answering J.J.'s question.

She put her hand out to touch Cal again, stopping just short of his sweater-clad shoulder. He'd shrugged it off once, but she didn't seem able to leave him alone. J.J. watched her face to see what emotions the cool reception wrought. She looked bewildered but showed no trace of anger—yet.

Doc's breath hissed as he drew it in. "That was a potent sedative. What did you do with those pills?"

"I gave them to Hazel," Colleen said defensively.

Doc got up. "I'd better tell them to check for that one too," he said. He pulled the door open and walked out, leaving J.J. to deal with the McFaile triangle.

They were left in silence, none of them knowing what to say. Colleen stood behind Cal's chair. She had settled for putting her hands on the back of the chair, where Cal wouldn't shrug them off. He seemed oblivious to her presence. Korine, however, glowed with indignation. J.J. knew he had to get one of them out of the room. Even someone as sensible as Korine could explode, given enough provocation.

"Cal," J.J. said, "would you excuse us for a minute. I'd like to ask Korine a few questions in private."

"Sure," he replied, rising. Colleen followed him out the door, a single anguished glance back at Korine betraying that she knew exactly how Korine felt about her—and didn't like it.

"Thank you," Korine said. No longer needing to hold herself back, her posture collapsed, and she sank into the curve of the chair. She pressed her hands against the edge of the table. "I thought I was going to kill someone."

J.J. smiled at the expression on her face when she heard what she'd said. "I know you wouldn't. Of all people, you'd be the last one I'd suspect of harming anyone."

"Maybe you don't know me as well as you think you do," Korine surprised him.

"Should I lock you up to protect them?" J.J. asked.

"I wouldn't thank you for trying. I'm willing to lay odds, though, that Colleen's the one who's been spying—spying for goodness' sake—on Dora and me. How can she do that?"

"I don't know. Looks to me like she's pretty infatuated with Cal."

"I noticed that." Korine's tone was dry.

"Hazel didn't happen to send that medicine home with Mrs. McFaile, did she?" J.J. asked.

"Not that I know of," Korine answered. "But, then, I wasn't allowed to see Dora after the accident until she walked in the back door with Cal."

"Point taken," J.J. said. "You going to be okay? Need a few more minutes?"

"I'm fine," Korine lied poorly. She stood up and collected her purse. "I'm going to go see Dora now. That is, if Cal will let me in the room."

"He'll see reason." J.J. hoped it was so.

He held the door for Korine, and the two of them walked to the cubicle where Dora lay, pale and fragile under a single threadbare sheet. Cal stood on one side of the stretcher, holding his mother's hand in his own. His cheeks were moist, although his eyes were dry enough. Colleen was nowhere in sight.

"Can I have a word?" J.J. asked Cal.

"What?" he said blankly, never glancing away from his mother's face.

"A word. With you. In private." J.J. was careful to keep the irritation out of his voice.

Cal showed no sign of having heard either the irritation or the effort to suppress it as he smoothed his mother's hand back under the sheet. He preceded J.J. out the door.

"Colleen go to help Doc?" J.J. asked.

"Colleen? I don't know. I think she said she had to go find something," Cal said. "You said you needed to ask me something privately. Here we are. Ask."

"How did you come to hire Colleen to do your checking up on your mother's affairs?"

Cal favored J.J. with a shrewd look. "I was up visiting. Mom and I had gone over to Juanita June's café. Colleen stopped by the booth. Offered to help with Mom in any way she could. She wound up sitting down, and I could see she treated Mom real well. I'd just talked to Clyde at the bank, and what he said seemed to back up Mom's stories about Korine. So I asked Colleen if she could keep an eye on things here."

"How did she report to you once she'd agreed to keep an eye out?"

Cal hesitated. "She came to Charlotte."

"Did she initiate a more intimate relationship with you?"

"That's not a crime. She's of age."

"That she is. She's even old enough to be accused of stalking a man in Asheville."

"What the hell are you talking about?" Cal's raised voice drew the attention of several people in the waiting area.

J.J. made shushing motions with his hands. "She was his mother's sitter. I don't have all the details yet, but he found it harder to break up with her than he imagined it would be."

Cal's blue eyes closed, then opened slowly. His forehead wrinkled. "She mentioned to me last week how well the three of us got along. She also told me that she'd be willing to come to Charlotte to help with Mom if I moved her."

"I don't think using Colleen would be a good idea."

"I caught that, thank you," Cal said.

The two men pressed against the wall to make room for a passing gurney. The orderly smiled and nodded his head, then maneuvered into the cubicle beyond Mrs. McFaile's. Doc sat in front of them at the nurse's station, leaning close over the phone.

Cal stared, unseeing, at the back of Doc's head. The rasp of the curtains being drawn around the new patient brought him back, and he took a step away from the wall.

"I need to talk to Korine for a little while." Cal held up his hand at J.J.'s protest. "I'm not disputing what you've said. As I explained to Korine earlier, some of the things Colleen told me didn't quite add up. We also need to decide on a plan if Mom stabilizes. First priority is going to be making her comfortable, of course, but we're not exactly sure what comes after that."

"I'm sorry," J.J. said. He clasped Cal's shoulder. The man's muscles tightened so that it was like putting his hand on a slab of pottery. J.J. took his hand away and offered it to shake instead.

Cal accepted the olive branch for what it was with a firm grip. "I know," he said. "You think Colleen did this to get closer to me."

"Don't assume anything," J.J. cautioned. "But we're working on 'putting away' the responsible party."

Cal nodded, then went to join Korine. J.J. stayed long enough to watch her uneasy expression relax as Cal began to talk to her. Doc was still ensconced behind the mauve counter, the phone tucked under his ear.

J.J. waited until Doc finished his conversation before he said, "Good news?"

"If you call finding out that once again a patient of mine has been poisoned with a drug I prescribed for her, then no, it's not good news."

"Did you call Hazel to find out what happened to the leftover medication?"

"She put it in her desk drawer," Doc replied. "It's gone now, of course."

J.J. stared. "She did what?"

"Desk drawer," Doc said savagely. "Says she feels awful about what has happened. She'll feel worse when I'm done with her. She's already lost two people out there to drug overdoses."

"I may charge her with criminal negligence."

"She locked her desk drawer."

"Yeah, just like Taggart's medication."

"I know. It's not a good situation."

"So I've discovered, time and again."

"What's going on with my ex-nurse and Cal?" Doc asked.

J.J. reached into his pocket and pulled out a peppermint. He rustled off the paper and put it into his mouth. "*Ex*-nurse?"

"I fired her."

"When?"

"A few minutes ago. Jett was just here looking for you and informed me about her last job. I don't need to tell you, she didn't have that one on her resume when she applied."

"I wish you hadn't done that," J.J. said.

"Should I keep a stalker on staff instead of using a collection agency?" Doc asked.

"No. I just didn't want her pushed too hard too fast. I'm still trying to figure some things out and would rather my suspects aren't feeling so strung out that they kill somebody, that's all."

"You think Colleen killed these people?"

"It's a real possibility," J.J. said.

"I'll kill her myself if she did. I don't think I can stand seeing another patient go," Doc said quietly.

J.J. reached into his pocket and handed Doc a peppermint. "I feel like I'm close, but we need more evidence. More details. The kind Judge Carrolton likes."

"Then go get them," Doc barked. The nurse behind him jumped, and the chart she was carrying showered down around her feet as it slipped from her fingers.

"Yessir," J.J. said. "Whatever you command."

Doc bent to help the woman with the papers. "Get on out of here."

J.J. went.

SYLVESTER'S HOUSE WAS on Elm Street, next to the Baptist Church. Even though it was close to midnight, there was a light showing through a window. Sylvester was probably still up. J.J. left his car on the street out front and walked up to the house. The light spilled out the window on the side of the house by the door, which J.J. took to be the kitchen. He veered around to check it out. His assumption proved to be correct. Sylvester stood over the stove, stirring something in the pot. As J.J. raised his hand to knock, Sylvester took a few steps to the door across from J.J. and shouted something.

A few seconds later, a small dog came skittering through the doorway. Ears up, tail frantically waving, he leapt across the floor to Sylvester's feet, where he groveled for attention. Sylvester reached down and patted the dog on the head, taking the time to scratch behind his ears and along his backbone before standing up again. He picked up the pot and carried it to the sink.

J.J. decided that he should stop playing Peeping Tom at Sylvester's kitchen door, so he raised his hand again and knocked.

Sylvester dropped the pot into the sink.

A few choice words later, J.J. stood inside Sylvester's door, with the dog so happy to see him that he peed all over J.J.'s right boot.

"Butch, I've told you not to do that." Sylvester grabbed a roll of paper towels and handed a bundle to

J.J. so that he could wipe off the leather. "But anyone who comes around this hour of the night deserves what they get." He picked up a noxious-smelling trash can from the corner and held it out for J.J.'s paper towels. "Butch is pretty good at tracking. Think your office could use one like him?"

J.J. eyed the piece of fluff tugging on Sylvester's shoelaces. He didn't ask how Sylvester planned to transform what was plainly a mutt of the poodle variety into a trained hound.

"I came to ask you a few follow-up questions about Taggart's death." J.J. didn't mention the stack of yellow paper on the counter. That could come later. He couldn't wait to tell Juanita June she'd been right on the money.

"Let me get these treats out for Butch." Sylvester picked up the pan from the sink, drained out the hot water, ran some cold water in the pot, then strained it again. He picked up the contents of the pot and placed it in Butch's dish. A meat of some kind, it smelled horrible.

J.J. took a step back.

The pup ran for the dish and joyously dove in while his master went to the refrigerator. Holding a pair of Bud Lights, Sylvester walked over to the table. J.J. shook his head.

Sylvester stowed one beer back in the fridge, then twisted the top off the other one. He tossed the lid onto the counter next to him and took a long swallow. Indicating with the bottom of the bottle that they should take a seat at the table, he asked, "What is it?"

"I need to go over with you what happened out at Shady Acres."

"I told you once. Can't you look it up?"

"I need you to tell me again."

"For crying out loud." Sylvester put his bottle down on the table with a thump.

"Start with where you were, and tell me exactly where everyone else was and what they did."

"I was in the parking lot. Taggart came tearing out of the bushes down by the driveway."

J.J. nodded.

"He stepped out into the road when he saw the old woman's car. She stopped. He went around to the passenger-side door and talked to her for a minute. Then he pitched forward. She drove over him. He died. End of story."

J.J. sat back in the chair, feeling more play in the joints than was comfortable. This piece of junk was in even worse shape than his office chair. He hoped it wouldn't fall apart under him. Hard to intimidate a witness when you're sitting on the floor on your butt.

He thought through the scenario. "And then after Taggart went down, Colleen Taylor came out of those same bushes and went over to help Taggart, right?"

Sylvester's face got a look on it that made J.J.'s day. It also made Sylvester's chair wobble under him. "You don't mean?" he said, obviously horrified. "The two of them were fooling around in those shrubs?"

"No," J.J. said. "Not that. But they did come from the same exact direction?"

"Yes," Sylvester said, then licked his lips.

"So, tell me again what you were doing at Shady Acres."

The puppy looked up from his meal, attuned to his master's emotions. He waddled over and sat under Sylvester's chair, eyeing J.J. uncertainly.

"Why?" Sylvester said.

"Does it have something to do with those flyers all over town about the Policemen's Ball?"

"I don't know where those came from." Sylvester's already small eyes narrowed even further. "And you can't prove that I do."

J.J. stood up and walked over to the counter and picked up the top sheet off the stack of flyers. "I wonder where you got these printed?"

"I told you, I didn't have a thing to do with them."

"Is that a fact?"

Sylvester's face turned an odd shade of pink. "You calling me a liar?"

"I'd never do that. But you may be a bit forgetful. I'd watch that if I were you. Forgetful folks are dying fast and furious right now."

Sylvester kicked the pup away from his shoelaces. "You can't threaten me. I've got a right to go where I want to go, and if I share a good joke with somebody, you can't make a big deal out of it." His eyes strayed to the stack of yellow paper on the counter.

J.J. knew that running a false advertisement through the post office was more than a joke, but he let it slide. He'd hand over what he had to the postmaster and see what happened from that point on. He was willing to bet that Sylvester owned the post office box listed on the flyer and that he'd been receiving money through it.

"Thanks so much for your help on this one." The heavy irony in J.J.'s voice went right over Sylvester's head.

"Anytime," Sylvester said sullenly. The man's dark hair fell over his eyes, hiding his expression as he reached down to pick up the puppy, who cowered back.

J.J. didn't blame the little guy. He'd cower too if an ugly face like that came at him.

Opening the back door, Sylvester let J.J. pass by him before speaking again. "Don't think I'm not aware that this is harassment. I'm not a criminal. I was in the wrong place at the wrong time."

J.J. put his hat back on his head and regarded Sylvester. "I appreciate your cooperation," he said. It hurt to be polite to this man, but he'd have the last laugh when he ran him in for obtaining property by false pretense.

J.J. felt a smile tugging at his lips. Inappropriate, under the circumstances. He'd better get out of there. It was way past time for him to turn in for the night.

SIXTEEN

J.J. SPENT MOST OF the next morning on the phone in his office. He hadn't slept well the night before. Janey hadn't called, nor had anyone answered the phone at Memaw's house when J.J. had finally given up restraining himself.

Every time his phone rang, he was sure it would be Janey calling to say that she was all right. So far, he'd been wrong every time. He'd spent about an hour doodling on a piece of paper, trying to figure out the patterns. He drew a triangle with the Asheville man and his mother and Colleen, another one with Cal, Colleen, and Mrs. McFaile. Colleen didn't have the same relationship with Jack and Olan Taggart that she had with the other two groups. It wasn't adding up.

She had opportunity; she had a history of violent behavior. He just couldn't trace a solid link between Colleen and Taggart. If she was involved with Jack instead of Cal, this would fit her pattern. But she wasn't. There didn't seem to be any love lost between those two.

Jack's alibi had checked out. Betty, his employer, had returned J.J.'s call—miraculously having received the message he'd left. She said she had called Jack at seven Friday morning to see why he hadn't shown up for work. She called again, fifteen minutes later, to clarify something so that his replacement could finish up the job Jack had started the day before.

Just to be fair, J.J. had checked out Hazel too. With those high-heel marks wandering all over the property, and the number of deaths at Shady Acres, someone out there may well be involved, and Hazel was as good a guess as anyone.

Her history included nothing criminal. When he'd called to check her employment record, the spokeswoman for the management company confirmed that Hazel was being replaced. She'd worked for them for nine years without a complaint.

After hanging up with the company, J.J. was glad he wasn't in that line of work. He thought that after nine years, the firm could have cut her some slack. Then he thought about the medication Hazel had carelessly tossed into her unlocked desk drawer. Maybe she was better off in another line of work, after all.

He shoved himself away from his desk. He needed to stretch. Ambling out to talk to Marlene, he found her surrounded by stacks of papers.

"Did Taggart's insurance policy come through yet?" he asked.

Marlene shook her head as she reached out to answer the ringing phone. She tucked the receiver between her ear and shoulder, picked up a few slips of paper, and shoved them at J.J. in dismissal as she took the message.

He glanced down at the notes as he walked to his office. The top one was from Jack Taggart, wanting J.J. to call him.

Settling into his desk chair with a grimace, J.J. picked

up the phone and called Jack's hotel and asked for room 59. No answer. He left his phone number on the voice mail.

Shuffling through the rest of the messages, he put one aside from Hazel Jurik. According to Marlene's note, Hazel had sounded excited on the phone.

"Marlene?" he called.

"What?" her irritated reply came back down the hall.

"Where's Leon?"

J.J. heard the sound of a chair scraping the floor, then footsteps down the hall. "He's over at the Penny Whistle having an early lunch. I paged him a minute ago." Marlene stood at the door. "You need a cup of coffee?" she asked, nodding toward the break room.

"No, thanks," J.J. replied, thinking of his wife yet again.

He picked up his cell phone and checked it. Still no messages. When she did call, he was…. No he wouldn't. He knew he would never let Janey have it, although he was so worried he could well let somebody have it before the day was through. He thumbed through the rest of the papers on his desk. Nothing there from the insurance company. The last message Marlene had handed him was from Mrs. Hawkins, asking him to call her at the café when he had a chance.

J.J. heard Marlene down the hall, scooping coffee out of the can. Within a few minutes the aroma of the fresh brew stuff snuck through his open door. He reconsidered stepping down the hall for a cup, then resolutely dropped his eyes back to the task at hand. Between the cravings for caffeine and nicotine, J.J. thought he was doing well to get anything done at all.

He picked up the note from Mrs. Hawkins again. Maybe

he'd join Leon over at the Penny Whistle for lunch when he was done. The iced tea there was strong enough to keep him going all day and half the night.

First he needed to finish tying up some loose ends. He punched in the number on the sheet of paper in front of him. Tri-Mutual Insurance Company was eager to take his call. Or so their automated answering system assured him.

J.J. wouldn't have thought that a small-town insurance agent would be so busy. After five minutes of pseudo jazz, a perky voice came over the line. "This is Lucinda Williams, how can I help you today?"

J.J. considered it his civic duty not to growl at the good people of Pine Grove, but this woman's forced cheerfulness grated on his nerves. He reminded himself to be cordial, identified himself, and said, "I need to check up on the policy you're holding for Olan Taggart."

"Mr. Bascom, sir, I really wish I could be of some assistance to you, but it is Tri-Mutual's policy that we can only provide that information to their policy owners."

"Ms. Williams, I'm a police officer conducting an investigation, not a nosy neighbor."

The girl's perky voice faltered. "I think you'd better speak to the owner? I've never, I mean—investigating? Like, he was murdered?"

The town's gossip mill hadn't gotten to this one yet. The horror in her young voice made J.J. feel so old he sensed new lines sprouting on his already weathered face. "Ms. Clarin would be good," he answered.

After a few more minutes of pretend music, a crisp voice came over the wire. "This is Anabel Clarin, how can I help you?" Her tone of voice made it abundantly clear that she didn't appreciate needing to do her employee's job. Or maybe it was having to deal with J.J. She'd been one of his more vocal opponents the last time his job had come up for renewal.

"I understand that Mr. Olan Taggart's life insurance policy was issued through your office," J.J. said.

"I'm so sorry, our confidentiality policy is to protect the families—"

"Ms. Clarin, Jack told me that he was going to call you and authorize you to talk with me. Now are you going to tell me what I need to know, or do I have to get the judge to give me a search warrant?"

J.J. heard the rustle of papers over the phone.

"Mr. Bascom, when I'm elected mayor, I can assure you that Pine Grove will put a premium on good manners in their public servants."

This was the first he'd heard that Clarin had political aspirations on her own behalf. After she'd supported Sylvester's aborted attempt to get himself elected to the appointed position of police chief, Anabel Clarin had crawled back inside her insurance agency and hibernated a while. Now, evidently, she'd decided she wanted to become the town's next mayor. J.J. didn't know which would be worse, the thought of this woman in office, or Sylvester as police chief, helping her get away with it.

"Ms. Clarin," J.J. prompted again.

"*Mrs.* Clarin," she corrected. "Let's see. I suppose everything is in order. I see there is a notation of a phone call from Mr. Taggart's son. Poor man."

J.J.'s hand tightened on the phone. Marlene passed his office door and did a double take when she saw the expression on his face. She draped herself against the door jamb, sipped from the brown mug with the message RED HOT MAMMA emblazoned on it over a picture of her and her baby, and listened, unabashed, to his phone call.

"What are the terms of Olan Taggart's policy?" J.J. asked. His voice came out a low purr.

Marlene giggled. He shot her a glare and waved her off. She looked hurt. Leaning over, she floated a fax copy onto his desk, then moved off down the hall toward her own desk.

"Let's see." Clarin ruffled through some papers, then started reading. "A usual policy for people of his stature. A hundred thousand dollars, paid to his beneficiary, Jack Taggart." She paused. "That's interesting." Her tone made it clear she wasn't pleased about this fact. "Young Mr. Taggart added a clause through one of my new associates about five weeks ago. A double payout if the death was accidental. *Was* it an accident?" The woman's voice sharpened.

J.J. would bet good money that whoever sold Jack that policy rider was going to lose his or her job. "You'll get a copy of the autopsy report," he replied. Then, because he was feeling spiteful, he added, "And thank you so much for all your cooperation, Ms. Clarin."

As he'd known she would, she corrected him, "It's *Mrs.* Cl—"

J.J. hung up before she could complete the sentence. To his disappointment, it did not make up for the irritation of the phone call.

He stared for a minute at the phone, then started to think. Jack had led J.J. to believe that the double-for-accidental-death clause was a surprise to him. But according to *Mrs.* Clarin, he had added it himself less than two months before. Leaning back in his chair, J.J. caught himself just before he went over backwards. Hands on the top of his desk, he leaned forward again.

He picked up the piece of paper that Marlene had left on his desk. "Son of a gun," J.J. said softly. It was a warrant from the Postal Inspector for the arrest of Sylvester Harris on charges stemming from illegal use of a post office box. Some days it paid to do favors for other people, because then you got to call them in. The little matter he'd settled quietly a few months earlier for the postmaster had served him well. That flyer was going to sink Sylvester.

Shutting the door to his office behind him, J.J. left a note on Marlene's empty desk, telling her that he could be reached on his cell phone. J.J.'s stomach rumbled as he walked to his car. Police work could be frustrating. But, at least, there were some compensations.

J.J. FELT LIKE an old-fashioned law officer in a Western film, entering the Penny Whistle Café at high noon. Sylvester greeted his entrance by shoving back his chair so fast it fell over.

"I am not going to jail," Sylvester informed J.J.

"Who said you were?" J.J. played innocent.

"That no-good postmaster turned me in for using the post office box for that prank I was playing on you."

"Prank?" J.J. raised one brow. He'd practiced it in the mirror that morning when he rehearsed his conversation with Janey about not calling. Skepticism personified. It worked pretty well on Sylvester.

"Really! I was only fooling. I wouldn't have kept the money."

"Be sure and tell that to the judge."

J.J. heard a few snickers behind him.

"I collected about $15,000 so far," Sylvester boasted. "Tell me that wouldn't come in handy for an outfit like yours."

The man had raised $15,000 through a scam like this? Juanita June folded her arms across her chest and tilted her head to one side, as Leon got up from his booth to join in the fun.

"You trying to bribe me in front of all these witnesses?" J.J. asked softly.

"No, of course not! I was going to give the department the money anyway." Every word dug Sylvester deeper into the mud he'd been swimming in.

An older man sat in the second chair at Sylvester's table, looking pretty uncomfortable. J.J. turned to him. "You a friend of his?"

The man shoved his chair back and stood. "I just this minute met him."

Sylvester stared a hole in the back of his not-friend's shirt as the man left the café. Leon whipped out his handcuffs and applied them to Sylvester's skinny wrists.

It was pure pleasure to see Leon drive him away and lock him up.

"I'd say I need to feed you something good to celebrate." Juanita June grinned up at J.J.

He followed her back to his booth, where Hank was waiting for him.

"Just wait right here," she said. "I think I have something in the kitchen you'll like." She walked away, ponytail bobbing, hips sashaying. The old Juanita June was back.

Mrs. Hawkins was with her when she returned. They each held the end of a long sheet cake. When they got to the table, they slid it in front of J.J. Emblazoned across the top of the buttercream icing was WELCOME TO THE FIRST ANNUAL POLICEMEN'S BALL!

"What is this?"

"Sarah Jane and I got to talking," Hank said. "It would be a shame to waste a good idea just because it originated with Sylvester. The council turned you down, and you still want another officer. I ran this idea past them, and they're all for it. If you can raise the money to pay a starting salary, you can hire someone."

"Are you kidding?" J.J. couldn't believe they were taking it seriously.

Mrs. Hawkins put her hand on J.J.'s shoulder. "Don't you worry. We're not counting on you to organize this. We're going to all chip in. When Janey gets home, we'd appreciate her help. Sarah Jane already said she wants to chair it. And we know her. If Sarah Jane returns her mind to a thing, it'll get done."

J.J. had trouble swallowing. "You're serious!"

"Well, if Sylvester can raise $15,000 on a scam, think how much we can raise through a legitimate event," Hank pointed out.

"Well, in that case," J.J. said, "anyone want a piece of cake? It's on me!"

The place erupted in applause.

A FEW HOURS LATER, J.J. tiptoed into Dora McFaile's hospital room. She lay curled sideways on the bed, the pillow damp under her mouth. Cal was slumped in the chair next to her bed, one hand on his mother's thin arm. His chest rose and fell gently, a soft rumble sounding on the inhalations.

J.J. had stopped by the nurse's station on the way in. They had told him that the woman was stable and seemed to be doing fairly well, considering her circumstances. Korine had stayed the night, then gone home to change and get a bit of rest. She planned to come back to relieve Cal so he could do the same.

Colleen sat on the other side of the bed. It occurred to J.J. that every time he had seen Colleen lately, she'd been weeping. The skin under her eyes was puffy and red. She barely blinked as she gazed at Cal's sleeping form. Her expression hardened when J.J. came in. She stood and leaned over the bed. She reached out one finger and stroked the old woman's cheek, then straightened and walked around the bed.

J.J. raised both his eyebrows and jerked his head toward the doorway. He followed Colleen out into the hall when she complied with his mute request. He quietly shut the door behind him.

"What are you doing in there?" he demanded.

"I spent nearly a month following that woman and making sure she was all right. I can't just stop caring about her."

Tears welled up in Colleen's eyes. Crocodile tears, no doubt.

J.J. crossed his arms. "Mrs. McFaile? Or Cal?"

"I know what that horrible man in Asheville said about me, but it isn't true. He was withholding treatment from his mother, and he knew I was about to tell her doctor. He had to do something to discredit me."

J.J. nodded. *Sure. And pigs can fly.*

Colleen pulled a large manila envelope from her purse. She looked at it a minute, then thrust it at J.J. "I know you don't believe me, but Grady was mistreating his mother. Here are copies of the photos I took and the journal I kept. I doubt if anyone will ever listen to me again, much less hire me, but I have to try."

"You always have this stuff with you?"

Colleen flushed. "I thought you might be needing to see the other side of the story sometime soon."

J.J. smoothed the flap on the envelope. Interesting that she was the prepared. "So why did you lie to Cal about his mother?"

"I didn't think I was lying. Mrs. McFaile was telling me the same kinds of things that Grady's mom had gone through. I guess I jumped to conclusions."

J.J. tucked the envelope under his arm. "I'll look at this and see what's here. Meanwhile, you stay away from this family, you hear?"

"Yes, sir," Colleen said sullenly.

As she walked away down the hall, J.J. called the station and asked to speak to Leon. He asked the officer to call Asheville and check on Colleen's version of her story. He still needed a little more evidence before he went for an arrest.

"What did she want?" Cal's quiet voice nearly stopped J.J.'s heart.

He turned to find Cal propped up in the open doorway of the hospital room. "Don't do that," J.J. complained.

"Sorry," Cal said, not looking sorry at all. "I had to play possum to keep her from talking me to death. If she hadn't left soon, I was going to 'wake up' and escort her out."

"Weren't you afraid that she might do something to your mother?"

Cal gave J.J. a strange look. "I was right there, what do you think she would have done?"

J.J. chose not to answer that question. "How's she doing?" He nodded at the sleeping woman.

"Not good." Cal closed the door behind him. "We don't know yet how much this will affect her." He looked away and blinked rapidly a few times. He swallowed. "I sent Korine on home to rest, but I expect she'll be back later."

"I suspect you're right. You going to get some rest yourself?"

"I'll rest later," he said, which answered J.J.'s earlier question better than anything Cal had said so far. He shifted his weight. "You any closer to an arrest?"

"Actually, I think I am," J.J. said.

"Good." Cal's eyes were hard chips in his rugged face. He looked toward his mother's door, and his whole being softened. "I did talk to Korine about the future. This changes a lot of things."

J.J. thought about all the reasons Korine had fought so hard to keep her mother-in-law in Pine Grove. After this, all of them were as insubstantial as snow in July. If Mrs. McFaile didn't know where she was, then there was no reason Cal couldn't take her wherever he wanted to.

"How'd Korine take it?"

"Like you'd expect. Quietly. She thought about it for a while, then she cried a little. Then she said, 'All right.'"

"You make things right between you yet?" J.J. asked.

Cal shot him a quick look.

J.J. didn't back down.

"I think so," Cal finally answered. "I did tell her I thought she'd done a good job with Mom."

"That's almost as good as an apology."

Cal shifted his weight again. "Listen, I'm going back in with Mom."

"You want me to bring you anything?"

"Not right now, thanks." He reached out and shook J.J.'s hand.

Giving the taller man a once-over, J.J. concluded that he'd been right about Cal. Once he got over his anger, Cal was a pretty good man. Mrs. McFaile had done a good job with her boys. "I'll let you know when I know something," he said.

"Good deal." Cal opened the door and slipped into the room.

J.J. heard him speaking soothingly to the sleeping woman as he shut the door behind him. He couldn't imagine how the man must feel. Cal had come to Pine Grove thinking he'd be taking his mother home with him and having months, maybe years of time to spend making her feel at home. She might never know that her son was taking care of her now. He thought about that some as he walked out to the car.

He examined his fear and resentment over Janey's trip home to see her grandmother. It wasn't fair of him to begrudge his wife's opportunity to reforge her bond with Memaw. The circumstances weren't so different from those of Cal and Dora McFaile. Time was short and family was precious.

J.J. resolved to call his brother that night and see if they couldn't find something to talk about. Since his sister had died, Rusty was the only close family he had left. He needed to take care not to lose him too.

SEVENTEEN

KORINE MANEUVERED HER CAR into a parking space next to a battered Chevy pickup late Monday morning. Everyone in Pine Grove must be sick; the lot was all but full. As she pulled her purse off the floor and slid the strap up onto her shoulder, the weight of it slapped her in the side. Hugging it tightly to her to keep it from throwing her balance off again, she grabbed the cardboard carrier with two huge double mochas—one for her and one for Cal—then pressed the button to lock her door.

The glass door to the hospital slid open. Korine took a big breath to steady herself before she went up to see her mother-in-law. The smell of the coffee escaped the cups as she walked down the hall, perfuming the air. She was really glad she'd stopped to get some. Hospital coffee left a good bit to be desired.

As she pushed the button for the third floor, a petite woman wearing green scrubs rushed into the elevator and hit the button for the second floor. She balanced on her toes inside the door, one hand fiddling absently with a pair of scissors snapped onto her belt. She threw a covetous glance at Korine's coffee, then sprinted off when the doors opened.

The hallway on three was deserted. Turning the corner,

Korine spotted Doc sitting at the desk. As she approached, he flipped shut the metal cover of the chart he'd been studying.

"That for me?" he asked, nodding at the coffee.

"Sorry. Didn't know you'd be here. The extra one is for Cal." Korine's purse slid off her shoulder. The weight of it tipped the coffee, and some of it spilled. She put the cups down on the counter, pulled her purse back up onto her shoulder, and mopped up the spill with a napkin.

"How is she?" Korine asked.

"Mmmm," Doc said. He looked down at the chart in his hands, up at Korine, then down the hall to Dora's room. "Fine. Much finer than I would have thought, actually. She's been awake some already this morning."

Korine half turned.

Doc reached out across the counter and caught her arm. "You might want to wait a minute or so."

"Why?"

"Jack's in there. Let Cal handle things for a change."

Korine looked at Doc. "What do you mean?"

Doc's eyes blinked behind his glasses. "I mean it's time Cal took on the responsibilities he should have been shouldering for years. Jack will get over this snit of his. He always does."

"What snit?" Korine pulled her sleeve out of Doc's grip. Smoothing out the cotton fabric, she waited for him to explain.

"Jack wanted an open-casket funeral. Olan was pretty torn up when Dora ran over him."

Korine's imagination summoned a picture she didn't want to see. She hadn't thought about the specifics. Naturally he wouldn't look very nice after Dora dragged him fifty feet along a roadway. Korine's purse clattered to the ground, scattering lipstick, wallet, and old grocery lists across the floor as she leaned heavily on the desk.

"Sorry," Doc said. He came around the corner and began to help her gather the bits and pieces to put them back into her bag. He picked up Dora's Bible, which Korine had thrown in at the last minute. "What's this?" he asked.

She reached out and took the book from him. It lay open naturally, as if the page had been looked at many, many times. Opposite the first chapter of Genesis was a hand-printed poem in red ink.

> Old woman, Old woman,
> You think you can hide?
> Your friends are near gone,
> Won't be long that I bide.

Underneath it all was a list of names, some of them softly crossed out with pencil. One name, more scored than the others, was Olan Taggart.

Korine let go of the leather-bound book like it was stinging nettle.

"Where did you get this?" Doc asked. His voice nipped at Korine.

"Off Dora's bedside table. I thought if she woke up, she might find comfort in it. She used to like to read a verse or two every morning."

"Used to?"

"Not for several weeks. Truth be told, I thought she was having trouble reading."

Doc reached past Korine to the open book on the counter. He used a pen to turn pages. She looked over his arm as he checked to see if anything else was written in it. When he turned to Job, they saw the simple admonition, "Keep your silence." It was made harsh by the gouges the writer had ground into the page with the red pen.

Korine read the Bible verse next to the note: "'He removeth away the speech of the trusty, and taketh away the understanding of the aged.'

"Dora was telling the truth about someone in the house," she said. Her voice shook with rage that anyone could have done this to the old woman. Korine pointed a finger at the passage. "She quoted this when J.J. was trying to get her to talk about Olan Taggart's death."

Behind her, Korine heard the door to Dora's room slam against the wall. She fumbled the Bible into her purse. If Jack was already upset with Dora about his father's death, he shouldn't see the horrible things written in Dora's Good Book.

Aside from a long hard stare as he passed by, Jack paid Korine no mind. His harsh footsteps hesitated after they rounded the corner, then she heard another door slam. He must have taken the stairs next to the elevator.

"Who could do such an evil thing to her?" Korine said.

Doc looked at Korine's bag as if he could see through the leather. "I know that handwriting." He carefully slipped his pen into his inside jacket pocket. He pulled out his hand and smoothed the worn tan corduroy over his heart. "Colleen did this."

"Colleen?" Korine said. She thought back to all the times Doc's nurse had been there when Korine needed help with Dora, a convenient angel of mercy. Once she discovered that Colleen was working for Cal—spying on them for him—all those coincidences were explained. It did not explain the malice behind these notations.

Doc walked over to the phone. "I'm calling J.J."

While he talked with the police chief, Korine went and looked out the window. As she watched the breeze whip the pedestrians in the parking lot, Jack Taggart strode out the front entrance and over to his car. The mullions on the window framed Jack as he paused, one hand on the open door. Korine stepped back, sure she could feel his hot gaze from where she stood. He lingered motionless, staring up at the building, for what seemed a long time.

Doc hung up and came to stand by Korine. "J.J.'s on his way over."

Pushing open the heavy door to Dora's room, Korine found Cal sprawled in the chair next to his mother's bed, both of them snoring gently. Hardly surprising. Korine was tired herself, and she hadn't stayed up with Dora all night long. He must really be exhausted if he'd fallen asleep that quickly after facing Jack down. It wouldn't hurt to let him rest a minute or two longer before she shared the latest news.

She placed the carrier with the second cup of coffee on the table behind Cal and took the chair on the opposite side of the bed. After setting her purse carefully on the floor next to her seat, she wrapped both her hands around her coffee and sipped. Hot caffeinated heaven. A minute later, Cal's snore quieted and Korine looked up.

He still sat sprawled in the chair, but his eyes were focused on her face. "What's wrong?" he asked, tension outlining the fatigue in his blue eyes. His face had congealed in the combative expression Korine now knew Cal only used to mask uncertainty. Obviously he thought she had come to take back what she'd said the night before.

"J.J.'s on his way over," she said. "Dora was right about someone being in the house. Colleen was more than your detective."

Cal's forehead furrowed. "What do you mean?"

Briefly, Korine explained about the notations in Dora's Bible.

Cal rose to his feet. His face flushed as the full impact of what his mother had gone through hit him. "I'm going to kill Colleen."

Korine rose too and caught at Cal's arm. "Wait," she said. "J.J. will make sure she gets what she deserves. You have responsibilities here now." She pointed to the bed. Noticing that Dora was now awake and watching the two of them with concern, Korine exclaimed.

Cal turned to look at his mother. The corners of his eyes drooped and he seemed to be having trouble catching his breath. He sniffed once, hard, then bent down and drew the white hospital sheet up under his mother's chin and smoothed it out over her shoulders.

"I'm sorry, Mom. Colleen won't bother you any more." As his weathered finger completed tracing the family heart on her cheek, the old woman smiled.

Reaching out one small hand, she touched her son's ruddy cheek. Finger trembling, she traced a heart on his cheek in return. She rested her hand against his cheek for a moment, then slid it down into his hand like a child seeking the comfort of a beloved parent. She closed her eyes and rested.

Jaw slack, eyes suspiciously moist, Cal's rough thumb smoothed the back of Dora's hand. Watching the man cling to his mother, Korine saw a stranger. Gone was the boy who had fought all his life with his older brother. Gone was the man who had abandoned his wife and children. The man in that room was a man who cared deeply about his mother, and who needed Dora more than Korine did.

It was Korine's turn to search for the right words to say. After a moment, she got up and walked around the bed. Standing next to Cal, she put one hand on his shoulder. "You're going to do a good job taking care of her."

Korine felt Cal's shoulder drop as he realized what she had said.

"You really meant it last night?" he said. "When you said you wouldn't try to stop me if I took her home with me?"

"Absolutely," Korine answered.

Cal's smile as he turned to hug his mother was all Korine needed to see to know that she had made the right decision. It wouldn't be easy for any of them. But it was right.

EIGHTEEN

Doc WAS WAITING for J.J. inside the door to the hospital. He told the police chief what he and Korine had found in Dora's Bible and led the way upstairs.

"Does Cal know?" J.J. asked.

"Korine went in to tell him."

"How's Mrs. McFaile with all this?"

"Korine said she was going to tell Dora that she didn't need to be afraid anymore, but who can tell what's making it into her brain and what's going right over her head. Dora's calm, if that was what you wanted to know."

J.J. led the way out of the elevator when they got to the third floor. Pausing in the doorway of Mrs. McFaile's room, he saw that Doc was right. The old woman was dozing peacefully. Her son clutched his mother's hand, while Korine's hand rested on Cal's shoulder.

Cal and Korine both turned and saw J.J. in the doorway. Slipping his hand out of his mother's, Cal stood. He and Korine looked at each other. Clearly, the differences between them had been patched up. Korine picked up her purse from beside a chair and walked past J.J. into the hallway. Cal went next. J.J. gently closed the door to the room as he followed Cal.

Korine had gone over to the counter and emptied her

purse. She collected the detritus and left the black leather-bound Bible on the counter.

Grimly, J.J. pulled his gloves on and gingerly turned the pages. With each entry, his anger grew. He closed the book and placed it in an evidence bag.

He turned to Doc. "You sure this is Colleen's handwriting?"

Doc nodded. He didn't look any happier than anyone else standing there. "I thought I was a good judge of character," he said.

"Don't," Korine said.

"It's not your fault," Cal said. Of the three of them, he looked the sickest. "I gave her the means to do this."

J.J. interrupted what was looking to become a blame-fest of large proportions. "She would have picked a victim somewhere. This one was a poor choice for her because she got caught."

"Not yet, she hasn't," Doc said.

J.J. nodded. "Leon's out looking for her now. I'll let you know when we pick her up."

J.J. SLAMMED THE DOOR to the cruiser. He thought about calling Leon to see how he was getting on with finding Colleen, but he knew the young man would have called if he'd brought her in.

Jett had stopped by and taken the evidence bag containing the Bible for a personal delivery to the crime lab. He'd promised to be as charming as he could be with the technician in his lab. It might even mean they'd have answers before the day was over.

J.J. started the motor. Traffic was sparse on the way to

the station. He pulled into his parking space and went inside. The hall was deserted. Good thing crime was light in this town, or he'd never be able to have time to investigate a murder.

He went into his office and pulled open his bottom drawer. He fished out the emergency pack of cigarettes and shook one out. Putting it under his nose, he drew in the scent of the tobacco. He stroked it, frowning, as his fingers shook slightly.

The cigarette dropped to the floor, shredded by the pressure from his fingers. Absently, J.J pulled open the center drawer to his desk and rustled open the peppermint package and took out a piece. He unwrapped the candy and put it into his mouth. He leaned down and swept the curling wisps of tobacco onto a scrap of paper and tossed the whole into the trash.

He stared at his hat on the coatrack until it faded into the background of his thoughts. He'd give anything to be able to say he knew beyond a shadow of a doubt that Colleen had killed Olan Taggart as well as terrorized Dora McFaile. There was still a nagging question at the back of J.J.'s mind about Jack. He just wished he could come up with hard evidence one way or the other.

There was the issue of Jack's alibi, which seemed genuine. The man's employer was clear as a bell about the time she'd talked with him. Jack had been in Charlotte when his father died. That didn't mean he couldn't have hired someone, like Colleen, but it made it harder to link him to the crime.

With the Bible evidence in hand, Doc's former nurse was currently J.J's favorite. He hoped the leather had picked up some sort of physical evidence from the girl. He shuffled the papers on the desk until he came to the envelope Colleen had handed him. He weighed it in his hand as if it would tell him of her guilt or innocence.

Despite her claim that the contents would explain everything to him about the situation in Asheville, it had left several gaps. There were aspects of that case that echoed disturbingly in the events in Pine Grove. He thought back to Mrs. Kohl's reluctance to hire Colleen, and the woman's missing necklace. Then he thought about Olan Taggart's pain and Dora McFaile's disappearing—and reappearing—jewelry.

He tapped the sheet in his hand. Colleen claimed that the son had given her a pair of pearl earrings, which belonged to his mother, in gratitude for the care she had provided. The son claimed that Colleen had helped herself to them as his mother slept. Perhaps most telling was the overdose this woman had been given just after Colleen had been fired. Again, each of the pair involved with the care had pointed a finger at the other one.

He picked up the phone and called the officer in charge of the Asheville case. A voice-mail message answered, so he left contact information and said that he needed to talk with the officer about Colleen Taylor.

He tossed the papers back onto his desk in disgust. Thinking about things was getting him nowhere. The phone rang, and J.J. picked up. "Bascom," he said.

"I can't find Colleen anywhere," Leon said. "According to her neighbors, she hasn't been home since early this morning."

J.J. tapped his pencil on the desk a couple of times. The

river rock Colleen had been fiddling with when he interviewed her Saturday gave him an idea where she might be. "Keep looking around town. I'm heading out toward Korine's and see if she's out there."

"Yessir," Leon said and then hung up.

J.J. left the heaps of papers lying on his desk. Not like they'd go anywhere while he was gone. He started the cruiser and went out to look for Colleen.

She wasn't easy to find. He finally spotted her Mustang parked in a pull-off by the river. parked behind it under a large, arching tree and called Leon to let him know where he was. He hung up and got out of the car. To his right, he could hear the river skipping over the smoothed boulders, the rushing noise carrying through the crisp evening. A soft trill signaled a bird's perch across the water. The sound dissolved into a flurry of wings as shut his car door. He walked across the sandy clearing and looked over the bank, not sure what he was going to find.

Colleen sat huddled on a rock by the frigid water. She tightened her arms around her knees but did not look up. Judging by the blue tinge to her lips, she'd been there a while.

J.J. turned up the collar of his coat and scrambled down the bank. With the sun close to going down for the evening, it was near freezing next to the swift water.

Colleen looked up at him—a single, searing glance—before her lashes fell over reddened eyes and she turned her head away. She put her hands down beside her and slid one foot forward. The toe of her shoe dislodged a small pyramid of stones at her feet. With a small cry, she bent over the stones, placing them carefully back in order. When she was done, she settled back, fondling the top stone instead of placing it back on the ground.

J.J. gingerly sat down on the edge of a rock close to Colleen. He made sure it was one which he could get up off of in a hurry if he needed to. It was ice-cold under his pants. Wet, too. He was going to have pneumonia before he got done with this case.

"Does Cal know about Asheville?" she asked.

"I didn't tell him. But I don't have to tell you it's over between the two of you."

Colleen hurled the rock she'd been caressing into the river. She shuddered and gripped her knees tightly with her arms. "I hate men." She put her head down against her knees and began to cry.

"You've got quite a collection there." J.J. selected one of the stones in the pile.

Colleen snatched it away from him. Stone sounded softly on stone as she replaced it carefully on the pile. He sat there, fingers still extended as if grasping the smooth dark surface of the rock as he stared at her. She was fast; he needed to be more careful.

"What's going on here?" J.J. said quietly.

"I keep choosing men who want to use me, that's what." The girl glared at him. She bent over and selected a slim white rock and tossed it to him. He caught it and looked down. On the bottom of the rock was Cal's name and the previous day's date.

Did she try to murder someone each time a man broke up with her? J.J. started to reach for the pile.

"Don't bother," Colleen said. "That's the only one that's marked. I've gotten to the point where I'm starting to forget who each one belongs to, so I decided to write on this one. It's a nervous habit, collecting stones when I'm upset. Each of these is for a relationship that didn't work out. That one," she said, pointing to an oddly shaped pale stone near the bottom, "is Leon."

She caught his startled look. "They aren't trophies. I keep them as reminders of what I learned with each man." Colleen pulled Leon's rock out. "For example, with this one…." She hurled the stone away into the rushing water next to her. "I learned that sweet faces don't always have good manners. He tried a little too much, a little too fast for me."

"You were playing with one of those when I was in your apartment."

"Grady." Colleen leaned forward, knees spread, and let her head rest on her left hand. Her right hand shifted a few rocks in the pile. Finally, she picked up the smooth palm-shaped stone. "I learned that I could live through my life falling apart after Grady."

J.J. digested that. Grady's mother had died in Asheville, and Colleen counted that as her life falling apart. "Which one represents when you learned to poison your patients?" he asked.

She cut her eyes up toward him, the rock in her hand unbalancing and falling to the ground. "I've never done that." She narrowed her eyes. "That's it. I don't have another word to say to you."

"You're not interested in who gave Dora McFaile an overdose?"

She shook her head. "I'm not going to help you try to find a way to make me guilty. I didn't do anything wrong—other than care. If you want to talk to me, I want to do it in the station with a tape recorder, my rights read, and my lawyer at my side."

J.J. stood up. Casually, before she could react in that quick way she had, he clamped handcuffs on her. Then he read Colleen her rights. He didn't know whether this would be the best time to mention Dora's Bible or not, but he sure as hell didn't want to spend any more time down on the river bottom while he figured it out.

J.J. followed Colleen up the bank. She had a little bit of trouble negotiating the incline with her hands behind her back, but safety was paramount. Poison might be her weapon of choice, but he wouldn't put it past her to try to wrap her hands around his neck for arresting her.

Colleen slipped. J.J. reached out and held her elbow to steady her for the last few feet. She snatched it back as soon as they got to level ground.

He put her in the back of the cruiser. "I'll send Leon or Jett down to get your car so no one runs off with it," he said.

Colleen's answer was to look away. After shut her door, she turned and rested her forehead against the window. Her breath fogged the glass, softening her features. Her eyes peered up at him through the mist, doe-wide and innocent.

J.J. slid into his seat and slammed his door. *Pretty is as pretty does,* he thought. *Colleen might very well be monstrous, indeed, inside.*

IT WASN'T UNTIL they had gotten halfway to the police station that Colleen spoke up again. "What are you charging me with?"

"We found the Bible," said, not really answering her question. He looked in the rear-view mirror to gauge her reaction.

Pale and shaking, she dropped her head back against the glass. "I didn't..." she mumbled.

"What?" J.J. asked.

"I didn't hurt anyone!" She leaned forward.

"You don't count giving Dora McFaile instructions to drive to Shady Acres hurting anyone?" J.J. observed mildly.

Colleen bit her lip.

"Administering an overdose. Now, that's a great way not to hurt someone."

"What do you mean?" she said.

"Olan Taggart. Dora McFaile. Maris Falkirk. And who knows how many others."

"I didn't kill anyone!" Colleen's voice rose. She looked down and shook her head slightly. Looking up again, she met J.J.'s gaze in the mirror. "You can ask Lyndsey Babbitt over at Shady Acres about Mr. Taggart. She hates me, but she'll still tell you that there was no way I could have given him that medicine. She usually works evenings, but she'd stayed over for the night shift. As soon as she saw me, it was like she couldn't get close enough. I suppose she wanted to get something on me to pass along to my patient's family."

"Why would she do that?" J.J. asked.

"She wants my private-duty jobs," Colleen answered. "Just ask her."

He intended to—as soon as he got Colleen settled in at the station.

J.J. WAS IN THE LOBBY of Shady Acres, waiting for Lyndsey Babbitt to come to work, when he hit a vein of luck.

"I don't know a thing about that post office box," the young woman said as she came through the door and noticed the police chief. The petulant voice proclaimed her to be none other than Babbitt. Her punk haircut stood straight up on end, like a startled porcupine, making her a dead ringer for the description of the young woman who had opened the post office box for Sylvester. There weren't that many girls with spiky pink haircuts running around Pine Grove.

"Is that so?" he said. "How about you sit down and we talk about it?"

"I'm gonna be late for my shift if I talk to you," she said. Her brows drew together and tears welled up in her eyes. Did all females know what crying did to him?

"Talk fast," he said.

"Sylvie asked me to open a box for him at the post office. I just picked up the mail and brought it home. I had no idea what he was doing."

Sylvie? J.J. shook his head, trying to clear it of the image of Sylvester and this young woman together, her whispering "Sylvie" in the man's ear. It was too much for , and he had to break out a peppermint from his pocket to cover his amusement.

"And what did he have to say about Olan Taggart?"

"What?" Babbitt squeaked. Her brows drew even closer together. "Sylvester didn't know Mr. Taggart. He was up here delivering—" She stopped short, realizing what she was about to say.

"Delivering flyers to you, wasn't he?" J.J. prompted.

"No," the woman said, eyes wide as she tried to see if he was going to swallow her story.

"I think you'd better tell me all about it," J.J. said.

Babbitt opened her mouth, then shut it again when she saw the resolve on J.J's face.

"How about we compromise?" J.J. offered. "You tell me Colleen Taylor's every move the morning that Taggart died, and I'll see what I can do for you with the postmaster."

Sometimes people were just itching to get things off their chests. Babbitt told him everything. She looked much happier once she got done.

"I'll walk back with you," J.J. said.

"Do you have to?" she asked.

"I know Carly fairly well. I can tell her why you're late."

"Great." The girl picked up her heavy handbag off the floor and slung it over her shoulder. She tucked her fleece zip sweatshirt under one arm. "Might as well tell her I'm quitting."

"Don't overreact," J.J. snapped.

As he followed her back to the unit, he wondered if she'd really quit just because she was late after helping him establish Colleen's innocence. looked down at the girl's spiked pink hair as he held the door open for her to enter the unit. It was too bad she knew everything there was to know about Colleen's actions that morning, none of which involved Olan Taggart.

J.J. was left with Jack, and the man had an alibi.

NINETEEN

"BABBITT," CARLY SAID. "You late again?"

"My fault, I'm afraid," J.J. said. "I didn't get to talk with Lyndsey yesterday when I was here, so I stopped her on her way in. I hope it didn't cause too many problems for you."

Carly gave a shrewd glance. Her full lips pressed together. Only the slightly deeper fold in the skin beside her mouth betrayed the fact that she thought there might have been more to it than that. Janey had always said Carly was perceptive.

"You arrested anyone yet?" she asked. Arms folded, she leaned her hip against the counter in front of the nurse's station. Babbitt had scurried on down the hall and stood holding the hands of an elderly man, who kept pulling away from her to swing his fists at the woman seated in the wheelchair in front of him.

"Haven't charged anyone with anything definite yet," he prevaricated. "You think she needs help?" J.J. asked, inclining his head toward the near-altercation down the hall.

"Lyndsey's good with them. As odd as it seems with her appearance, she oozes calm to these folks. Frankly, even if she is late now and then, I wouldn't want to see her go.

"How does she get along with Colleen when she's out here?"

Carly threw back her head and laughed. "Listen to you!" she said. "Those two can't stand breathing the same air. Funny, though, Lyndsey's been following Colleen around lately. Guess she took our talk to heart about the possibility that Colleen's the one who's helping herself to the things that keep turning up gone."

J.J. looked down the long hallway toward Babbitt. She hadn't mentioned that when she said she could vouch for Colleen's movements the morning Taggart died.

"We'd sure love it to be her." Carly's tone was dry. "It would be really bad if it was somebody who works here."

J.J. looked down sharply at the nurse.

"I know, you're workin' on it." She smiled up at him, face soft with laughter. She sobered. "Don't you worry, if it's one of us, we'll find out who did it and make sure they don't get a chance to do anymore. If it's Colleen, then you'll let us know. Now, I got to get to work. Tell Janey to call me when she gets back. I want to hear how things went back home."

J.J. left the unit and walked back down the hallway toward the exit. He didn't like the way this was feeling to him. As he rounded the corner, he ran into someone.

"Sorry," he said, putting one hand out to catch the person he'd nearly knocked flat.

Hazel rubbed her shoulder and smiled at him. "Don't worry. You're not the first one to bump into me at the corner. I'm thinking we might need a mirror there so people can see around the bend."

J.J. smiled. "You have a minute?" he asked.

Her smile died. "What's going on?" she asked. She reached up and smoothed her bangs back behind one ear.

"I just had a long talk with one of your employees back on the unit where Olan Taggart lived. I need to ask you a few questions about some things she brought up."

"I don't know," she said, smoothing her hair again. "I've got a huge amount of work to get done."

"Won't keep you long," J.J. said, indicating the hallway toward Hazel's office. He focused in on the woman as they walked. She was paler than she'd been when he'd rounded the corner. "It's about Jack Taggart," he said.

She missed a step, then stopped short.

"Don't worry, he hasn't been back bothering the staff again. Just a few things I want to double-check with you."

Hazel turned to face J.J. "We don't need to go back to my office for that. I don't know Jack well enough to do much more than say I'm glad I won't have to deal with him anymore."

"In a job like this one, isn't there always someone like Jack?"

"Always," she sighed. "I suppose I ought to be glad they fired me. Now I'm forced to look outside the nursing home industry for a job."

"Do you know yet where you'll go?" J.J. asked.

Hazel looked away from him down the hallway. She shrugged one shoulder as if to say it didn't matter to her. The pinched expression around her eyes told J.J. that this wasn't the case. "Probably Charlotte, but I've got an interview lined up for Chattanooga next week."

She looked up at J.J. and saw that she hadn't fooled him a bit. "Okay, so I'd rather have stayed here. I like the town. I'll be sorry to leave it behind."

"It grows on you." J.J. thought back to his family's reaction when he told them he was leaving East Texas to move to the mountains. They couldn't understand how he could leave Texas. He couldn't explain the feeling that as soon as he hit the foothills of the Appalachians, he knew he'd finally found home.

J.J.'s cell phone vibrated against his hip. "Sorry," he said, flipping it open. "Bascom," he said into the phone.

Leon said, "We found out who was breaking in at the Kohls'."

J.J. waited.

"You know how we had Colleen come in and let us print her so we could rule out her prints on that medicine bottle of Taggart's?"

"Yes," J.J. said slowly. "They were a match?"

"Yep. Can I pick 'em, or what?" Leon sounded almost proud of the fact that another one of his ex-girlfriends was involved in a crime.

J.J. thought it over, then simply said, "Good work."

Leon hung up without even mentioning the fact that he should be off duty by then hung up the phone to see Hazel staring at him.

"What's going on?" she said.

"Taggart's case." He sidestepped the obvious answer.

"What is it?"

He raised his eyebrows and tilted his head to one side. Everyone wanted to be the first to know when someone was in trouble. "I can't discuss it with you right now."

Hazel tried another tack. "You said you had some questions about Jack. Still need to talk with me?"

"Yes, actually." J.J. could be obtuse when he wanted to be.

He pulled out his pad and turned to the page containing

his questions about Jack. "Jack said he wasn't up here much, but he was attending that support group meeting, wasn't he?"

She frowned. "I suppose he might have been. I didn't have a whole lot to do with that. The social worker runs it. They had it on Wednesday so the families could consult with Doc while he was here. He does rounds on the clients here Wednesday afternoon. Some of the family has to travel a ways to get here, you know."

"Could we ask the social worker?"

Hazel gave an odd look but indicated an office door about twenty feet down the hall. "Frank should be in."

Frank turned out to be a short black man in his fifties, who had an easy smile and the shiniest bald head J.J. had ever seen. He waved Hazel and J.J. into his office and leaned back in his chair to consider J.J.'s questions. "Jack started coming to the support group a couple of months ago. After the first time, we kept him and his daddy apart as best we could. Get too close and we'd be hearing bagpipes for days." Frank laughed when he saw J.J.'s confused look. "Olan Taggart's way of working off steam was to play his bagpipes," he explained.

J.J. turned to Hazel. "Janey said you had to confiscate his bagpipes the day before he died."

"Sure did. You would believe how bad he was about it that day when—" she stopped.

"Yes?" J.J. prompted.

Hazel ignored him and concentrated on Frank's face.

"Jack wasn't here that day, was he?" asked.

When she still did not answer, Frank jumped in. "That would have been Friday, right?" he said. "Support group's on Wednesday."

"The only time he ever played them was after Jack had been here," Hazel said.

"You sure?" J.J. asked.

Both Hazel and Frank nodded. "You could set your calendar by it," Frank said.

"So much so," Hazel offered, "that the nurses would hide the mouthpiece the day the group met so they wouldn't have to deal with taking it away from him once he got started."

"So why was he playing them the day before he died?"

Hazel reached up as if to touch her hair again, then folded her hands in her lap.

Frank looked sharply at her. "What is it?"

"I was just wondering," she said. "What if Jack *was* here?"

Frowning, he said, "Jack's entitled to visit his dad." Tapping out a neat tattoo on his knee with a chewed-up pencil stub, he raised one eyebrow at Hazel.

"Well," she said, "Jack usually tells us when he's coming. So if he came up that day, why didn't any of us see him?"

J.J. spread his hands. "As much as I'd like to think you've just cracked this case wide open for me, I think Judge Carrolton will not consider bagpipe playing as hard evidence."

Frank smiled. Hazel just looked more worried.

"Did Jack make any friends in the group?" J.J. asked.

Frank thought that one over before replying, "Well, he used to stop and have coffee with folks after the group session. Sometimes he'd come in here to talk about his daddy's care. There wasn't any one person in the group he was particularly friendly with."

"You think Jack killed his father?" Hazel asked.

J.J. stood. "Somebody sure did," he said. "Jack's a good guess right now."

Frank stood up and walked around his desk to shake J.J.'s hand. "Even though I can't say as I think Jack could kill anyone, we'll ask around here and see if anyone saw him. They may have and didn't speak up before."

J.J. handed Frank one of his cards, flipping it over to point out his cell phone number scribbled on the back.

Hazel walked the police chief out to the front door. "Even if Jack was here on Friday, Mr. Taggart didn't die until Saturday," she pointed out.

J.J. slipped his sunglasses on and pushed open the front door. "I know that," he said. "And I'm keeping it in mind. But if we can find a witness who can put him at the scene within twenty-four hours, we might have to seriously consider him as a suspect."

The door shut behind him, closing off a stunned look on Hazel's face.

J.J. thought about the case as he drove back into town. He didn't even tap his fingers on the steering wheel like he usually did, he was so deep in thought. He pulled in at the station, got out of his car and locked it, then went inside.

It was cold, so he twisted the dial on the thermostat in his office. Once in his chair, he lifted the receiver off the phone and punched in the number for the Best Western. When the desk clerk answered, J.J. asked for Jack's room.

"Mr. Taggart checked out this morning," the receptionist said in a husky voice. "I guess he's taking his daddy home to be buried?"

"I guess so," J.J. said slowly. He hung up and thought a

minute more. Jack might have gone to stay with a friend locally, but he also might have had to go home to work; he ought to have checked with J.J. first to let him know how to get in touch with him. People tended to go on about their business even though they were part of a murder investigation.

He looked at his watch. If Jack had checked out that morning, then he should be home by now. J.J. fiddled with the papers in front of him, uncovering Jack's home number. He called.

Jack picked up after two rings. "Hello?"

Static poured through the wire. The connection was horrible.

"I'll call you back and see if we don't get another line," J.J. said.

At the same time, Jack said, "Hang on, let me pull off the road and see if that doesn't clear this static."

Then the connection was lost.

As J.J. stared at the paper on his desk with Jack's phone number on it, he felt his lips curl in an expression that was most definitely not a smile. He mentally kicked himself in a hundred different directions. Jack either had call forwarding on his phone, or he didn't bother with regular service to his home. He had no alibi to speak of, after all.

TWENTY

A few days later, J.J. sat in his office.

"There's Captain Daniel Bailey on the phone from the Mecklinburg County Sheriff's Office," Marlene yelled. "They picked up Jack Taggart this morning."

"You got him," J.J. said after he fumbled the phone to his ear. At least Jack was in custody. Colleen had disappeared as soon as she made bail. He was still pissed about that. He reined in his frustration to listen to the good news.

"Taggart was driving around," Bailey said, "picking up hospital linens. Said he was afraid he'd lose his job if he didn't go back to work."

"What did he say when you arrested him?"

"The usual."

"'Innocent. I want my lawyer.'" J.J. sighed. All they needed was a little more evidence. What they had in hand was enough to bring the man in for questioning, but perhaps not enough to convict. And J.J. wanted him convicted.

"We got a search warrant and went through his house," Bailey said. "Sad story. The stack of medical bills for his father was higher than I would have imagined."

J.J. swiveled in his chair and got up to look out the window of his office. "He mentioned it was expensive." Ironic that Jack's need to get back to work had led J.J. to break his work-related alibi.

"We found the pin you mentioned."

"Really?" That was good news. Carly had been positive that Olan Taggart was wearing it the night before he died. That put Jack up there even closer to the time of death.

"And we found a pair of scrubs rolled up in the corner of his closet," Bailey added. "Some gray hairs on them that weren't his."

"You don't say? Lab's got them?"

"As we speak."

Hopefully it would turn into solid evidence. J.J. started to smile. The memory of Dora McFaile's car sitting on the asphalt at Shady Acres came to mind. A slight man dressed in scrubs inching closer to the prone figure on the ground.

"Son of a gumshoe!" J.J. said.

"I beg your pardon?"

"Captain Bailey, would you believe I actually saw him at the crime scene and didn't recognize him? Never saw his face."

"That so? We'll let you know if there's anything else interesting down here."

"Thanks," J.J. said. He leaned over his desk and hung up.

Sitting back down in his chair, he sighed the last of his reports on the case and shuffled the papers until the edges lined up. Colleen hadn't counted on being caught: she'd left her fingerprints in all sorts of interesting places. The Kohls' house. Dora McFaile's bedroom. Inside drawers of patients at Shady Acres. Then there was Mrs. McFaile's medicine bottle and the Bible. Colleen had graduated from stalking to attempted murder.

She and Jack may have both drawn their inspiration from Maris Falkirk's death, but it had been too much to ask to find evidence that they were working in tandem. J.J. smiled down at the paperwork in his hands. Jack's file wasn't yet complete, but once the lab ran tests....

He picked up the manila folders and walked them out to Marlene's desk, where he took great pleasure in placing them in the to-be-filed stack.

"Going home so soon?" Marlene asked when she saw that he was wearing his coat.

"Janey's getting back tonight, and I've got a dinner planned that will knock her socks off."

"Tell Juanita June I said hello."

Marlene's parting shot brought a grin to J.J.'s face as the door to the station closed behind him. She knew him so well. He walked the few short blocks over to the Penny Whistle and picked up the steak dinner he'd special ordered.

Janey had sounded good on the phone when she'd called an hour before. Tired, but happy that she'd gone for the visit. There were still issues to be addressed—the biggest one was Memaw's resistance to Janey's marriage to J.J.

The trip had produced some positive results, however. Janey had managed to talk her grandmother into moving out of her house and into a nice retirement home, and they were talking again. It was a start. More important to J.J., his wife sounded grateful to be leaving Memaw and coming home to him.

He put the foil-wrapped containers on the backseat and headed home. Steak, flowers, fire in the fireplace, murder suspect in jail. He was more than ready for a celebration.

TWENTY-ONE

A FEW WEEKS LATER, Korine looked over J.J.'s desk at him and said, "I thought Jack killed his father."

"Yes, he did," J.J. replied. "But Colleen thought it was such a great idea that she borrowed it and used it to poison Mrs. McFaile. Her fingerprints were on the bottle you found next to the bed. Remember how Colleen reached for the medicine bottle in the hospital?"

Korine nodded, the vision of Colleen's sweater-clad outstretched arm flashing into her mind.

"Her prints were all over your mother-in-law's room in addition to the bottle," J.J. continued. "She was the one who drugged Mrs. McFaile."

Korine leaned back in her seat. She exchanged glances with Cal, who sat next to her. "Start over," she said. "I'm not following you."

"Colleen wasn't real stable." J.J. ran through the story about river rocks and how she would keep one for every boyfriend she felt had done her wrong. "So I started looking up some of those old boyfriends. Without exception, she had engaged in some sort of stalking behavior. With you, Cal, she was using your mother to discredit Korine so Colleen would have a reason to get closer to you."

Cal shook his head. "I'm sorry, Korine. I believed all that crap she told me."

"Some of it was true," J.J. said.

Korine nodded. "Dora was paranoid. She did miss things. It got a lot worse, though, after Collleen started sneaking in and moving her stuff around."

"How did she get a key?" J.J. asked.

"I gave it to her," Korine said bitterly. "She helped me out one day when Lorraine's daughter wasn't feeling well and I had to go to work. Then she went down to Klein's and had a copy made."

"Which was when Mom's lock obsession started?" Cal guessed.

"You got it." Korine frowned. "So why did she send Dora over to Shady Acres? Did she know Jack was going to kill his father that day?"

J.J. sighed. "My theory is that she just wanted Mrs. McFaile to go over to Shady Acres so that she could 'discover' her driving and call Cal. As upset as Jack was by the condition his father's body was in, I seriously doubt they were working together."

Cal stood, followed by Korine. "And Colleen?" she asked.

"She's dead," J.J. said heavily. As much as he wanted Colleen to have to meet justice face to face, this wasn't the way it was supposed to be. "She was down by the river in Asheville where she used to go to pick up those rocks. A couple of kids saw her go in. She was standing too close to the edge when part of the bank collapsed. Colleen won't be bothering either of you anymore."

KORINE WRAPPED THE QUILT closer around her. Cal had declined to stay for supper, saying he wanted to get back to Charlotte before the weather got too bad. Korine couldn't blame him. The forecast wasn't pretty if you were going to have to drive in it.

While it was definitely cold, the old porch rockers were large enough to allow her to tuck her feet up under her and really snuggle in. She took a cautious sip from the steaming mug of hot chocolate that Buster had brought out for her. They sat next to each other on Korine's front porch, watching the first snowfall of the season.

The snow had begun early that morning and continued on through the day. Even the tracks made by Cal's truck as he left had been covered. The hush that fell on Korine's small corner of the world drowned out the pain of the empty room upstairs.

Dora was gone from Pine Grove, taking with her the many memories she might still have shared with Korine of Charlie and his childhood. Cal had placed her in a care facility in Charlotte that was more than adequate. Korine had been to visit and found that Dora actually seemed happy there.

Korine raised the warm earthenware mug to her lips and sipped. She smiled as she felt Buster lightly brush the marshmallow smile away from her mouth. His hand stole under her blanket and held her hand.

"Penny for them?" he said.

"I was admiring that bluebird house you put up for me over there," Korine said. "I like having something to look forward to in the spring."

"You cold?" Buster fussed with his own blanket, then stuck his chilly fingers back into hers.

"Sure," Korine laughed. "But I love to watch it all come down."

"Well," Buster said, standing up and folding his blanket under his arm. "I'm not near warm enough to stay out here. Mind if I go inside for a bit?"

"Not if you don't mind if I stay here," Korine said. She really didn't want to go in just yet. She knew when she did that she would hear Amilou and Janey clearing Dora's last remaining things out of her room and packing them away.

The night before, at Janey's birthday celebration, Korine had jokingly said that if her friends didn't come do it for her, it wouldn't get done at all. Amilou, Janey, and Buster had surprised her, showing up in Buster's truck early that morning so that Korine wouldn't have to face it alone. They'd sent Cal and Korine off to talk with J.J. about Colleen while they worked.

When the pair had gotten back, Amilou and Janey presented Korine with a new commission for the landscaping company. The home that Dora lived in wanted a birdwatcher's area. Amilou had suggested that she, Janey, and Korine give this to Dora for Christmas. They would plan it now, then put it in once the ground thawed out again. Korine had fiddled with the plans a bit after Cal left, but she couldn't quite settle. Which was why she was sitting in the cold, watching the snow come down instead.

Buster stood up to go back inside. "I'll check on you in a bit and see if you haven't frozen to death."

Korine didn't answer, but she smiled at him, and pulled the mug up close to her face and breathed in the steamy sweetness. She stared out at the bluebird house, rising squarely up on its post out of a small drift of snow. What she saw was the look on Dora's face when they'd led her into her new room.

Cal had taken Dora's bedspread and a few of her favorite pieces of furniture to the home. The place didn't allow rockers, so they'd adapted one of the rockers from Korine's kitchen into a regular chair. In a small shadowbox outside her room was a photo of the house in which Dora and her husband had raised their family. Next to it was an old snapshot of Dora holding Cal in her lap, Charlie leaning in over her shoulder. With those things to spark her memory, she would always know that room was hers.

Dora hadn't loved her new home, but she was as happy there as she had been at Korine's. Cal said she felt safe there; and indeed, from what Korine had seen on her visits, they took good care of her.

Korine drank the last of her hot chocolate and stood up. She slipped one hand out from under the blankets to open the front door, then went inside. Rinsing her mug in the sink, she smiled at the sound of feet overhead.

The first few times she'd heard footsteps after Dora left, she'd been frightened. Now that she knew Colleen wouldn't be back to bother her, she would be free to enjoy the sounds of the house settling in around her, enfolding her in those happy memories. She looked around the kitchen.

Olmstead was asleep under the remaining rocker, tail curled around her fluffy belly. The stray cat, which Korine should probably get around to naming, sat watching the tail tick-tock back and forth on the Felix the Cat clock. The lingering aroma of cinnamon and sugar, from the fresh schnecken that Mrs. Kohl had sent with Buster, mingled with the smell of coffee and hot chocolate, and made Korine sigh.

It was still home. She'd weathered the changes after

Charlie died. She'd weathered her son's move to Savannah and the surprises which that had brought to her life. She would weather this change too. The house was now hers and hers alone.

A large thud overhead, followed by an indignant voice cursing whatever had fallen, interrupted Korine's maudlin thoughts. There was a pause, then the clatter of footsteps coming down the stairs.

Amilou angled her way through the kitchen door and staggered across the room. Korine opened the back door and stepped out quickly to let Amilou out the porch door as well. She took the box and put it in the bed of Buster's truck. Janey and Buster followed with the last of Dora's things. Buster closed the top on the bed and locked it.

"Do we have time for a little something from the bar before we all have to get ready for tonight?" Amilou said.

"I made some hot buttered rum," Korine said.

The group quickly made their way back inside. Buster poured himself what he called "hot buttered coffee," since he'd be driving that night.

"To home," Amilou said, raising her mug.

"I can do that," Korine said. "With hopes that our families find happiness in their homes—wherever they are."

Janey's eyes had tears in them. Memaw was settling into her new home in Louisiana, Dora in her new home in Charlotte. Amilou, Buster, and Korine all had their houses to themselves, no matter how much each of them wished they still shared them with people from their past. But they weren't any of them alone.

Amilou leaned over and put one hand on Korine's arm. "We got everything done. You've got your guest room all set and ready to go for when Chaz or Dennis wants to come home."

"Thank you," Korine glanced up as the Felix clock struck six. She cleared the frog out of her throat. "I guess it's time to change and head out to the First Annual Policemen's Ball."

Buster, Amilou, and Janey pulled on coats, scarves, and gloves and headed out.

"Wear that red dress," Buster whispered in Korine's ear as he left. "I'll be back to pick you up at seven."

She gave him a quick hug, then watched the trio drive away.

She rinsed the dishes, dried them and put them away. Wiping her hands on the tea towel, she decided she could no longer put off going upstairs to get dressed for the party. The room wouldn't bite her as she went by.

At the top of the stairs, she stared. They'd left Doras's door open. The bed was neatly covered with the faded quilt Dora had made for Charlie and Korine when they got married. Lying on top was Dora's pink suitcase, open as if she were just inside the room, unpacking for a stay.

Korine put one shaking hand up to her face, then stepped forward into the room. Lying inside the case was a scrapbook. MEMORIES, it said on the cover. Reaching down with both hands, Korine picked up the book and opened it. On the first page was a copy of Dora's portrait as a young girl. Smoothing her shaking hand over the page, Korine hesitantly turned to the next page. Dora on her wedding day. Page after page of wonderful memories of a life fully lived. The last picture was one of Dora leaning on her broom in front of Korine's porch, hand shading her eyes as she looked off over the yard toward a flying bird.

A note was taped to the inside of the back cover.

I thought you would like a copy of this. I did it for Mom so that we would have something to talk about when I go to visit her. I'll always remember what you did for her.

It was signed simply, *Cal.*

Korine hugged the book to her and looked out the little window that Dora had looked out so many times. She sighed and put the book back down on the bed. Snapping together the latches on the suitcase, she put it in the closet under the empty coat hangers and shut the door.

She went into her own room and pulled out her new red velvet dress. It might clash with her eyes, pink from crying, but she didn't mind at all. She pulled off her sweatshirt and began to dress for the Ball.

HARLEQUIN®
INTRIGUE®

WE'LL LEAVE YOU BREATHLESS!

If you've been looking for thrilling tales of contemporary passion and sensuous love stories with taut, edge-of-the-seat suspense—then you'll love Harlequin Intrigue!

Every month, you'll meet six new heroes who are guaranteed to make your spine tingle and your pulse pound. With them you'll enter into the exciting world of Harlequin Intrigue— where your life is on the line and so is your heart!

THAT'S INTRIGUE—
ROMANTIC SUSPENSE
AT ITS BEST!

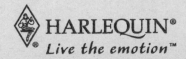

HARLEQUIN®
Live the emotion™